PRESS RELEASE

AMAZON FEATURED AUTHOR

Amazon Shares a Selection of Customers' Favorite Books from Indie Authors

October 15, 2018 at 9:00 AM EDT

Top Picks To Add Self-Published Books to Your End-of-Year Reading Lists

Kindle Direct Publishing Helps Authors Reach Readers Around the World

SEATTLE--(BUSINESS WIRE)--Oct. 15, 2018-- (NASDAQ: AMZN)—Hundreds of thousands of independent authors are finding their audiences through self-publishing with Kindle Direct Publishing (KDP). More than ever before, authors are reaching new readers directly and cultivating communities as they grow their writing careers on KDP. Readers also relish the value and entertainment from these authors. On average, 20% of books on this year's Amazon Charts Top 20 weekly lists are self-published.

"We launched KDP in 2007 with the first Kindle, and since

then hundreds of thousands of independent authors have chosen to self-publish their books, earning up to 70 percent of their royalties and retaining the life-long rights of their work," said Charles Kronbach, Director of Independent Publishing Worldwide for Amazon. "In 2017, thousands of KDP authors earned more than $50,000 in royalties, and more than a thousand earned more than $100,000. We are inspired by the success of these writers and how they are delighting readers."

Below is a curated list of top-selling books on Amazon from independent authors and why customers love them (average customer rating as of October 2018):

• **John Ellsworth's** *30 Days of Justis (Michael Gresham Series)* (Thriller). Overall rating: 4.6 stars. "I could hardly put this book down. First book I have read by John Ellsworth. I cannot wait to read more. Well written and holds your attention!" – Ann C

THE LAWYER

JOHN ELLSWORTH

COPYRIGHT

THE LAWYER

PROLOGUE

S everal months ago, I took a last look around my office before I walked out for the last time. I felt like a married person losing a spouse. This place was my home for thirty years, for better or worse, in sickness and health, in good times and in bad. It was the previous six months that had qualified for the bad: six months and a mere eight new clients. My partners voted me out of the law firm that I had founded when I was fresh out of law school. "Don't take it personally," managing partner Everett Evans told me, "it's only business." Yes, but until that moment it was *my* business and now you say it's not? Just shove me out the door? "Article Eight—" he began, but I shut him off. I knew all about Article Eight of our Partnership Agreement: the right to vote out a non-producing partner, emphasis on *non.*

I had no explanation. New work had just vanished, and I was kicking myself every morning while I shaved and had to look into the eyes of the man who chose law over medicine and dentistry. If your customers have insurance, you're golden. If they don't have insurance—you're a lawyer. A doctor wouldn't dream of taking on a patient who has no insurance. Lawyers—lawyers do it every time a new case walks in.

Suzanne Strunk—my secretary—appeared with yet another cardboard box to hold the final artifacts that could prove I had once been a member of the firm. My framed certificate proving my good standing in *Illinois Attorneys for Criminal Justice*, my certificate for finishing Trial Lawyers College in Reno, my certificate of membership in Rotary. All three listed the name of my law firm. Plus the small stuff from the middle drawer in my Italian desk, including a stack of unused business cards with my law firm's name in raised letters. It all went into my box and then I stood upright and clapped my hands together, scattering the imaginary dust my life had collected.

Suzanne closed the two steps between us and fiddled with my necktie. An old habit of hers, one that I allowed very rarely, for Suzanne was happily married, and married women shouldn't be touching other men intimately like the necktie thing. I mean to me, it's intimate. To someone else it's housekeeping. The tears in her eyes overflowed and she touched my face with her hand. "I'm going to miss you, Michael."

That was six months ago.

To everyone's amazement, it turned around almost overnight and I have prospered.

I have prospered because I stumbled onto the case of the *United States of America v. James Joseph Lamb.* Suddenly, my name was in all the newspapers, I was seen on TV, and my phone started ringing off the hook.

Saved by the murder of a judge's wife.

It's a terrible thing to prosper off something like that. But nobody ever said the world was going to be Disneyland.

Because it isn't.

Not where I work.

I'm a criminal lawyer.

1

" *Chicago Tribune, May 31*

Twenty-five-year-old James Lamb goes on trial today for murdering the wife of Federal Judge Francis Pennington. If convicted, Lamb will be facing the death penalty. He is defended by Attorney Michael Gresham of Chicago. Attorney Gresham says he will prove Lamb's confession came only after Lamb was savagely beaten by the FBI. The government says Gresham's claims are predictable and imaginary.

—*Keenan J. Harshman, Reporter*

FBI Special Agent Nathan Fordyce takes the witness stand, smiles at the judge and then frowns at me. I step up to the lectern. Fordyce's eyes never move off of me. I am the lawyer who can speak black into white and night into day—Michael Gresham, consummate wordsmith. The other side of the equation is that Fordyce is the shooter you would want on your side in a firefight. His role is to send my client off to die with a needle in his skinny black arm. My role is to convince the jury that my client's confession was coerced and that my client's low IQ made it impossible for him to orchestrate the murder in the manner they claim. My heart goes out to this young client and his predicament. I can and will prove his diminished capacity during the course of the next several days while the jury listens and prepares to vote.

"Mr. Gresham," the judge says with a note of impatience, "please proceed with your examination." It is the second time he has addressed me.

This is a pre-trial motion to suppress. The jury is not in the courtroom, and that means the gloves come off. There is no requirement that I treat this witness compassionately, as with a jury watching. Trial begins in fifteen minutes; Judge Amberlos is drumming his fingers on the arm of his chair.

A deep breath, for I am anxious and terribly frightened for the young man whose life is in my hands. I gather up my courage and I begin.

"Agent Fordyce, I want to start by discussing how you obtained James Lamb's confession. First, you have claimed it was freely and voluntarily given. However, your partner, Jim Burns, assaulted Mr. Lamb to make him confess. Isn't that true?"

"No such thing."

"Mr. Lamb has promised me he was assaulted. Not true?"

"Your client has a very vivid imagination, counselor."

"It's imagination, is it? Imagine this with me, Mr. Fordyce. Imagine my client came away with four new gold teeth after you took him into custody. Imagine very cheap gold teeth, incidentally. Cemented in his mouth by government dentists because your partner knocked the white ones out of his head with a police sap. Does that ring a bell with you?"

"No bells, counselor. Again, your client is very creative."

I turn and look down at my client. "Mr. Lamb, please smile for Mr. Fordyce."

Lamb slowly looks up at me. "Huh?"

"Stand up and smile for the FBI. Then turn around and show Court TV what your new, FBI-approved, government smile looks like."

"Objection," cries the Assistant U.S. Attorney.

"What's the basis for your objection?" asks Judge Amberlos.

"Prejudice."

"Overruled. Mr. Lamb, please show us all your smile."

Lamb stands and does a slow 360, his lips curled away from his teeth.

"Is that what they call a grill, Mr. Fordyce? I am referring to my client's funky teeth."

The FBI agent looks puzzled. "A grill? Are you talking about the gold dentures the rappers wear?"

"I am. Isn't that the look my client has now?"

"If you say so, counselor."

"Thanks to you and your partner?"

"Thanks to your client resisting arrest, counselor."

"Please sit down, Mr. Lamb," says Judge Amberlos to my client.

Out of habit, I glance around the courtroom. I am wondering what the TV audience thought of that little display. The courtroom is noisy as the Court TV people pan their camera and whisper along the back wall. Behind me, a tripod crashes to the floor. We all turn to look. Judge Amberlos says nothing. We were shocked when he allowed the network's motion to bring a camera into the courtroom. That never happens in federal court. But neither does a trial over the killing of a judge's wife.

Then I see that he's still there on the front row, sitting on the U.S. Attorney's side of the courtroom. His name is Francis S. Pennington Jr., and he is a District Court judge. It is his wife that my client is accused of murdering. Pennington has appeared at every court date, beginning with the initial appearance and throughout the standard motions defense lawyers file. He sits still as a statue, a lump of immutable truth: his mate is gone. It's an odd thing, in a way; word around the courthouse has it that she was unfaithful. Of course, there's always gossip like this. I don't know what to make of it. But as I look him over, I can only wonder. He never moves his eyes from the young black man named James Lamb with the up yours grill in his mouth. Who could?

James Joseph Lamb is a wiry man with a perpetual squint from a lifetime of looking for cover just before a South Chicago drive-by. As if the new gold teeth aren't enough to deal with in front of a jury, there's also the prison tat: the mandatory two blue teardrops beneath the left eye. Not an attractive package even for our racially mixed jury, which in all likelihood will see nothing in my client that is worth saving from the needle. But there's a hitch. The ability to plan and execute this murder far exceeds Lamb's mental abilities. His IQ is pegged one point above what the psychologists categorize as having an intellectual disability. "Why are they saying I killed someone?" he asks me. "It's complicated," I tell him, which, I am sad to report, satisfies him.

Judge Amberlos says, "Mr. Gresham, was there more?"

"Yes, thank you, Your Honor."

It is time to confront the illegal search and seizure.

"Mr. Fordyce, when you arrived at my client's apartment, did you knock on the door?"

The agent hesitates. We both know it's a trap.

"I knocked on the door."

"Who answered the knock?"

"Your client. Mr. Lamb."

"James Joseph Lamb answered your knock?"

"Yes."

"Did you say anything to him?"

"I asked if we could come inside. My partner and I."

"What did he say?"

"He said no."

"What happened next?"

The special agent shifts his weight in the witness chair. He looks at the Assistant U.S. Attorney, Bob LaGuardia, who is sitting back, his face raised to the ceiling, his eyes closed. Bob is not your typical prosecutor: he is courteous, thoughtful, and slow to anger. In fact, he is affectionately known around the U.S. Attorney's office as Bob "No-Guns" LaGuardia, for the fact he doesn't subscribe to courtroom shooting matches. No-Guns is a plodder who is fair, and juries love the guy. He woos with sugar and it works: he is 55-0. He leaves Fordyce hanging.

Special Agent Fordyce continues. "What happened next was his girlfriend pushed past him and said we could come in. It was raining, and we were standing on the porch getting soaked. I guess she felt sorry for us."

"You guess she did? But she didn't tell you that?"

"No, she just said to come inside."

"So at this point, the defendant had said you couldn't come inside, but his girlfriend said you could, correct?"

"Correct."

"Mr. Fordyce, why were you there?"

"We heard your client was dealing drugs with a federal fugitive. We wanted to come inside and ask him some questions."

"Isn't it true you could have asked your questions from the porch?"

"No, it was raining, and we were getting soaked."

"So you are suggesting there's an exception to the U.S. Constitution's prohibition against unlawful search that allows unlawful search and seizure when it's raining?"

Fordyce looks up at Judge Amberlos.

"Judge, do I have to answer that?"

"Listen to the question and try to answer, please," says the judge.

"Isn't it true you wanted to get inside to plant the gun you found at the murder scene?"

"No. We just wanted to talk."

"You just wanted to talk? Well, your story is that you did much more. In fact, your report says you wound up searching and finding the gun used to kill Judge Pennington's wife. Is that correct?"

"Yes."

"How many guns did you take inside my client's apartment that night?"

"Two. One. I mean one apiece. My service weapon and Agent Burns's."

"So you brought, at least, two guns inside. Are you sure it wasn't three? You're sure you didn't bring the Pennington murder weapon with you to the party?"

"It was two guns total. No need to bring a third. Your client supplied that from under his mattress."

"How did that happen? How did you wind up under my client's mattress?"

"Once we were inside we smelled the strong odor of marijuana. We noticed a pipe in the ashtray on the coffee table right there in the living room. It contained a green leafy substance. So we searched the whole apartment and found the gun in the process."

"Now, when you were outside on the porch, could you see this pipe?"

"Objection. Asked and answered," says LaGuardia. No-Guns has stirred. An eyebrow may have raised.

"Overruled."

"Please answer. Could you see the pipe from the porch?"

"I don't think so."

"Well, *did* you see the pipe from the porch?"

"No."

"Did your partner?"

"I never asked."

"Long story short, at the moment you entered my client's living room, you were unaware there was marijuana there, correct?"

"We had our suspicions."

"But you had no evidence your suspicions were accurate, correct?"

"Yes."

"Do you know whether the girlfriend was on the lease?"

"We found out later she was not."

"So, when she consented to you entering, she didn't actually have legal authority to ask you inside, did she?"

"Objection! Calls for a legal conclusion." It is a good objection. I had thought I'd catch Bob napping. But no such luck.

"Sustained. Mr. Gresham, you know better than that."

I do know better.

"Let me rephrase."

"Please do. And move it along. The court is of the opinion you have about exhausted this line of questioning. The jury is waiting, and so am I."

"Rephrasing, you later learned the girlfriend was not on the lease, correct?"

"Correct."

"And she was not a tenant there, correct?"

"Not exactly. She was staying there off and on."

"Counsel," says Judge Amberlos, "I'm going to stop you right there. The jury is anxious, and I'm sure you want argument."

"I don't get to finish my questions?"

"I've heard enough, Mr. Gresham. I'm ready to rule against you. But on the off-chance you can astonish me with your oral argument, please proceed. Please astonish me."

"May it please the court," I say, launching into the ten-thousandth motion to suppress argument of my thirty-year career. I proceed to pound the latest Constitutional law cases, search and seizure rules, opinions and dissents, and Seventh Circuit case law. Then I sit down with a confident look on my face. My knowledge and grasp, while perhaps not totally astonishing, have been compelling. I am convinced that I will prevail. I must prevail: without the planted gun that killed Judge Pennington's wife the government has only the confession. And it was coerced; we have the newly installed gold teeth to prove it.

Bob LaGuardia launches into his counter-argument. He is soft-spoken and intelligent—but in the end, he knows he has a clinker, and he becomes subdued. The visiting girl-friend, who wasn't on the lease, had no legal right to consent to the officers entering the room. Both of us know the judge should suppress.

Judge Amberlos has proved amazingly consistent. Over the past three months, as we've developed this case, I have lost each and every motion I have filed. Judge Amberlos has handed the government win after win after win, until yesterday, when lightning struck, and the judge ruled my client could eat his lunches in the courtroom during trial rather than being returned to the holding cell where the noon fare is bologna and bread. Now he will get real food, the same food the jury is eating, purchased and served by the same U.S. Marshals who oversee the jury as they come and go to lunch. This, I kid you not, is the one motion I have filed that has been granted. The right to eat fried chicken instead of bologna. But the sad part of all this is that my client, with his mental disability, was deliriously happy when I informed him we had won the motion to eat in the courtroom. He began fiercely pumping my hand and throwing his arms around me for a gratitude hug. Which underscores this salient factor: Lamb places so low on all known psychiatric scales that he hasn't understood that we have lost the eighteen other motions I have filed to save him. The stuff that matters just didn't win out. Especially when I argued my motion challenging his competency to stand trial. In the end, we lost that too, which means the government is drawing ever nearer to succeeding in its quest to execute a man who is one point above the cutoff for mental retardation. One IQ point and there would have been no trial; my client would have been adjudicated incompetent and placed in a facility for long-term penal care. One point and we wouldn't be here.

But we are.

With two words the judge rules: "Motion denied."

My client's confession will be presented to the jury. The gun will be allowed into evidence.

I cast a sad look at James Joseph Lamb. Wearing a suit three sizes too large for him, a suit out of my closet, he understands little of what's being done to his life. I have defended him previously, maybe ten years ago. That was in Judge Pennington's court. Lamb pulled a dime on that one and was out in sixty months. Now, the Assistant U.S. Attorney will tell the jury that Lamb, once he was released, murdered Judge Pennington's wife as payback for the prison time, and here we are.

"You may take your seat," the judge tells Special Agent Fordyce. On his way past my table, Fordyce pauses. He wants to say something to me but restrains himself. The FBI needed a quick conviction for this terrible crime and Nathan Fordyce, and his partner have accommodated them. He exhales and passes me by. He sits beside Bob LaGuardia at the prosecution table, stretches out his arms and legs, and inhales a deep lungful of air, the free kind that you can only get outside of prison walls.

"Bring in the jury, we're ready to start the trial," Judge Amberlos orders the bailiff, and I swallow hard. Because I am Irish Catholic and fifty-five and still believe in such things, I pray a quick prayer for God's pursuing grace. That's what you do when the U.S. Government is trying to execute your client.

It is only going to get worse, and I am left hoping for that grace.

It cannot arrive too soon.

2

Judge Amberlos settles the jury in the courtroom and tells them they're now going to hear the attorneys' opening statements. He reminds them that the statements are not evidence, that they are merely commentary by the attorneys on what they believe the evidence will be. The jury is to weigh the evidence at the end of the trial against what the attorneys said in opening. Did the evidence prove what they said? The jury should pay close attention.

Bob LaGuardia goes first. He tells the jury that James Lamb broke into the home of Judge Francis Pennington Jr. and murdered his wife in cold blood. There was premeditation, there was planning, there was a carefully constructed plan of a cover-up as he wore gloves so he would leave no prints and he wore a hair net and scrubs, so there was no hair or fiber. Moreover, there was no DNA, so he knew what he was doing. Finally, he timed it so the judge was gone downtown to the federal court, where he had several years before sentenced Lamb to ten years in prison for the stabbing of a

U.S. Marshal. While motive isn't a necessary element of proof, LaGuardia explains, there was motive: Lamb was in a rage at the judge over being sent to prison. Judge Amberlos has ruled that the prior conviction for the stabbing is admissible to show state of mind in the Judge Pennington murder, so LaGuardia can parade that conviction before the jury. It is done over my strong objections and, yes, my motion to suppress, which, like the one today, was also denied. The result: Lamb is an accomplished killer with a compelling motive, and he deserves to be convicted of First Degree Murder and put to death.

The look on the jury's face when I stand to address them can be reduced to one word: skepticism. They have just been turned inside-out by the government. If there was any lingering doubt about the guilt of my client, it is now vanquished with LaGuardia's opening statement. I don't want to reveal my full hand, but I take care to explain that what the jury heard about Lamb's careful planning and execution would have been the work of someone with twenty more IQ points than Lamb had. I promise them that I will produce records of his inability to pass the GED while in prison on Judge Pennington's sentence and of his IQ test of that same period. Arms are folded across chests as I talk. Body language experts would point out to me how the jury leans as far away from me as possible while I stand at the rail of the jury box and address them. But I don't need an expert to point that out; it is clear they are listening without hearing. They won't even make eye contact. James Lamb would die by their vote if they cast their ballots now. For the record, I despise the death penalty. In thirty years I have lost one client to it, and I sat in witness of the most horrifying spectacle of a human being choking to death on toxic fumes that I still have nightmares about it. If the public could witness one such violent death—even by the needle—the death penalty would become a relic pointing to the past barbarism of our time, much like the torture machines of medieval days.

Then we are off and running. LaGuardia calls Special Agent Nathan Fordyce back to the stand. Fordyce is all-FBI: a muscular man, someone who probably played meat-grinder football on a defensive line in college, and who will come across as earnest, sincere, and fair, especially in how professionally he has been investigating Lamb.

LaGuardia reviews the Lamb confession with Fordyce, the Who, What, Why, When, and Where of how the confession came into existence. Then he moves it into evidence. I make a note on my exhibit list that the jury now has it.

The confession is passed around to the jury. It is a short one. It reads:

> *Voluntary Confession of James Lamb*
>
> *I, James Joseph Lamb, do freely and voluntarily say the following:*
>
> *1. I have been given my Miranda warnings and understand them and do freely and voluntarily waive Miranda;*
>
> *2. I admit that I took a gun and shot and killed Veronica Pennington on November 4, 2014;*
>
> *3. I murdered her because Judge Pennington sent me to prison for a crime I didn't do, and I paid him back.*

4. No one forced me to say these things, and I consent to this being used in a court of law at any time and any place.

/s/ James J. Lamb Date: November 7, 2014.

The jury reads the confession with keen interest and makes notes as it passes among them.

Watching all this from the witness stand, Nathan Fordyce is the exemplar of fair dealing and honest police work. He neither smirks nor scowls at me when no one is looking. He is calm, cool and collected and we both know he's lying. And he is supremely confident: not only is there the confession but they also found the gun that killed the judge's wife under Lamb's mattress. Open and shut case.

LaGuardia breaks the silence once the confession has made its rounds.

"Now, Agent Fordyce, going back to the scene of the crime, I want to walk you through what you did once you arrived."

"All right."

"What time did you and Special Agent James Burns arrive at Judge Pennington's house?"

"May I look at my Activity Report?"

"Please do."

He scans over his report and then looks up.

"Our supervisor tapped us on the case at one-twenty-two that afternoon. The judge had just gone home after his morning court and his lunch and found his wife murdered."

"So your supervisor assigned you to investigate?"

"Yes, Burns and I are assigned to RHD—"

"What's RHD?"

"Robbery-Homicide Detail. That's our permanent assign-
ment, and we were the only RHD's in the office, so we got
the tap. We headed downstairs to the car pool, climbed into
our vehicle, and activated our emergency lights. We ran
north on Lake Shore Drive to the near north side."

"That part of Chicago people call the Gold Coast."

"Right. It's a beautiful home, and when we arrived, there
were three black-and-whites pulled in the driveway. We
badged the cops and went inside."

"Who did you speak to?"

"Sergeant Carmody. He told us—"

"Object," I interrupt. "Hearsay."

"It's preliminary," says Judge Amberlos. "I'll allow it."

"He told us the scene had been secured, and no one had
been allowed inside since the first responders on the scene.
They had talked the judge into coming outside."

"Where was the judge?"

"He was in the backseat of a black-and-white. The EMT's
pulled in right after us and made sure he was okay."

"Was the judge ever a suspect?"

"No, why would he be? He was downtown in his own
courtroom."

"So he was cleared?"

"Of course. So Agent Burns and I told the CSI photographer what we wanted. That was first before anyone entered the scene."

"Describe what you wanted."

"Well, the judge's wife was on her back on the floor with one leg drooped up and over the piano bench. She was wearing a thin gown of some sort and it was open down the front. Her breasts were showing. We were interested in her positioning, number one, and interested in the four bullet holes in her body—three in the chest and one between her eyebrows."

"And what about the judge's son?"

"The judge's son was in his room in his bed. He was taking his afternoon nap as he was only a year old."

"Describe what you saw in his room."

"No mess, no fuss. Sound asleep. I touched his pulse just to be sure.

"What did you do next?"

"I went back into the family room and told the CSI where I wanted extra effort."

"Where was that?"

"I was looking for any distribution of the mother's blood inside the family room."

"Meaning?"

"Meaning put the area under special lights and try to find

footprints that maybe tracked her blood away from where she was sprawled out. We might get a trace on some suspect's shoes, and I wanted to know as much about carpet print as we could find. Plus shoe size."

"What else?"

"Latent prints. Always."

"What else?"

"Well, I wanted all bullets recovered from the walls in case any rounds had passed through her body. Later I would be glad we found the spent bullets and casings because we were able to match those items with the gun we recovered from the apartment of James Lamb."

The jurors look up as one. The murder weapon? In the defendant's possession?

"That was the gun you found during the search and seizure."

"Right. We searched his apartment on information he was dealing drugs with a federal fugitive. Once we found the marijuana we searched the rest of the apartment. We found the gun under the mattress in the only bedroom. Forensics had it matched forty-eight hours later."

It continues, each answer burying the death needle in Lamb's arm. We stop and break for lunch and then we're off and running again. The direct examination continues for another three hours. Fordyce describes the murder scene, the bodies, the ballistics, the autopsy—everything to give the jury the twenty-thousand-foot view of the case. He uses dozens of photographs to indicate what he means by the blood, the wounds, the fatal shots—any and all gore and grief he can describe.

When he is finished, he has just described a blood bath. Which, in fact, it was.

The mother's head wound had bled profusely as part of her skull was blown away; the shots in her chest had missed her heart, and it kept beating long enough to pump blood all around her torso. Bloody footprints led all around the room —forget the special lights to find them; they were everywhere.

Finally, it comes my turn to cross-examine. It is just after four o'clock.

"Mr. Fordyce, were my client's fingerprints found on the gun you say you discovered in his apartment?"

"No."

"Were my client's fingerprints located at the Pennington residence where the murders occurred?"

"No."

"So for all we know, you could have found the gun at the scene of the crime and later planted it in James Lamb's apartment under his mattress, correct?"

"Except that's not what happened, counselor."

"That's what you say. But what proof do you have that it wasn't you moving and hiding the gun?"

"You have my word. And my fingerprints aren't on the gun."

"You were wearing gloves at the murder scene?"

"Yes."

"And you were wearing gloves at the search and seizure in my client's apartment?"

"Yes."

"So your prints wouldn't be expected to be found, would they?"

"No."

"So the absence of any prints from your fingers would be normal, correct?"

"Yes."

"By the way, you've shown the jury the confession that you say my client freely gave. Was that confession captured on video?"

"No."

"But you have video capability in the interrogation room where you obtained the confession, correct?"

"Yes."

"So. Why not video?"

"I didn't think it was necessary. Your client immediately said he did it and would sign a statement. There wasn't any issue about voluntary or not. So we wrote it up, and he signed it. It all happened in about fifteen minutes without video. It happens."

"So you're saying it's common to obtain confessions and not record them on video?"

"Very common."

"Who was in the interrogation room when my client confessed?"

"Me and my partner."

"James Burns?"

"Yes."

"Describe what was said leading up to the confession."

"I reminded Mr. Lamb that we found the gun at his place. We asked him whose gun it was. He said he bought it at pawn. We asked him where and he didn't remember."

"Describe where you were sitting."

"Lamb was at the head of the table, and Burns and I were on each side. Your client wanted a cigarette and we gave him one. There're ashtrays there. We asked him if he needed anything to drink or if he needed to use the restroom and he told us no, that he was fine. So I then said, look, you can't tell us where the gun came from, you have a prior felony conviction, and you're on parole and can't even have a gun, so we know you've violated your parole, and you're going back to prison on that alone. So why not just tell us what happened at the judge's house?"

"What did he say?"

"He takes a deep drag and blows smoke at the ceiling. Then he jerks forward in his chair and says, 'All right. All right. So I went there, and she opened the door, and I pointed the gun at her and forced her back inside. It was the family room. I told her to sit down on the piano bench. Then I shot her. I looked in the rest of the rooms. I was looking for the judge himself.'"

"My client told you that?"

"He sure did."

"So what happened next?"

"There's a computer and printer. Burns types it up and prints it out and your guy signs. That's the sum and substance, counselor. Case closed."

"He was placed under arrest at that time?"

The witness smiles. "Well, I wasn't going to set him free."

"No, I suppose you weren't. What puzzles me is that less than three hours later the FBI Agent In Charge holds a press conference and tells the world that the Pennington case has been solved, that there's been an arrest and a confession. Why so fast to get the story out there?"

"People were scared with a killer running loose, and I guess the government wanted to tell them the case had been cracked."

"You were at the press conference?"

"Me and Burns both. Check the video, counselor."

"You must have been feeling quite proud. Was it then that you leaked the confession to the press? The reason I ask, it showed up on CNN that same night."

"I honestly don't know how that happened. It didn't come from the FBI, that much I can tell you."

"Well, who else would have had it?"

"U.S. Attorney, clerk's office—I don't know. Haven't you investigated, counselor?"

"Apart from the gun, wouldn't it be fair to say that the only connection between my client and the murders is the confession?"

"I suppose."

"You suppose?"

"Yes."

"Well, was his hair found there? Or any fiber from his clothing or apartment?"

"No."

"Did you find blood on any of his shoes?"

"No. We took them all into custody."

"But there was no blood."

"No. Correct."

"Any fingerprints?"

"No."

"Any DNA in any of the sinks, traps, victim's skin, gun?"

"No."

"No prints on the gun and no DNA?"

"No."

"So the only link between James Lamb and the murder is the confession?"

"There was the gun under his mattress."

"Which I believe you planted there, Mr. Fordyce. Which leaves the confession."

"Free and voluntary. It has his signature on it, counselor."

"Can my client even read?"

The special agent looks at me. It is a very fundamental question. His eyes move over to the AUSA, whose head suddenly jerks up. What? His look says. Can he read?

"I assumed he could. He looked at the confession."

I shake my head. "But did you ask him if he could read?"

"No."

"So, for all you know, he didn't even understand what he was signing?"

"His lips moved. That meant he was reading, far as I was concerned."

"His lips moved. And that means to you that he was reading?"

"Yeah. Lots of people's lips move when they read."

"But again, you didn't ask him if he could read?"

"No."

"And you didn't ask him whether he understood what he was reading?"

"No."

"That is all for now, Mr. Fordyce. Your Honor, I reserve the right to call Mr. Fordyce during the defense's case."

"So noted. Ladies and Gentlemen, we'll break here for the day. Please remember the court's admonition that you are not to discuss the case with any person, avoid all newspaper and TV accounts of the case, and immediately report to me if anyone tries to discuss the case with you or in any way influence your vote. Thank you. We're adjourned for the day."

I take the elevator downstairs without talking to the reporters who have crowded into the car with me. They are pushing mikes in my face and repeating the same question: "Is your client prepared to plead guilty if they give him life and waive the death penalty?" That's all they want to know. For myself, I'm wondering the same thing, but the problem is, no one from the U.S. Attorney's Office has made such an offer. This one appears headed to the table with the straps and the silver needle.

Down the sidewalk, a hundred steps is where I find my SUV waiting at the curb. Inside is Marcel Rainford, my investigator, and driver, who has been in attendance in the courtroom for much of the day. He's there to be my eyes and ears to what's going on in the courtroom while I'm busy and can't keep attuned to the general mood, whispers, and strategies between cops and AUSA's, and all the rest of the minutiae that bubbles up.

I climb in the backseat and reach up front. He places two cigarettes and a yellow Bic lighter in my hand. That's my daily limit. They're bad for me and all that, yes, I know, but the stress of criminal law will kill a fifty-five-year-old much faster than a couple of cigarettes. At least, that's my story, and I'm sticking to it.

"Hey, Boss," he says. "That went down hard."

"Yes. We got our ass handed to us in there today."

"Tomorrow's a new day."

He backs out of our slot and puts it in drive. We begin picking our way to my home on the near north side of Chicago.

Marcel has been with me almost fifteen years, and we go back to when we got called up to go to Iraq during Bush Two's misadventure. I served ten months in-country in the JAG Corps; Marcel served two tours as General Dumont's logistics officer—meaning, basically, he was a bodyguard who didn't get to shoot anyone because he was guarding a four-star Army general. We both came out frustrated, but we had gotten to know each other at beer call, and we had hit it off. When we returned to the states, I had a law practice to try and revive, and Marcel had no place to go so he tagged along, got his investigator's license, and began working up criminal cases for me. It worked out well, and here we are.

Like me, Marcel is unmarried. His sad story is a deceased wife with colon cancer. My story is a wife who ran off with a younger man to have a baby late in life. Which leaves the two of us alone to commiserate, something we do at beer call on Wednesday nights. My limit is two beers, and Marcel, who has graduated beyond beer, usually sips a JW on the rocks. I don't know his limit; he's usually ordering a third about the time I'm heading home.

After Sue Ellen had left me, I was filled with shame. So many times she had asked—begged—for a baby and I had refused. It was never the right time, and the money situation was always in flux. Those kinds of excuses. She finally got

tired of waiting and went after the lifeguard at her tennis
club. She ran him to the ground, seduced him, and
convinced him that a forty-five-year-old woman has more to
offer a thirty-two-year-old man than his peers. They started
rendezvousing; she wasn't coming home some nights, and it
was a quick downhill from there. As for me, I haven't been
seeing anyone. There was a fitness trainer at my gym that I
considered asking for coffee until I noticed the fat diamond
on her finger when she took off her workout gloves. That
would have been ugly. Am I lonely? Well, I am alone, and
there are times I am dying for someone to tell about my day.
But that's about the worst it gets. The rest of the time I keep
myself busy defending criminals and planning how to pay
Sue Ellen's alimony.

The alimony is a whole other story.

Marcel drops me at my house, backs his personal car out of
my garage, and we say good night.

I inspect all the rooms inside my house—the inner man
needing someone to talk to and, of course, finding no one
there to listen. I wonder if it will always be this way, this
silent and small when I come home at night.

I fight down the old divorce pain. Grown men embroiled in
life or death trials don't have time for personal angst while
the heat's turned on high. Finally I settle on a TV show
where contestants sing and judges turn their backs on them.
But even this makes me realize I am no different from those
contestants.

Nobody ever said this would be easy.

3

I'm up early the next day, take my four-mile jog, shower, and dress, and then Marcel drives me downtown to my building on LaSalle Street on the Lower Loop, and we park underground. It is eight a.m. when I arrive. Court starts at ten. He goes off in search of fresh bagels while I head upstairs.

I bellow as I enter my office, "Morning, Mrs. Lingscheit! April Fools! This is the perfect day for us to run off together and tell the law to bite it!" Evie Lingscheit, a large-boned Germanic woman, knows I will never leave law because I don't earn enough to run off. She's doubly certain it wouldn't be with her if I did.

She is speaking into her headset and holds up one finger.

I'm not broke, not even close. But I have very high overhead, which is all about my ex-wife's alimony. A bellicose divorce judge gave Sue Ellen everything she asked for, including fun money of $7500 per month. A week later he told my lawyer, at a Bar Association social, he did it because he loves cheerleaders. How he knew Sue Ellen had been a cheerleader on the Longhorns' spirit line, I'll never know. But he gave her enough alimony that she'll never have to work again—as long as she remains unmarried. Sue Ellen has since bedded but not wedded three suitors that I know about. RAH-RAH-SIS-BOOM-BAH!

"No calls, no drop-ins," I tell Mrs. Lingscheit as I lunge past her desk.

Mrs. Lingscheit responds to me, "Good morning, Michael."

She points behind me.

My heart falls. Sue Ellen Gresham is sitting in our small waiting area with the younger man who stole her away from me.

They are all smiles.

"Good grief," I manage, "the smiling couple."

"We need to see you, Michael," my ex- says. She looks ten years younger since our divorce. "Your drop-ins beat you here."

"Funny lady," I shake my head.

"How are you sir," says the boy scout. I don't respond. I have no clue how to speak to the kid who wrecked my marriage. So I turn back to Evie.

"Ten minutes first," I tell Mrs. Lingscheit, holding up all fingers. She nods and my ex- puts her nose in the air, but there is tacit agreement. Ten minutes is fair; otherwise, it's an ambush, as they are unscheduled drop-ins.

"Ten minutes," I smile at Sue Ellen and close my office door behind me. My phone message light is blinking. I hit PLAY.

The voice of Arnie, my older brother, gushes over the line, "Michael, oh boy oh boy have I got news for you! I've met this guru—granted she's only nineteen—but the things she knows about me! I haven't even said a word, and she's given me my entire history! How's she do it, Michael? It's a miracle. And she has predictions and warnings for me. Anyway, we're at a hotel on Wacker that shall remain nameless and we are passing certain items back and forth, and we are inhaling. I was calling to say I won't be able to make lunch today because I have a deposition and my paralegal tells me the other lawyers have voted to have lunch catered, so we don't have to break. I'm telling you, Michael, this girl—her name is Esmeralda—she's going for her nursing degree by day and meeting men at night to pay her tuition. We're lucky we had our parents back in the day, Michael because tuition has gone through the roof. Did you know I was high pain-tolerant, Michael? Esmeralda has helped me see that. Anyway, Michael, I might not need Dr. Allington anymore because Esmeralda looked over my paperwork and—"

The recording runs out, and I am left dangling. But only for a moment. When Arnie refuses to take his meds, this is the kind of call I get. The other type of call I get will be from his partners at his law firm begging me to help control my brother. What can I do? Arnie's actual diagnosis depends on which psychiatrist he is seeing. Sometimes he is bipolar, and that explains his mania. Other times he is agoraphobic, and that explains his refusal to leave his apartment for days, hanging out in his pajamas and refusing to shower. Other times he is suffering from a dissociative disorder that explains the new personality my brother suddenly has speaking for him. I don't know; maybe he's all three. My mother is in a nursing home, and my father is long dead and there are no other siblings, so Arnie falls to me. Which is fine; truth be told, I all but worship my brother. One day, science will solve the mysteries of Arnie's psychology, but it hasn't done so yet.

I walk to my desk and sit down slowly. Having received the phone call, I gird myself for the follow-on bizarre behavior that is sure to come when he's refusing to medicate. Something is coming. Storm clouds are forming on the horizon.

~

I BUSY MYSELF with other calls, return two, and just allow Sue Ellen and her playmate to generally cool their heels. Then my curiosity gets the better of me, and I buzz Evie. "Send them in."

Sue Ellen enters my office with a haughty flourish. She is wearing a yellow dress with red roses in honor of this spring day. A thin white cardigan takes away the nip in the morning air. Her hair is yellow and goes well with the dress, and she is wearing platform heels that display just how beautiful a woman's legs can be. Sue Ellen has a fantastic body, a great smile (her dad is a dentist), and the personality of a homecoming queen. She was a runner-up in the Miss Texas pageant, where her talent was ragtime piano. Tales of how much the Phi Delt men loved her piano playing in college plagued me through our time together. Sue Ellen was always very quick to share her body. Thank goodness I no longer have to wrestle those demons.

Young Stuff (I refuse to learn his real name) brings up the

rear, sitting beside Sue Ellen as she pats the chair next to hers, indicating her preference for his roost.

"So, Michael," she begins, "how have you been? You're looking good!"

"Thanks, I feel good."

"Well, that's just wonderful!"

"Except for the first of the month when I have to write your child support check."

"Child support?"

"Well, in the paperwork it's actually called 'alimony.' But we don't need to kid ourselves about that."

She begins to frown, thinks better of it, and tilts her head at me. "I do thank you for keeping your promise. You always were a man of your word. That's what I'm hoping Eddie can learn from you. Consistency."

Consistency. She says it like it's a code word capable of sending men to war. What she really means, though, is that I didn't file an appeal from our divorce. I didn't, and it's too late now. I took it like a man. Mainly because I was so damn hurt by her betrayal of me with Young Stuff that I couldn't gather the energy I needed to write the appeal. It just wasn't there. But now my IRA is almost depleted and paying her every month is all but impossible. She doesn't know that. Yet.

"Well, Sue Ellen, I just can't stand the suspense. What can I do for you?"

She leans forward. "You're going to like this, Michael."

"That would be good."

"We want to have a baby."

My first reaction is predictable; I tip-toed around having a baby with her when she was mine—much to my later regret; I'm all but shut down before she even launches into her spiel.

"A baby? You're forty-five, Sue Ellen. Do you mean you want to adopt?"

"Eddie is only thirty-two. He wants his own family of his own children. Not adopted children. His own."

"So. What would my role be in your conception? The very fact you're here telling me this means you need something from me. It's not high-IQ sperm you're after, is it?" I immediately regret it but my feelings are hurt, damn it. If Sue Ellen's having a baby it should be with me.

"I went to a fertility doctor. Here's the process. Eddie's sperm goes to the laboratory, and they mix it with some younger woman's eggs. The eggs are then implanted inside of me. There are lots of shots and growth hormones to make me ready to accept the implant and grow it."

"Do you really want growth hormones? Don't those cause cancer?"

"There is a risk with everything, silly. You took a risk when you drove to work. How did you know you wouldn't get side-swiped and die? You didn't. But you took the risk. Well, that's how I feel. I don't think my body is going to sideswipe me if I inject it. Instead, I think it will love me back and give us a baby. Our own family."

"Again, what's my role?"

"We're short on funds."

"You need money from me?"

"I'm hoping you can advance one year of alimony payments in a lump sum."

"That's ninety thousand dollars. One, I don't have it. Two, even if I did, I wouldn't do it. It's not a good investment for me."

She leans forward and places her elbows on my desk. She points a long, enameled fingernail at me.

"That is where you are wrong. It's the best investment you'll ever make, Michael. Because if you do this one thing, I'll sign an order for the judge saying you never have to pay me another dime."

I am stunned. This is almost too good to be true. And I know in a flash that I will do it. I don't have the money, I don't know how to get the money, but I will get it. This, I will do, and then I'm free! Seriously? I will jump through rings of fire to get this chance. But I keep my cool.

"Well, it's interesting," I say. "It deserves some thought. Can you give me a few days?"

"We need the money by the first. That's four weeks. If we can't get it by then, I'm putting the house on the market, and I won't ever speak to you again if I have to sell our"— meaning hers and my—"house."

"You're threatening me that you'll never come here again to borrow money from me?"

"I'm threatening you that I'll never marry. You'll still be paying me when you're eighty-five and I'm seventy-five. That's a solemn promise, Michael."

"Well, there is that," I say. "Okay, I'll talk to my bank. I'll see if they'll give me a home-equity line of credit. If they will, we'll meet and talk and go over an order for the judge. If they don't, I will try elsewhere, but that is very iffy. My best chance is Bank of America."

"Michael," she purrs, "I can always count on you, can't I? You're still trying to make my life good."

"Why would I want your life to be anything else but good? Of course, I'll try."

Not to mention I just might wind up free of you and free of the millstone around my neck.

Two sharp knocks on my door and Mrs. Lingscheit comes bustling in.

"Sorry to interrupt. Michael. We need to talk immediately."

"All right," says Sue Ellen, "we're out of here. I'll expect to hear from you in the next week or so, Michael."

Young Stud reaches across the desk to shake my hand. Grudgingly I accept. His hand is warm and sweaty. Just as I hoped.

When we are alone, Mrs. Lingscheit turns to me and begins.

"Arnie is in trouble. He's at the Willis Tower. Here's the address. He's supposed to be in a deposition. He showed up in handcuffs."

"Whoa up, woman. How do we know this?"

"Sam Shaw called. He's furious."

Sam Shaw is the managing partner of Arnie's law firm. I am already calculating. Court doesn't begin until ten this morning as the judge has other cases to process between nine and ten o'clock. I might have time to take care of this before then.

I throw on my blazer and hit the door.

It's faster to walk than grab a cab, so I make my way from LaSalle down to Wacker and head north to the Willis Tower. As I walk, I call Sam. He updates me: another attorney on the scene called him and gave us what happened. He describes the event. I have to ask him to repeat it.

As the Willis Tower elevator doors part, I take a deep breath.

Cleaning up after Arnie is never fun.

4

Ever since we were playing Tonka trucks, my brother has been a study in spotty mental hygiene. I am younger than him by five years and have followed his career in and out of the offices of mental health professionals for almost fifty years. His inner life seesaws between mania and psychosis; he takes meds for these things only because his outer life goes to hell the minute he stops and it frightens him. Until it doesn't. Like me, he is a lawyer. He runs the litigation group at Eden Shaw Robles, a 400 lawyer firm in downtown Chicago.

According to Sam Shaw, Arnie arrived at the depo room handcuffed to a teenage girl all of nineteen years old. She was thought to be a prostitute. There was a scuffle at the door. The girl tried to pull away so she wouldn't have to go inside. Arnie outweighed her by a good hundred pounds, so he won the moment and dragged her inside.

Everyone stared. She was wearing black toreador pants, mukluks, a tank top, and had one arm through a wind-breaker. The arm with the handcuffed hand couldn't go through the windbreaker, so the windbreaker was hanging half off and half on. Arnie was decked out in a rumpled suit with his jacket likewise at half mast.

"Hell of a night," Arnie said as he breezed past the knot of lawyers at the near end of the conference table. With all possible aplomb, he strode to the far end of the room. Our source says that Arnie was pulled up short when the girl suddenly plopped in the chair at the head of the table. My brother's eyes were dilated, and his speech was staccato. "Whatcha-gonna-do-with-that?" he shouted at his cuff-mate, who had sourced a black mascara applicator and was attempting to sharpen her appearance.

Juan Carlos Munoz Perez, the second wealthiest man in Mexico and the CEO of MexTel, picked just that moment to enter the deposition room. This was Arnie's client. He effected a grand entry, resplendent in a silk three-piece. He was accompanied by two bodyguards lurking behind sunglasses. He looked neither right nor left but proceeded along the table to take his place beside his lawyer—my brother—only to find his seat *ocupado* by the young lady of the streets. Perez's eyebrows shot up, and he hissed, "*¡Salir de mi silla, puta!*"

"She can't get out of your chair, *Señor* Perez. She's-she's-she's-with me! Come sit on my right."

Perez leaned to his attorney's ear and yelped loud enough that everyone heard, "Who is this *puta*?"

"Someone I met last night. It's a long story and shouldn't concern you. My staff is on the way with a key. Maryanne?" Maryanne, Arnie's paralegal, had frozen up once she realized her boss was handcuffed to the girl undergoing makeup reconstitution.

"Sir?"

"Call Georgia. Ask her where the hell the key is!"

"Yes, Mr. Gresham. Right away."

Maryanne headed for the building lobby where she could get cell service. She called Sam; Sam called my office, and here I am to save my brother from himself.

He is still sitting at the head of the table when I arrive. His left arm is resting beside the teenager's arm. With her free hand, she attacks her eyebrows with silver tweezers. The other attorneys are mostly silent in the presence of the Mexicans, while others are scattered up and down the hallway, phones stuck in their ears. Arnie is staring at the ceiling, distancing himself from the scene he has created. The Mexican CEO is at Arnie's right, arms folded, eyes closed, drumming the fingers of his right hand on the table. He smacks his lips and shakes his head. "*Puto culo*," he mutters, "*¡Pendejos!*" His bodyguards are focused on everyone's every move, chilling all ordinary deposition chit-chat.

I speak enough gutter Spanish to know this is one miserably unhappy client.

"Arnie," I say, and he lowers his eyes. They look like glazed icing.

"Michael!"

"Arnie, I need to speak with you outside."

"Did you bring the key, Michael?"

He lifts the handcuffs to show me in case I missed.

"Please, come on outside."

We retreat to the lobby end of the hallway, Arnie and me, and his cuff mate, standing just inside the revolving outside door. She stands off to the side and gives me a long, edgy look. I want to backhand her but of course, that's a jailable offense. Besides, none of this is her fault; this is all Arnie.

"Could you pretend not to listen?" I ask her.

She turns her head away, popping her gum.

"Arnie, you flushed your meds, didn't you?"

"Oh, Michael, this girl has helped me see things about myself I never realized before. All that money for doctors and medications and groups? Totally unnecessary. Did you know in high school I never had one date? All those times I told mom and dad I had a date I didn't really. I was going out alone to meet up with other geeks like me from the Latin club, and we would go to someone's house and play video games. Did I ever tell you how lonely I was? Well, Esmeralda says I am a visionary, that I have an ancient soul. That I have this uncanny ability to see things for what they really are, like Neo in The Matrix after he takes the green pill. Or was it the red pill? I forget."

"He had the choice of a blue pill or a red pill," says Esmeralda. "The blue pill, the story ends. The red pill, he gets to see how deep the rabbit hole goes."

"And he took the red pill," Arnie asserts. "Oh, Michael, I want that red pill! The things I've seen in the last twenty-four hours. I have no business practicing law. It is time for me to rehab my poor life."

I can't hold back. This kind of talk makes me crazy. "That's called abandonment of client, Arnie. Lawyers get disbarred for abandoning clients. Maybe we should talk to Sam Shaw and see about getting you some senior help assigned to the case. Someone to help until—"

"You're not following me, Michael! I walk away now and never look back!"

"No! I'm going to continue this deposition, and we're going to talk to Sam."

"NO-NO-NO-NO-NO! Michael, you aren't listening!"

"I am listening, and I believe you. But there's a way to make this work. We can't just walk out. Medications, okay?"

I've helped abate my brother's frolics-and-detours over the years. This train jumps the track every twelve months or so. The secret is to keep him close by while you move him along toward your goal.

"Medications are a form of spirituality," I whisper. I wink at him. He winks right back. Now we're co-conspirators; progress is possible.

"If you say so, Michael. But Esmeralda is coming with me."

"Wait here, Arnie, I'm going back in and make the announcement on the record. We're continuing."

"NO-NO-NO-NO-NO, NO continuance! Get Sam to send someone over to take my place. We're going to fly out today, Michael."

I look at Esmeralda. She shrugs and smiles.

"Wait here. Don't move a muscle!"

Back into the depo room, I hustle. "All right, everyone, we're on the record. I'm Arnold Gresham's brother, Michael, and I'm sorry to inform you Arnold is sick, and we're going to have to continue today's deposition."

Pandemonium. Everyone is pissed and promising to seek sanctions against Arnie, his client, and his firm. Perez is fuming, and his bodyguards are ready to pounce on someone, anyone.

Whatever; I return to the lobby and discover Arnie and Esmeralda have left. A panicky feeling hits me; I check outside, where I see him standing on the sidewalk, sharing a joint back and forth. Illinois doesn't have a pot-for-personal-use law. We jail people for possession. I make a break for the door.

"Ditch the joint!" I scream at my brother, and his teenage seer responds by casually flicking it to the sidewalk. I grind it beneath my shoe, scraping it to a black ash, and walk to the curb and start flagging for a taxi.

On the taxi ride back to Arnie's firm in the Congress Building I call Sam Shaw for the second time that morning and advise him to clear the decks, that we've had another meltdown.

"Not this time, Michael," he spits at me over the phone. "The partners aren't going through this again. He's your brother; you make this work!"

"We need to work together, Sam. He needs a senior member onboard."

"He needs to take his goddamn medications, Michael!"

"Of course, he does."

"You tell the bastard we're calling his home mortgage, and he can sleep on the streets!"

"I'll tell him."

We stop on a red. I turn to Arnie to ask him about his mortgage, and he suddenly pops open his door and drags Esmeralda into the street. They dash for the sidewalk. She turns to wave at me as they disappear into a Walgreen's.

ATM, I'm guessing.

5

"No," I cry, but the light changes and we are moving.

I slam my hand against the backseat, crying, "NO NO NO NO NO!"

The cabby's eyes catch mine in the rearview. He shakes his head and continues speaking into his cell phone.

At the Congress building, I step out and pass a five to the driver. He doesn't acknowledge me, of course, just weaves off into the crawl of eastbound traffic.

Sam Shaw hustles me into Arnie's office and shuts the door.

"What the fuck, Michael?" he growls at me.

"Hey, I don't work for you. What the fuck yourself!"

"All right. Let me calm down."

"Yes, that would be good."

"Your brother is representing MexTel. Juan Perez is Carlos

Slim's CEO. All Mexican telephone conversations go through his office. He left the depo in a rage, and his thugs raced him over here. He's down the hall in my office, threatening our firm with a malpractice lawsuit. I'm not exaggerating about how important this man and MexTel are to this firm. Your brother has represented these people for three years on this one case. We've billed over twenty million dollars in fees; this represents almost five percent of our total billables. That's enough to pay the bonus of every partner in our firm three years running. Are you beginning to get a feel for the case, Michael?"

"I'm sure it's his meds, Sam. We need to track him down and—"

"Track him down? I thought you were bringing him."

"I was. He jumped out of the cab."

"And what the hell is this about handcuffs and a young woman. Is that even true?"

"With my own eyes, Sam. This is a classic Arnie meltdown, and we can have him back in his office in forty-eight hours if you'll just give me some help tracking him down and getting him back to his condo."

"How can I help? You need the FBI for this. Not a building full of civil litigators."

"We need to cover the airports. He said something about flying out."

"Where was it left with everyone at the depo?"

"Well, I went on the record and explained that Arnold was sick and wouldn't be able to represent his client today. They were pissed and threats were made. You need to get someone on the horn with every one of those folks and soothe ruffled feathers. Someone with some charm."

"I'm thinking Melinda Settlers. Are you still dating her, incidentally?"

"No. That was months ago, Sam. One time."

"Okay, look. I'm going to turn you over to our head investigator. He can set up the search. But I need you on standby for when we track him down. You have to take the lead with him, Michael. He doesn't listen to anyone else. Not on this planet, at least."

"Of course, I will. But for right now I've got to get back to Judge Amberlos's court. Trial begins in twenty-five minutes."

"Leave your cell number with the desk out front, please."

There is nothing else to say.

My brother has probably crashed and burned here for the last time. Unless I can pump new life into him and get him back on track in the next forty-eight. That just might squeeze him through the tiny window of opportunity to salvage his career that right now is all but closed.

"Later," I tell Sam.

We shake on it. But then he gives me a terrible look, the desperate face of a cornered brute.

That's how guys in 400 lawyer firms do things with little guys like me.

6

80-89 IQ.

This is the I.Q. range most associated with violence. Most violent crime is committed by males from this range. The causal mechanism between crime and below-average I.Q. is that lower I.Q. levels inherently tend to go with having less impulse control, being less able to delay gratification, being less able to comprehend moral principles like the Golden Rule, and being overstrained by the cognitive demands of society.

IQ and Real Life: The Most Dangerous Slot, P.J. Cooper, M.D., *Psychology Today, March 2001*

I arrive at the Everett Dirksen Court Building twenty minutes later. Downstairs is a familiar cafeteria where I can crawl off alone and steal a few minutes in which I just might consider my own life and time. I check my watch. 9:50 a.m. The line is empty, so I score a quick black coffee and a plain cake donut. Both are ingested by 9:55. I roll around in my head the notion of being free of Sue Ellen. That is one task I will definitely take on. I call Evie. Get me an appointment with my mortgage rep at Bank of America, I tell her, ASAP. She confirms.

I am on my way upstairs and who should I meet head-on as he's leaving the restroom but Judge Pennington himself. We haven't spoken since the last time I appeared before him, which was six months ago before I took the Lamb case. I know he recognizes me, and I know he sees me but still he looks right through me. "Morning, Judge," I say and open the door to the courtroom to allow him to pass through. "How could you?" he says through gritted teeth as he passes me by, entering the courtroom ahead of me. He heads for his saved seat directly behind the Assistant U.S. Attorney. I take my seat at counsel table, and sixty seconds later Judge Amberlos enters from his chambers' door. He is all black robes, red eyes, and hands that shake as he presses the TALK button on his desk microphone. "Bailiff, please bring in the jury."

The jury returns and quietly take their assigned seats. They look at the judge. One woman breaks off and looks across directly at me. She purses her lips and shakes her head. "How could you?" her look says.

The judge nods at Bob LaGuardia. The TV camera swings from its focus on the American flag and finds the AUSA, who stands to speak.

"The government calls Kimberly Clements."

The witness is sworn and seated. She is a large-boned, intelligent-looking woman wearing black slacks and a green blazer with gold buttons. She gives the jury an FBI Academy nod and smile and looks back to the Assistant U.S. Attorney.

LaGuardia begins. "How are you employed?"

"I'm a forensic specialist with FBI's Evidence Response Team."

"How long have you had that job?"

"Five years."

"What do you do in that capacity?"

"Our job is to respond to crime scenes as well as process evidence that is sent to us. Make photo arrays and develop latent prints—that sort of thing."

"Do you have any specialized training?"

"I have a bachelor's degree in biology. I have a master's in forensic molecular biology. I have taken a number of courses in advanced forensic science."

"Directing your attention to November second, twenty-fourteen, were you told to respond to a crime scene in the eleven hundred block of North Decansis in Chicago, Illinois?"

"Yes, I was."

"What did you do when you first arrived?"

"The first aspect of our job is to document everything as we find it. So I photographed the crime scene as I found it. Outside and inside. Then the detectives had special shots for me to take so I did those too."

"Then what did you do?"

"I made a videotape of the scene. Then I called in our homicide reconstruction unit to assist me in preparing a sketch of the scene. After that, I proceeded to search the scene."

"What were you searching for?"

"Any evidence of what happened and any evidence that might have been left behind by the perpetrator."

"Tell us about gunshot searches."

"I was looking for expended rounds from a firearm, any kind of fragments from a bullet that may have, you know, hit somewhere else and fragmented or may have exited the victim's body. Along with that, just any, you know, tire marks, shoe impressions, anything like that."

"What if anything did you find?"

"Bullet fragments, cartridge casings, shoe impressions in the carpet and outside on the sidewalk—very slight, toe and heel from tracked blood. Also tire marks on the driveway."

As the direct-examination proceeds, all lead fragments, bullet casings, video, stills, and drawings are marked and admitted into evidence without objection from me. This is typical, necessary forensic testimony that does nothing to convict my client.

But maybe it can help to exonerate him.

Then it's my turn to cross-examine. This CSI has spoken to me previously when I went to the crime lab and bought her lunch so we could talk. She knew better than to speak to me and so I nibbled around the edges of her workup. In this manner, I got everything I needed. So today I am ready for her—thanks to the assistance she gave me over tuna sandwiches and potato chips.

"Ms. Clements, were you able to determine shoe size from the heel-toe prints you found in blood?"

"I was."

"Tell us the size, please."

"The subject wore a size thirteen."

"How did you determine that."

"I measured the bloody prints with a ruler.

"And did you examine the shoes taken from my client's closet in his apartment pursuant to the search warrant?"

"I did."

"What were those sizes?"

"All tens, except a pair of flip-flops and they were just marked medium."

"Did you bring those shoes with you today pursuant to my subpoena?"

"Yes, I did."

The shoes are marked and admitted without objection. I break off then, for I know what's coming.

LaGuardia asks, on re-direct, "Ms. Clements, the defendant's size might be ten, but that doesn't mean he was wearing a ten on the day he killed the victims, does it?"

"No, it doesn't."

"That is is all."

Then it is my turn again.

"How many times in your five years have you identified cases where a defendant was wearing a shoe size other than his or her normal size?"

"Never."

"Now, please review all notes, drawings, diagrams, reports, and photographs and then look over and tell the jury what items connect my client, Mr. Lamb, to the murder scene."

"I can already tell you."

"Please proceed."

"Nothing I'm aware of connects him."

"No DNA?"

"No."

"No fingerprints?"

"No."

"Nothing at all?"

"Nothing."

"That is all, Your Honor."

The witness is excused.

I look around, trying to discern who the state's next witness might be. Again, Judge Pennington's eyes lock on me. "How could you?" they say.

A skinny man with a ragged beard enters the courtroom, a U.S. Marshal on either side of him. He is dressed in shiny slacks and an open-throated wine red shirt. There is a yellow and green toucan tat on his neck and his eyes are rheumy, fighting to focus on a room larger than the prison cell where he's apparently spent his last decade. I can guess who he is as he was listed in the state's disclosure of its witnesses.

My client squirms in the seat beside me when he sees the man cross in front of him on his way to the witness stand.

"Max Kittredge," he mutters to me.

I nod. Of course, it is. Lamb's cell mate from Marion, one of the most notorious of all federal prisons. Lamb and Kittredge doubled up in a nine by twelve for several years, sharing every thought, every feeling during all those sunless days and starless nights. I have no doubt why he's here, and I sit back, waiting to get kicked in the groin by this opportunist.

After he tells the jury his name, his address (U.S. Penitentiary, Marion, Illinois) and his age, Kittredge is asked why he is in prison.

"For stabbing a little girl."

"For stabbing her?"

"Well, she died, actually."

"She died because you stabbed her?"

"Yes."

"How long have you been in prison?"

"Fourteen years, six months, twenty-five days plus change."

The Assistant U.S. Attorney, standing at the lectern, drops his head to his notes.

"While you have been incarcerated there, did you at one time share a cell with James Joseph Lamb?"

"Yes."

"Do you see Mr. Lamb in the courtroom today?"

"Yes."

"Please point him out."

The witness points at my client.

"Let the record reflect the witness has pointed out the defendant," says the AUSA.

"So noted," says Judge Amberlos.

"While sharing that cell, did you and Lamb ever discuss why he was in prison?'

"Yes."

"Why was he in?"

"He told me he was there for stabbing a U.S. Marshal."

"So you two were both in for stabbing someone?"

"Evidently."

"Did you and Mr. Lamb ever discuss the judge who sentenced Lamb to prison?"

"Yes."

"Do you know his name?"

"Judge something Feathertop."

"Would Francis Pennington ring a bell?"

"That was it," says Kittredge, pumping his fist up and down. "That was it!"

"Did Mr. Lamb ever say he had any animosity toward Judge Pennington."

"No. He only said he would like to kill the guy."

LaGuardia looks at the jury. Their looks say they understand his six-year-old's command of the King's English.

"Mr. Lamb said he would like to kill Judge Pennington?"

"Just about every day. Until I was sick of hearing about it."

"Did he ever talk about murdering the judge's wife?"

"Nope. Not a word about that. Just the judge."

The prosecutor turns the witness over to me.

"Mr. Kittredge, who did you say you wanted to murder?"

"What?"

"Well, when you and Mr. Lamb were discussing killing people on the outside, who was it you wanted to kill?"

"My ex and my dad."

"Anyone else?"

"No."

"Did you ever, in fact, kill them?"

"I ain't been out."

"Do you think you'll kill them when you get out?"

"I don't know. I guess I hope I don't."

"You guess?"

"Yessir. I surely hope I don't, or I'm bang right back in the hoosegow."

"I see. Now, what special favors has the government promised you to come into court and say these things today?"

"Special favors?"

"You know, like shortening your remaining time in prison."

"Oh, that. You see, I come up for parole in nine months. They said I could speed my parole to next month if I would testify."

"So they're moving your parole up by eight months?"

"Yessir."

"Is that why you came into court and said these things about your old cell mate?"

He looks at Lamb. Lamb returns the look. Kittredge breaks off eye contact.

"Yessir. I was hoping to get out early."

"So that's why you said these things."

"Yes."

"Did you ever think Mr. Lamb was actually going to kill the judge?"

"Yes. No. I don't know. Everybody in Marion talks shit. You know how it is."

"All right. Have you spoken with Mr. Lamb since he got out on parole?"

"Nossir."

"That is all, Your Honor."

"Mr. Kittredge," LaGuardia says without waiting, "have you told us anything today that wasn't true?"

"Nossir."

"So even though you might get some help with the parole hearing date, you're not just lying to make that happen?"

"Why would I do that?"

"To save eight months?"

"No, eight months ain't shit. I can sleep for eight months. No, I ain't lying."

"That is all, Your Honor."

The witness is excused, and the U.S. Marshals attach them-selves to him again before he can walk out through the gate. The trio disappears through the outer courtroom doors.

That wasn't so bad; I'm thinking. The usual tat-rat. Happens in all cases where there's been even just one day of incarcer-ation. The prosecutors always bring in a rat with the whole confession. Never fails.

We break for lunch, and the deputies prepare Lamb to eat at counsel table. Marcel and I meet out front on the sidewalk and decide to head back south to an Arby's. We pull in, and order and Marcel stirs his Coke with his straw.

"Damnedest thing," he says to me.

"What's that?"

"Your brother. What you told me about him taking off with some young señorita."

"Yes. Those were the good old days. But they ended when we were nineteen, for the love of god."

"Your next witness is Special Agent Burns."

"James O. Burns."

"Yeppers. What's he got to add that Fordyce didn't already tell us three different ways?"

"Time will tell. You talk to Evie lately?"

He looks crossly at me. "What if I did?"

"Nothing. I mean sure, she's my secretary, but in answer to your question this morning, would I give a damn if you ask her out? Actually, I think it would be good for both of you."

"Really? You wouldn't pitch a hissy?"

"No. We're all adults. If I can put up with your foul moods I suppose she can too."

"Sorry if I got a little miffed this morning. I thought you didn't want me asking her out."

I spread my hands and shrug.

"Each to his own."

~

IT IS THE AFTERNOON SESSION, and Agent Burns has just advised the jury of his role in the case, pretty much going back over ground Agent Fordyce has already covered. I'm fighting to stay awake after the huge roast beef sandwich and chocolate shake I downed at lunch. I know better, but I did it anyway.

My ears perk up. We're onto new ground here.

"Tell us about the arrest of James Lamb."

"Like I said, we arrested him after we searched his apartment and Special Agent Fordyce found the gun under the mattress."

"What were you arresting him for? You didn't know the gun had been used in the commission of a crime at that point, did you?"

"Actually, we did. See, he was out on parole, and one condition of parole is that the parolee shall not possess a firearm. Hiding a gun under your mattress is being in possession of a firearm. So he had violated his parole, which is the same thing as a crime. Or maybe it's not, but either way, he had to be arrested until the prosecutors decided if they would violate him or not."

"Did they violate him?"

"No. We got the report back on the gun—it matched the murder weapon in the Pennington case—they filed murder not parole. So, here we are."

"When you arrested Lamb that night, did he cooperate?"

"No, sir. He was on speed."

"Describe that."

"Talking a hundred miles an hour, couldn't sit still, ideas coming and going through his head like comets."

"What happened next?"

"Agent Fordyce brings out the gun and nods at Lamb. I ask him to stand and put his hands behind his back. He asks why, and I tell him we need to go downtown and ask him some questions. He immediately extends his hand toward me and pushes me back. There's a coffee table there, and I trip and hit the floor. Lamb's laughing, which is irritating. But still, I get up to my feet and ask him again. Very nicely, hands behind your back. He reaches for me again and this time, I'm ready. I carry a lead-filled sap in my coat pocket. I whip it out and rap him a good one across the mouth. I was aiming for his nose—that's where the blood spurts always stop them cold. But I got his mouth instead. Broke off four teeth, I think it was. But he immediately bends over and turns his back to me, hands behind for cuffing. I throw the cuffs on him, and we take him down to our ride. That's exactly what happened."

Bob LaGuardia studies his notes, reviews the Activity Reports from the agents, and tells the judge he's concluded his direct examination of the witness. Now it's my turn.

"Mr. Burns."

"Special Agent Burns, sir."

"What, your first name is 'special'?"

"My title is Special Agent."

"All right, Mr. Burns."

"Your Honor," LaGuardia starts to complain.

"'Mister' and last names are sufficient in this courtroom," the judge tells the witness. "Please proceed with your examination, Mr. Gresham."

"Mr. Burns, you're saying, I take it, the defendant deserved to have his teeth knocked out?"

"No, I'm saying he was resisting arrest. That's why I rapped him."

"Actually, you didn't say he was resisting arrest. You said, and I wrote it down word-for-word, 'He reaches for me again,' and I'm wondering why you assumed his mere reaching toward you called for a sap across the teeth. What's that sap weigh, about one pound?"

"About that."

"And in your book, reaching out to you is the same as resisting arrest?"

"It sure looked that way. The top of that coffee table was glass, and I was afraid he was trying to shove me down on it."

"But you said he was reaching. You didn't say he was shoving."

"Reaching, shoving: what's the difference?"

"Well, one might be to hold out his hands to surrender to the cuffs, the other might be to push you down on the coffee table. The truth is, you don't know whether he was surrendering or he was resisting by the mere act of extending his arm, do you?"

"I could see in his eyes he was coming for me. He was speeding."

"Did he tell you he had taken a methamphetamine?"

"No, but I know the signs."

"So a person who's taken a meth pill and extends a hand toward you deserves to be hit in the mouth with a pound of lead?"

"That isn't at all what happened."

"No? But that's what you just told the jury. So there was more you haven't told us about?"

"I spent eight years on the streets. I know when someone is attacking and when they're only surrendering. That's all I can tell you."

"So let me see if I understand you. My client lost his teeth because he was resisting arrest, correct?"

"That's correct."

"Now you're sure this didn't happen down at the police station when he refused to confess to you?"

There's a momentary pause, slight, but you felt it.

"No, it didn't happen down at the station. It happened in his apartment. Just like I said."

"That will be all, Mr. Burns, thank you."

The AUSA then calls Beulah Wetmore, secretary to Judge Francis Pennington. Her sole reason for testifying, it turns out, is to establish the foundation for the admission into evidence of a letter allegedly written by James Joseph Lamb to Judge Pennington while Lamb was in prison for stabbing the U.S. Marshal. I have seen the letter before and Lamb told me he had written no such letter, so I offered to have

the handwriting analyzed and then he came clean and said
that yes, he wrote the letter but when he did it he was under
the influence of some drug they were putting in all of the
prisoners' food. Highly unlikely, I thought and still think so
today. The old saltpeter tales of chemical castration. Were
they ever true? Damned if I know.

She finishes up her testimony and the AUSA moves the
letter into evidence. I object on the grounds the handwriting
hasn't been validated as my client's handwriting; LaGuardia
says he's calling a handwriting expert next to validate it. I
withdraw my objection, stipulate that it's Lamb's handwriting, and the letter comes into evidence. It is passed around
to the jury, which eats up another half hour. By the time
they are finished reading, it is half past four and LaGuardia
says he has just one more witness but he'd rather wait until
in the morning to begin. I don't have any problem with it
because I believe I know what's coming and that would be
Judge Pennington, who's going to tell one hell of a horror
story about his dead wife when he got home and found her
that terrible day. Those are images I'd rather the jury not
take with them tonight, so I agree to call it a day.

We are adjourned.

I walk off the elevator on my floor, hit the restroom, and head for my office.

Even as I approach the door, I don't have a great feeling. My sixth sense is kicking in.

As I pass through the door to my office, I see why.

Four Latinos wearing expensive suits and gold watches are waiting impatiently to see me. I shoot a look at Mrs. Lingscheit, who only shrugs and raises her eyebrows.

I stop and give them a look. They must all buy their hair product from the same lube shop.

"And you are?" I ask, looking from face to face.

"Mr. Gresham, I am Roberto Aguilar, and I am a lawyer from Mexico City. This gentleman on my left is Juan Carlos Munoz Perez, the CEO of MexTel. MexTel provides ninety-nine percent of the communications services in Latin America."

I nod and consider my next move. I actually intend to hurry on over to the U.S. Attorney's office, but I've got a very strong feeling this is more about Arnie, and I need to deal with it for his sake. I hold up one finger and turn to Mrs. Lingscheit.

"Tell the Schmidts I'm busy for about ten minutes when they get here? Then interrupt me."

She understands, because there are no Schmidts. "I will."

I turn back to my visitors.

"Gentlemen?" I say, raising my arm and inviting them into my office, "Please follow me."

As a unit, they stand and follow into my lair. Four chairs, four visitors. Mrs. L closes the door behind us.

"All right," I say as I remove my blazer and hang it on the back of my chair. "What can I do for you gents?"

Again, Aguilar speaks. "Your brother is Arnold Gresham, and he has been representing MexTel for several years now. It is a case of groundwater pollution that several thousand people are claiming MexTel should be responsible for. There are billions of pesos at stake. At a twenty-five to one rate of exchange, generally speaking, that makes this a billion dollar case in U.S. dollars."

I nod appreciatively. "Go on. How can I help?"

"Señor Perez tells me you came to the deposition this morning and took your brother away. He was handcuffed to a young lady. We have spoken to Mr. Sam Shaw at your brother's firm and we have somewhat of a clearer understanding what that was all about. But at this moment, we are left with our—as you Americans would put it—our ass hanging out. Sorry to be so blunt, but there you are. Your brother's got our entire case up here"—he touches his head with his finger—"and we cannot afford to lose him off the case. Mr. Shaw agreed. Mr. Shaw will have the second-in-line senior member of the litigation staff assigned to the case immediately, but that doesn't solve our problem."

"I don't understand. The case gets more staffing, and you're covered. Why is Arn—my brother—such a key to all this?"

"Because a file is missing. It's an in-house file, and it cannot be turned over to the plaintiffs. If it is, we face a massive loss. An unacceptable loss. Now let me be blunt."

He leans forward conspiratorially.

"These other two gentlemen with me, whose names you don't want to know, are security agents with MexTel. They are here to make sure our in-house file is preserved as secret."

I feel my gut drop. Security agents, hell. These guys are enforcers. That's why there are no names for me. That's why he didn't introduce them. I size them up. One has a banana nose, and his hair is shaved down to his skull. He favors a diamond earring in his left ear and a thick black mustache on his top lip. The second man fingers the buttons on his coat nervously and, as he does, I swear I can see a shoulder holster barely hiding beneath his left arm. Great, I'm thinking, just what Arnie needs.

"So where is this file?" I ask. The best thing I can do is run down the file and turn it over. If Arnie has it, I'll pry it loose from him before they get to him.

"We have tossed his condo. It's not there."

Astonishment crosses my face and attorney Aguilar nods violently.

"Oh, yes, my people have been there and have gone through everything. Including his laptop and iPad. Nada, Señor Gresham."

"How big is this file?"

"Not very big. Less than fifty pages."

"And what is it comprised of?"

"Groundwater test results from twenty years ago."

The picture is fine-tuning right before my eyes. MexTel evidently had notice of some bad stuff it was doing to the groundwater in Mexico and, I'm betting, buried the test results. Simple, but it always is something that simple in these huge cases. There's always the flimsy gas tank of the Ford Pinto, or the skimpy rubber of the Goodyear tires, or the cancer-causing side effects of a jillion pharmaceuticals manufactured and sold on the hurry-up. So the companies play hide-the-ball with the citizens they've injured, and litigation goes on forever because of it. And Arnie knows all this and has lifted their groundwater test results and jumped ship with them. For just a fleeting moment I am proud of my brother. But just as immediately, I am also fearful for him. These people will stop at nothing to get their documents put back in the bag. I have no doubt, not with a billion USD at stake. I'm going to have to find Arnie and get this stuff back to MexTel before they find Arnie and pry it loose from his cold, dead fingers.

"Groundwater test results? My brother has no use for that.

Let me contact him and he'll turn those items back to you. No problemo."

Aguilar sits back, wraps his hands around a knee, and smiles curiously at me. "And how do we know you can do this? Do you even know where he's gone off to?"

How can I tell him I last saw Arnie headed into a Walgreen's? That's probably not going to seal the deal.

"I do know where he's gone. Give me a full day and I'll make contact with him and get your documents back to you."

"Six o'clock tomorrow night. Or else—" Aguilar smiles.

"Or else what?"

"Or else there's no going back. It will be all over for your brother."

"Hold on. Are you threatening him?"

Aguilar again nods violently.

"Yes, I am. Make no mistake. It is a huge threat. The worst kind for him—and for you too, now that you know about our file."

I slide down an inch in my chair. It honestly hadn't occurred to me that I would become a player in Arnie's troubles. But here I am. I curse my brother and hugely regret saying I would track him down. The truth is, he could be anywhere from the Bering Sea to Aruba right now, and I would have no way of knowing.

"All right. Let me get to work on it now. Thanks for coming in."

No sooner have we said our goodbyes, and fingers been

pointed at me, and threats underscored, and a noisy exit been made, than Mrs. Lingscheit buzzes. It's Sam Shaw, and it absolutely cannot wait. I pick up line two.

"Sam? Michael here."

"Holy shit, Michael, are they there? These guys are whack jobs! And the biggest whack job of all is Perez, the CEO. He came in and demanded access to Arnie's office so he could review his file."

"You didn't let him in, I hope."

"Dream on, dreamer. Of course, I let them in. I was polite and only too happy to help. I did everything I could to keep my firm and me, personally, off their radar. Your brother is bringing our world to an end if he doesn't get in here and undo this mess!"

"Easy, Sam, I'm working on it."

"You didn't tell them that?"

"Yes, I did. I had to tell them something, else they were going after Arnie to take him out. Of course, I told them I'm on it. And I am. So let's start with what we know."

"We don't know jack. Arnie's gone off somewhere without his medications handcuffed to some floozy who's going to test out the theory that American Express Platinum has no limits. God only knows what she's going to cost the firm."

"Cost the firm? Arnie's Amex card?"

"Firm card, Michael. Wake the hell up, brother."

"Can you cancel the card?"

"Tried that. Turns out Arnie has gotten himself on the

account as co-obligor. We can't get him off, which means we can't get us off. But that's the least of our problems. What the hell do these thugs want that they think Arnie has?"

"A file. A dangerous file that could destroy their company."

"You mean an actual, physical paper file? Not a computer file?"

"I don't think it's ever been digitized. I don't think it exists on any computers."

"So that's what that was," Sam says. His reference is oblique, spoken more to himself than me.

"You just lost me."

"We've checked his emails. He's calling together a status meeting of all attorneys on the case in order to turn over documents he's just located. That's what his last email said. It was sent from his phone."

"He's turning them in?"

"Bingo. Your brother is a whistleblower."

～

TWO HOURS LATER, I have called everyone I know who has any dealings with Arnie. His ex-wife, Madeline, laughed me off and chided me about mixing medications and Arnie in the same sentence. She hung up on me, still having herself a grand laugh. That helped my mood. Neither of his secretaries knows anything. His four paralegals know nothing about any file he might have pulled and taken with him. They tell me their document list checks against their actual file documents. It's all there, they maintain. Nothing missing. Of course, Arnie would have kept the file off somewhere else; probably locked in a desk drawer off-limits to everyone. Then I call Arnie's grown, married daughter in Dallas, and she says she hasn't talked to her dad in five years. He used to call her every night and talk for hours, but since he started taking his meds he's been withdrawn and distant. I can offer her no explanations, but I do apologize for being such a loser of an uncle myself. I've lost track of her, and it almost makes me want to cry when I admit it to her. She tells me not worry, that she knows about my divorce and what I must be going through. She promises she'll reach out to me more, too, and we hang up.

Just in time for Mrs. L to buzz. She has Arnie holding on one.

"You bastard," I say when I pick up. "Where are you?"

"No need for you to know that, Michael. I'm just calling to give you a little tip on something."

"What would that be?" I am holding back. I don't want to cause him to hang up on me.

"Well, I'm preparing to divulge certain test results on MexTel. And the gentlemen who own that company are going to be very hot. So you need to watch your step."

"They've already been to see me, Arnie. I'm in it up to my ears."

"Oh, no! I should have called you earlier. But we just got in."

"Got in where, Arnie?"

"Not over the phone, Michael. Your lines are bugged. Remember? This guy owns the entire Mexican telephone system. No telling what kind of in he has with AT&T and Sprint and the rest of those miserable, money-grubbing public utilities that are so good at screwing us all. Don't get me started. But wait, now I'm getting the big picture. They're going to use you to get me back! They're going to threaten you to get their file back! You've got to get away, Michael. Will you come and join Esmeralda and me? It's the best I can offer."

How can I say this? My brother is so—so—I am livid. And I am literally without a next move.

"Arnie, I have a life here. I have clients. I don't want to come to where you are. I don't want to hide from the Mexican Mafia."

"That's not a wise choice, Michael, but I know how you can get, so I'm not going to argue the point."

"Look, Arnie. All these guys want is their file back. Let's return their file and they'll go away. Then you and Esmeralda and I can all go on with our lives."

"That's impossible. We can't let them off scot-free. They've introduced carcinogens into the drinking water of seventeen impoverished Mexican villages. They've killed dozens of people, sickened hundreds of others, and hundreds or maybe thousands more are going to die an early death because of them. Think of something else. The documents are staying with me. Until I turn them over to plaintiffs' counsel."

"Please tell me you're not really going to do that, Arnie. That's the worst possible—"

"Michael, you're not hearing me! I'm done with the old life!

This girl—this seer—has helped me understand my life with all the blinders off. Chemical handcuffs—that's what she calls the drugs the doctors have been pushing on me. Chemical handcuffs. Have you ever heard a sadder turn of phrase? They've robbed me of my middle years, Michael. Kept me bound up in chains. Thank the powers that be for Esmeralda. I'm telling you, Michael, I really think I'm falling for this one. Yes, I am! I'm head-over-heels in love, Michael!"

"Oh my God."

I can only sit here and shake my head. This is the worst I've ever heard him go on. How many days has it been now without his meds? Two? Three? He's definitely at his bottom. I least I hope this is his bottom.

"Arnie," I begin. "I need you to hear this. It might be the last thing you ever hear from me if you don't listen."

"I'm listening, Michael. Just don't try to get me to medicate again. If you go there, we have nothing to discuss."

"Just shut the f—shut the hell up! More than any other time in our lives together, I need you to trust me. I need you to do what I say. For once, you cannot trust your own mind. Your mind is lying to you. You need to rely on me—just this once. And come home. Bring the file, don't turn anything over to anyone, and get on the next plane and come home. We'll work it out with the firm, with the doctors, everything else. Only, please. Come. Home."

"No can do, Michael. We're ordering room service and some-one's knocking. Have you ever had lobster that's so fresh it's never even been on ice? That's how fresh tonight's meal is, Michael. I really wish you would reconsider and come and join me."

"I don't even know where you are."

"Come to Cozumel. When you get there, call me on my cell. I'll tell you where to go next."

"Hold on. You're using your cell?"

"Of course not. MexTel can find me in two seconds if I roam on my cell. Give me some credit, Michael."

"Then why did you tell me to call you on your cell?"

"I'll get your number from my cell when it rings. I won't answer it. I'll call you back on a landline."

I'm no phone geek but even I see the gaping hole in his process.

I try again. "But I'm not coming to Cozumel. And you're not coming back. I'm screwed, Arnie. I'm screwed because I'm your brother."

"Oh, Michael. You need a good night's sleep and a day away from the office."

"Please, Arnie."

"It's our food, Michael. Gotta go. So long for now!"

The line goes dead, and I replace my phone. I hang my head and a full-on shudder works its way up my spine and shakes my shoulders. Tears come to my eyes—not because I'm fearful, not because I give a damn about MexTel and their legal problems. The tears are for my dear, sweet brother.

You can't put the genie back in the bottle when there's no longer a bottle.

Mrs. L comes bustling into my office.

"I saw the light go off on your phone. Arnie's loose again?"

"He is. Watch everything you do and say very carefully."

"You look tired, Michael. You need to go home and get some rest."

"I'm going to, I promise."

She gives me that suspicious, Germanic iron-clad stare-down. She doesn't believe a word of what I just told her.

The truth is, I don't either.

A good night's sleep with my bedroom door unlocked is way down the road.

---

66 *Chicago Tribune, April 2*

Judge Francis Pennington Jr. grew a thick beard last year. He then took a vote among his staff. His secretary voted yay, his court clerk voted nay, his paralegal voted nay, and his office manager voted yay. Judge Pennington declared the jury was deadlocked and kept the beard.

Two days later his wife was brutally murdered, and the beard disappeared the next day. Close friends say he had aged ten years.

66 *Keenan J. Harshman, Reporter*

F rancis Pennington Jr. is called to the stand by the Assistant U.S. Attorney. He is a tall, lanky man whose stiff bearing and frozen face don't entertain any nonsense from the litigants and lawyers who appear

before him in the U.S. District Court in Chicago. But today
he is a witness here, not a judge.

He walks from the gallery down through the swinging gate
and ambles toward the witness podium and chair in one
fluid movement. One sees that here is a man who is accus-
tomed to appearing almost regal in courtrooms while
distancing himself from the riffraff that roam public buildings. His skin is patently white and taut across his face, and
his eyes are a cloudy blue that remain filled with pain from
what he encountered that terrible day when he found his
wife slaughtered in her own home.

The Assistant U.S. Attorney wastes no time in getting to it,
for the judge's testimony about the scene he walked into is
counted on to energize the state's case and send James
Joseph Lamb straight to hell.

"Directing your attention to March 2, 2014, tell us what you
were doing that day," says LaGuardia from the lectern,
where he has positioned himself and where he is standing
half-facing the witness and half-facing the jury as if they
have formed a common circle. Their grouping is one of
inner-circle confidentiality; my client is not allowed inside,
and neither am I.

The judge clears his throat and nods but just barely.

"Well, I finished up my calendar that morning in federal
court. Then I met with two colleagues—two magistrates
who had performed magisterial tasks on several of my cases
—over lunch. We talked about those cases and eventually
had it all said and done, and the after-lunch coffee was
drunk so I went down to the basement where we park. This

is a secured area not open to the public and guarded by the U.S. Marshal's service."

"What happened next?"

"I arrived home—maybe twenty-five minutes later. The garage door opened, and I pulled in and climbed out of my Volvo. Then up the stairs and inside through the mud room, where I stopped to change out of my work shoes into my moccasins. This is a particular habit of mine as I like to shift gears physically before interacting with my family. It sands away some of the sharp edges I must maintain downtown."

"So you're in the mud room and changing shoes. When do you first become aware something is wrong?"

"I called out my wife's name—Veronica—and she usually comes to meet me with a coffee or Ginger Ale. But today she doesn't answer. So I proceed through the kitchen into the family room and from there on it's all a jumble in my mind. I see her lying on the floor, on her back, one leg up over her piano bench. At first, I think she's fainted, so I rush to her. Then my mind accepts that I am looking at bullet holes in her bare chest and that there is a massive bullet hole in her head, between her eyes. I served in the military during the first Iraq War, and I know mortal wounds when I encounter them. So my next thought is my son. I run into the hallway and charge down to his room. Next thing I know I'm standing over him and he's peacefully sleeping. I am so relieved I vomit. It's all too much for me, and I am crying and out of control and I know that the life I cherished is over. I put my hand in the center of his back and jiggle him so slightly and his eyes open. He sees me and smiles. I am suddenly lucid. The killer. He could still be in the house. So

I go on alert and begin sifting through the other rooms in the house."

"Did you keep a gun of your own?"

"Yes, I have a small gun safe in my closet. I went to it and realized I couldn't remember the combination. Later on, I realized how distressed I must have been because the combination is three twists consisting of the date of my graduation from law school. Simple, yet vanished from my mind. The next several days were like that where I didn't know what month it was or where my office was. Of course, I was pretty heavily sedated by my doctor so maybe that's part of it. Veronica's mom helped with my son."

"So what did you do once you had searched the house."

"Well, the search only took maybe five minutes. I was angry and reckless, tearing from room to room without a gun of my own. If I had found the perpetrator I have no doubt, he would have gunned me down too. But he was gone. So I went back into the family room and sat down beside my wife. Then my son called out. I couldn't have him walking in on this scene so I went back to his room and shut the door with me in there with him. I had my cell phone so I called nine-one-one. I explained the situation, and they immediately dispatched. Two police cruisers were first on the scene, and one of those officers took me and put me in the backseat of his squad car. Another officer took my son and put him in a second car. He stayed there with him. Then his partner went into the house and returned with a cold can of Ginger Ale and a banana. They were given to my little boy."

"What happened next, Judge Pennington?"

"It seemed like we sat in the squad cars forever. Finally, a special agent came and opened the door. They wanted to swab my hands for gunshot residue, which they did. Then they asked whether I had a gun and I said I did, and I gave them the combination to my safe. The combination had come to mind now just as quickly as it had fled before. Then the special agents left me alone in the squad car. I didn't realize at the time that I was a suspect, and they were keeping me in the patrol car as a person of interest. Then they returned to tell me my gun was still inside the gun safe, and they finished checking my ID and found out I was a sitting U.S. District Court judge, and they let me out of the squad car. They turned my son over to me. We returned to the kitchen and sat there for an hour until Elizabeth Franks, my family doctor, came walking in. She checked me over and left me a small, unlabeled bottle of tablets. Take one every four hours. And here's another pill. Take it for sleep. I thanked her, and she squeezed my hand and told me how sorry she was. By now Veronica's father and brother and mother had arrived. Angelina, the mother, took my son outside and they looked at a book out on the porch. Her father and brother were distraught, and my father-in-law came into the kitchen without speaking to me and sat at my table, weeping. My brother-in-law Harold Ramous was enraged and suspicious of me until the Special Agents pulled him outside and told him what they knew so far."

"Did he calm down after that?"

"He did. He came into the kitchen and hugged me and said how sorry he was. I told him I was sorry for him, too."

The witness pauses and asks for water. The Assistant U.S. Attorney quickly pours a glass of water from the pitcher on his table and hands it to Judge Pennington. As he testifies, I have been watching the jury, and they are mesmerized. These are people who have never talked to someone who came into a murder scene, and they are hanging on every word. I can tell that they are wondering how they would be reacting in such circumstances. It is crucial testimony, painful to hear, and I don't interrupt.

LaGuardia then takes the judge through his wife's autopsy, the funeral, and memorial, the feelings, and emotions of it all. By the time Judge Pennington has finished with his testimony, there isn't a dry eye among the jurors. I notice that now they are looking at me and at my client with severe, angry eyes. I try to avoid eye contact. I am not your enemy, my body language says. And neither is my client, who I make an effort to re-humanize by clasping him on the shoulder at one point and whispering to him. He is not an animal, I am broadcasting, and he is not the one who did this terrible thing.

Judge Amberlos calls a recess before my cross-examination. I interrupt the adjournment just long enough to say that I have no questions for cross-examination. Judge Pennington's shoulders slump, and he leaves the courtroom. But I know: he'll be back. And his presence will demand of the jury that they point their finger at my client and tell the court my man is guilty of this terrible crime. It is an unspoken link between Judge Pennington and his supporters, the jury. My jury, the jury I have cultivated and handled so carefully—they are gone from me, and we are no longer on the same page. They belong to the victim and her husband.

My client is alone, with just me, while everyone else, including the trial judge, wishes he were dead. It will be my job to distract them and re-program them enough that they move in their minds from a common finding of guilt and disgust toward my client to a place where they can actually believe he is not guilty of this thing. That, I am telling you, is the most difficult task I have ever faced in a courtroom and I wonder if I am up to it.

Truth be told, I hate my client as much as the jury does right now. Blindly, even knowing he's not guilty, I have voted with the jury and against him. It is a compulsion, a spell we are all experiencing, the need to see justice done and someone put to death.

Even I will need to be re-programmed. Luckily I am capable of that. As a lawyer, I have long ago learned to lie to myself, to deceive my mind into actually believing that red is green, that day is night and vice-versa. No matter how damning the evidence and testimony, I can pull myself around to denying it all.

Plus, I know deep down that my client is innocent. James Joseph Lamb, while bordering on retardation and disqualification as a contributing member of society, was and is incapable of doing such a terrible thing. He is constitutionally incapable. He doesn't breed death in his bones.

He is not—and I will not let him be cast as—death come 'round at last.

9

J udge Pennington has finished with his testimony, yet, when we start back up, LaGuardia tells Judge Amberlos that he needs to recall him to the stand for a short series of questions. I do not object. To do so at this point in front of this jury would be tantamount to opening my veins and bleeding out before them. It would be suicide to object.

I will see, in the days to come, whether I can pull my client into the jury's inner circle. If I can, he will walk out of here a free man. If I can't, he will die some midnight in the next several years.

Judge Pennington walks back up to the witness stand, steps up onto the podium, and re-assumes his seat. He has collected himself, dried his tears, and is ready to answer again.

"Judge Pennington," LaGuardia begins sonorously as if this might be more than a short session, "tell the jury what you have experienced since the murder of your wife."

I almost object but restrain myself. It isn't time for that. The jury is still in the judge's pocket, and they want to hear what he has to say. It would, as I've said, be suicide for me to try to deprive them of that corporeal real estate.

"Sleepless. Can't eat. Can't think straight. I've even lost bowel control a few different times."

The jury looks at him in astonishment. Did he really just say that?

"Anything else?"

"Rage. Extreme rage. I want to kill the man who did this to my beautiful wife. Did you know she had just taken up watercolors? She was learning to paint a common drinking glass." The judge is weeping now, and the jury joins him. Even I, the most jaded of anyone present, cannot keep the tears in my eyes from running down my cheeks. I cannot even imagine what Lamb, stoically staring straight ahead, must be feeling.

"You said you want to kill that man. Of course, you can't and you won't. So how would you tell this jury to help? What can they do?"

This is unusual, this question, but I again restrain myself.

"I would like to ask the jury to find James Lamb guilty and sentence him to death. An eye for an eye."

"All right. Nothing further, Your Honor."

Judge Amberlos peers down at me, and I swallow hard.

"No questions," I say.

"Very well, the witness may step down. May the witness be excused?"

"Yes."

"Yes."

"The witness is excused. Ladies and gentlemen, I think this is a good place to take our lunch break. We're forty-five minutes early, but I expect we can all use a little time away from the courtroom right now. We'll resume at one sharp. We're in recess. Remember the admonition."

On the east end of Schaumburg, south side of Washington Street stretches the Golden Years Home. As I walk inside and pass the reception desk and admin offices, I have the choice of right or left. I turn left, end of the ground floor corridor, and then right. Down four doors on the left is 1012.

Mom.

Her name is Anita Elizabeth Allbright. Which is a misnomer, because she is no longer bright at all. She is eighty-five and suffered early onset Alzheimers. Where mom was once a two-fisted drinker and legal secretary and, later on, a half-days volunteer at A.A. Central, she is now a frightened old nursing home resident who often doesn't know Arnie or me. Whenever I see her, she has either just lost something or just found something, usually the TV remote or her hearing aid.

Mom is tall—like me—and slender, also like me. She possesses a head full of hair that is still more brown than gray, although it had more streaks than two months ago when I'd last seen her. Yes, thanks to my trial calendar, it has been two months. Her eyes are brown and moist and all-innocence—a far cry from the lunatic who gave me life and then mostly abandoned me until I was out of law school, and she suddenly decided to retire at sixty and needed "a little help" financially each month. We became fairly good friends for the first two years of her retirement, but then the Alzheimer's took over. Her doctor called me, and I moved her into the Golden Years. Now I try to see her at least twice or three times each month and have managed more or less that frequency.

I knock three times on her door and then let myself in.

Jeopardy is re-running on the Golden Years in-house channel, and the contestants' clothing indicates the show was probably filmed back in the eighties.

"Buenos Aires!" shrieks my mother at the flat screen. "Goddam fool!"

"Mom," I say, "it's Michael. What's this about Buenos Aires?"

"Who?"

"It's me. Michael."

"No thank you, not today."

"It's your son, Michael. I'm here to take you to lunch."

Without taking her eyes off the screen, she flings her right arm out and feels around on the TV tray beside her recliner. She locates her upper plate, and pops it into her mouth. Then she turns and has a look at her son.

"My God, you look familiar."

"I should, I'm your son."

"Keep telling 'em that, big boy. Somebody's sure to bite."

"Mom, do you want to slip on your shoes? I'd really like to take you someplace for lunch."

"Today I'm eating in the cafeteria. It's taco Sunday."

"No, Mom, it's Thursday."

She taps the screen on the iPhone I gave her. Evidently she mastered the calendar app and took the time to enter the Golden Years lunch and dinner menus.

"Just like to be forewarned about the food," she chuckles. "This way I'm never disappointed."

"Well, I'm glad that works for you. But I was thinking more like the Red Dragon Inn. We could have one of their great pork tenderloin sandwiches and those onion rings you love."

"Who says I'm in love? With you?"

I sigh. All the air goes out of me as I see how distant she is today. There is little use in taking her out. Plus I have the trial starting up again in two hours.

"Come on, mom, let's hit the cafeteria. It's eleven o'clock. They're serving now."

"Can you wait while I get my shoes on? In a big hurry are we?"

She scowls and slips into her house shoes. They are the L.L. Beans I got her last Christmas—along with a few necessities like sweaters and underthings that Sue Ellen picked out. They look good: fleece-lined, deerskin house shoes that she selected from the catalog herself. She curls her toes and bounces her feet against the carpet.

She looks up at me and scowls then looks from side to side.

She stands, stretches expansively, and walks out the door, headed for the cafeteria.

"Wait," I say, "I don't think you have your lowers in."

Back into her room she clomps and returns with a complete set of teeth. She clicks them together and says, "Happy?"

Into the cafeteria, a place with that industrial cafeteria smell.

She precedes me through the lunch line, coming away with four fish sticks, mashed potatoes, green beans and corn, a napkin wrapped around two forks, and iced tea. My selections are the same, but I get a fork and a knife. We scan around for a place to sit—it is jammed, for eleven o'clock. We can only find a four place table with two chairs already taken. The two residents—guys in their eighties, I'm guessing—don't respond when I ask if they would mind company.

Mom sits down heavily, takes a bite of fish she holds in her fingers and chases it with a drink of iced tea. She doesn't chew properly, and chokes, and for several moments I'm thinking Heimlich. But no, another two gulps of iced tea seem to do the trick.

"So, mom," I say, "how have you been feeling?"

Whereupon she removes her lower plate and studies it. Satisfied, she pops it back into her mouth and resumes chewing her second bite.

"I said are you feeling pretty good?"

"I'm feeling fine," she says. "And I know you, Michael, so don't act so disappointed."

"I'm happy you know me. I love you, Mom, and I need you to know that."

"Well, I always loved you and your brother, too. I was never a great mother all the time, but I tried. Goddamn it, Michael, I tried!"

"I know you did, mom. Let's just let all that old stuff go. What matters is now. We get to spend time together; we get to tell stories and talk about the good times we did have. So let's enjoy it."

"Are you trying to hide something from me?" she asks in a new tone.

"Yes, mom, I'm trying to hide my real name from you. I'm really Mick Jagger of the Rolling Stones."

"You're covering something. I know you, Michael."

"You do, mom. But I'm really not covering up."

"You look different. Are you older, son?"

"No, mom. Just a little worse for the road wear."

"Michael, would you get another lemon for my tea?"

"Sure, mom."

I stand and hurry back to the line, where I reach between two seniors and two-finger a half-lemon out of a bowl. I wrap it in a napkin. Then I return and pass the lemon over to her. She unfolds the napkin and plunks the lemon into her tea.

I am casually chewing when I notice.

She has removed her upper plate and placed it on the dinner plate of the man directly to her left. He is sitting head-down, pushing potatoes onto his fork with a dinner roll, and isn't objecting.

For a moment, I don't know what to do.

So I watch as mom tries to take another bite of her fish stick and can't do better than gum.

"Excuse me, mom, but is that your denture on the gentleman's plate?"

"Damn fool has taken his teeth out," she says. "Utterly revolting. I think I'm going to toss my cookies, Charles."

"Whoa up, mom, but I think that's your own denture. Why don't you pick it up and have a look."

"Have a look? What's that gonna do?"

"I mean, can't you tell your own plate by looking?"

"You have to put them in your mouth. What if you're wrong, and you have me putting that old fool's teeth in my mouth?"

She begins crying and I reach across and take her hand.

Then I retrieve the denture from the gentleman's plate and wrap it in my napkin and stand and walk around to my mother. I help her up, bring her food plate along, and walk her back to her room. We arrive with her flatware and her food plate. As well as her dental plate, curled in my right hand inside a very damp napkin.

I help her into her chair and move the TV tray in front of her. Then I place her fish sticks plate on the TV tray. Taking her dental plate to the sink and unrolling the napkin, I proceed to clean the plate with one of those funny toothbrushes denture wearers use. I then take her denture to her and hold it out. By now The Price is Right is fully underway, and I don't even try to interrupt.

She casually seizes the denture, expertly inserts it into her mouth, and doesn't miss a beat of her show.

She is happy, she is engrossed, she is chewing and seems to savor.

What more can I ask than to see my mother's needs met?

I ask myself that question as Marcel backs his pickup truck out of the visitors' lot with me riding shotgun.

What more could I ask?

We have an hour to get back downtown to court.

~

RECORDS CUSTODIANS ARE CALLED to testify after lunch, and we are subjected to three hours of testimony that will allow into evidence all medical, criminal, crime scene, and court records the prosecutor wants to put before the jury. I am willing to stipulate them, but LaGuardia wants to pass them one-by-one to the jury so that they see them twice: now and once again in the jury room. I fight sleep and stare straight ahead, concentrating on ignoring the stale prison air my client is exhaling beside me. His air bears the scent of kung pao chicken with heavy garlic, and cigarettes. I move as far away as I can and shift positions so my back is more or less to him.

Finally, at five o'clock we are in recess. The court has personal business tomorrow, so we will resume trial on Monday. The jurors' faces reflect displeasure with this announcement because it means delay and more inconvenience in doing their public duty.

I tell Lamb I will see him before Monday, and I am gone.

Time enough tomorrow to continue this death march.

Time enough tomorrow for me to try to bring it to a halt.

11

After dinner, I get a call. It is the Cook County Sheriff's Department, and it is important I come see my client tonight. There is nothing I can do but suit up and show up.

It is 8:30 by the time I get back out to California Avenue. I park in the visitors' lot and walk up the sidewalk to the entrance.

The jail is busy; regular visiting hours are underway, and the lobby is crowded. I wait in line and finally get to flash my bar card and driver's license to the woman behind the bulletproof glass. Wearing the liver and brown uniform of CCSD, she is all business and ramrod straight in her chair. She is surrounded by CCTV screens and keeps her eyes bouncing between the screens as she helps me.

"Who you here for?"

"James Joseph Lamb."

Her eyes flip down to her computer screen, "Lamb, Lamb, Lamb, here we are. Uh-oh, he's in Cermak, sir."

"Cermak Hospital?"

"Uh-huh. Right next door."

"Why's he in the hospital?"

"You'd have to ask him that. The computer don't tell us."

I hustle back the way I just came in and move down the sidewalk to the entrance of Cermak Hospital. Like the jail, it also begins and ends with a woman sitting at a computer screen behind bullet proof glass. A microphone allows us to talk.

Cermak Hospital is one of a kind in the United States. Every day it provides healthcare to the twelve thousand detainees at the Cook County Jail. It offers primary care, specialty care, dental and mental health services. In the back is a complete medical laboratory. On this end is a 129-bed infirmary. It is the largest single-site correctional health service in the U.S., I am told, and it's heavily guarded from end to end. Getting in to see Lamb in the hospital is no less difficult than down the street in the DOC.

I am admitted to the place, and a jailer takes me to my client.

The beds themselves are contained within small fenced enclosures, each one large enough to accommodate a bed and two chairs. The fencing is actually vertical straps of steel to which the inmate/patient is at all times chained. We pass a dozen such enclosures, and I am reminded of dog kennels.

The deputy stands aside and ushers me inside the second-to-last cove. James Lamb is lying beneath a sheet, and his head is propped up on a pillow. He has a tube going into his nose and has a tube inserted in the large vein on the back of his left hand. He is right-handed and is holding a Superman comic book.

"Is that all you can find him to read around here?" I ask the deputy.

She smiles wickedly. "Counselor, it's what he asked for. Bright guy, this one."

She steps back into the corridor where she waits for me. I doubt we'll be speaking privately with her standing right there, but I nod to Lamb and start in any way.

"So. What the hell happened?"

Lamb's face and forehead are badly bruised, his eyes—while able to read—are all but swollen shut. One ear has a bandage covering it. His hands are battered and bruised as well.

"Fell down," he says nonchalantly. "Shit happens."

"You fell down in your cell?"

"Fell off the top bunk. Splat! Thought I was paralyzed."

"The deputy mentioned they were investigating a fight you started. Any truth to that?"

"What? Get outta here. I don't start fights; I finish them."

He turns a page in the comic book and his eyes come to rest on its pages. His lips move.

"So how long will you be in here? We've got a trial going on, you know."

"Couple of days. I'm pissing blood. Prison doctor says I have a lacerated something—kidney? Does that sound right?"

"Was someone kicking you in the back?"

"Naw. Like I said, I fell outta bed, Mr. Gresham. Must've landed on my back."

"Right. Somehow I can't feature how that would lacerate a kidney, but I'm not a doctor."

"No. You're a lawyer. I'm down with that. You're doin all right by me."

This is the most I've ever heard my client talk. I previously thought his mostly silent affect was because of his low IQ. But he doesn't sound all that low IQ right now. There's even a hint of sarcasm in what he's saying and how he's saying it. Low IQ doesn't do sarcasm. At least not that I'm aware of.

"So what's my outlook, Mr. Gresham? You goan get me off?"

He flips a page, and I am treated to a passing view of Superman prone in the sky, his cape trailing behind.

"I don't think they have a case against you, except for that damn confession you signed."

He opens his mouth and displays his gold crowns. "Beat it outta me. No two ways about that."

"Well, that's what we're going to argue to the jury."

My cell phone goes off. I quiet it.

"Hey," he says, "can I use that to call my girlfriend?"

"James, do you see the deputy standing right outside? You think she won't hear?"

"So? What they gonna do? Put me in jail?"

This one requires a belly laugh, and he winces as he over-does it.

"No," I say, she's gonna put me in jail if I let you use my phone. That's called contraband and giving a prisoner contraband is a very serious crime."

"Well, could you get a message to my girl?"

"I could try."

"Could you tell her that I'll be out of here before much longer, and we can get down on the baby thing."

"Baby thing?"

"She has my baby. Her baby, but I'm its dad. You follow?"

"I do. So, tell her you can soon get down on the baby thing? Got it."

We chat for another five minutes about nothing in particular, and then I leave the cell. The deputy has moved to the other end of the hall. I should have let James use my phone; I'm thinking. But she quickly walks the length of the hallway and speaks into her shoulder mike. We then retrace our steps back to the entrance of the ward. The door buzzes and I am out.

It is a cool April evening, and a light breeze is moving clouds overhead. A few patters of raindrops can be felt in the spaces between the overhanging trees along the sidewalk. I hunch my shoulders and pick up the pace to my SUV.

The parking lot is filled with headlights and moving cars, in and out, and people talking as they come and go, some of them angry and acting out because a loved one is in jail. I click my door lock and climb in.

As I exit the lot, a car parked along the street starts up and falls in behind me. I think nothing of it. But then, two turns later, when it's still on my tail, and I take a left and it follows me without its blinker, I begin thinking something of it. I'm not alarmed; I know Fordyce and Burns are interested in me —I'm a bad guy because I'm defending Lamb. Or, the MexTel thugs could very well be out following me to see if I might lead them to Arnie. That's possibility number two. Possibility number three is that I'm paranoid because I'm drained right now. That's the door I choose to walk through.

The rest of the drive home I pay no attention. Once I'm safely in my garage, and the door is lowering, I exhale and allow myself to slump and slowly drag inside.

I check my messages; nothing there. Then I go into my bathroom and brush my teeth, take my cholesterol pill, and pull off my suit. In my bed five minutes later, I am falling asleep, and it's the first time all day I've felt really good.

Then I remember Lamb is on trial tomorrow, and he's in the hospital. I need to notify the court.

Into my office I go, wearing my robe, and sit down at my laptop. I log into my office network, pull up all the necessary emails of all parties I must notify.

Then an email arrives from the Circuit Court. No trial tomorrow due to Lamb's hospitalization. They're one step ahead of me, and I'm glad. I can always use a day off during a trial.

Finally, at twelve-thirty, it's lights out.

I toss and turn in my bed, unable to sleep. My mind bounces from James Lamb to Arnie to Sue Ellen. Finally, I climb out of bed and go into the family room and stand staring out of the back window at the newly mown lawn. I lean and crack open a side window and the grass smell transports me away. It is real and pure and hopeful.

With that fragrance lingering, I at last find peace. Just as I am drifting off, I hear my laptop chime on my nightstand. Email announcement.

Without looking, I already know.

Arnie has reached out.

12

I t is my habit to check my office email before leaving home each morning to go to work. I check this morning's and, lo and behold, there is a new email from Arnie. It's multi-addressed to me, and Sam Shaw, Roberto Aguilar, Juan Carlos Munoz Perez, three in-house attorneys with MexTel extensions in Mexico City, and Hon. Sylvia M. Prather, Judge, U.S. District Court, Northern District of Illinois.

Great, Arnie's getting everyone on the same page as only the unmedicated Arnie would ever deign to do. This is not going to be good, I'm thinking, as I read on.

The gist of the email is that Arnie is calling a settlement conference—usually the judge gets to do that—unilaterally, at which he is going to provide everyone with "documents that will change the course of the underlying litigation, documents that place a smoking gun directly in the hands of the criminal conspiracy at MexTel, documents that will elevate me [Arnie] to a position of ultimate trust among the federal bar of the Northern District." Then he adds, with a flourish thought humorous only by the writer himself: "Who knows? I may even be spontaneously appointed to the federal bar to mediate all controversies including truth, honesty, and the American way." Superman language, directly out of the old TV show intro.

I am dumbstruck. The crazy son of a bitch is actually going to turn over records that have been hidden—he has been the chief hider—that will ruin his client. Great. Whatever it means to the litigation, I am suddenly filled with great apprehension for Arnie's safety. Now MexTel has a compelling reason to hunt him down and silence him forever so that its secrets are never revealed. If they weren't desperately seeking Susan before, brother, they certainly are now.

Into the kitchen I go, in panic. I pull open the refrigerator and pour myself a large glass of orange-pineapple juice. Then I return to my home office and my laptop and read through the email again. This time much slower. He is definitely greasing the skids for MexTel. He has, in effect, signed his own death warrant if ever any lawyer did.

I consider the bigger picture. Today is Friday, April 3. He has set the settlement conference for Monday, April 6, at ten a.m. in Attorney Conference Room A just outside the courtroom of Judge Prather in the Federal Courthouse on Dearborn Street. That leaves me from noon today until Monday morning to hunt him down and get his medications down his throat and hide him somewhere they will never think to look. Left to his own devices, Arnie's own notion of a safe hiding place will be the five-star hotel in whatever city he has lodged himself. MexTel and Sam Shaw will know this; all they need to do is look over his expense accounts to see that he has always considered no hotel too upscale for him, no five-star restaurant too pricey. Of course they've never cared before either; he has carried their water and so far they haven't had to pay one dime in damages for the Mexicans they've killed and given cancer. But that "so far" ended at 6:04 a.m. this morning when his email was blasted out to all the players in the case. Now they definitely care.

Where will they begin looking? Meaning, where should I start looking? Arnie has spent three years in vexatious litigation over MexTel. Most likely he has no other case assignments during those three years because the one case is full-time for several lawyers. What does this point to? For one thing, Arnie's travel has been restricted to Chicago and Mexico City, where MexTel is headquartered. And maybe side trips to the offending groundwater sites throughout Mexico where the populace was poisoned and killed. But those places can immediately be erased, because, while Arnie may be ill, he isn't stupid. He knows he would stand out like a carrot in a jar of pickles if he were to decide to be the only Anglo living in Boulavares City, Mexico, or wherever the hell else he might have visited. Those places I can forget about. That leaves Mexico City and Chicago.

I recall our last conversation. Come to Cozumel and then call the number he used. Why do I need to go to Cozumel? I wonder. Why can't I just dial it now?

Which I decide to do. I fish my cell phone out of my jacket pocket and go back over the recent calls list. There it is; the number he called me from. I punch CALL.

It rings once. Twice.

Arnie answers on the third ring.

"Michael? Are you calling me from Cozumel?"

"No, Arnie, I'm—"

Dead.

The bastard hung up on me.

I love the guy, I really do, but right about now my patience is all gone.

Still, he is my brother, and someone has to save him.

I wonder if I should send Marcel after him. Marcel was at one time an agent of Interpol, the international police agency when he was a much younger man living in Warsaw before he came to the U.S. as a political refugee. His Interpol training has served him—and, indirectly, me—well. He can find anyone, anytime, anywhere in the world, inside of twenty-four hours. All I've ever had to do is give him a name and last-known, and he's off and running, returning with the game slung across his shoulders usually in just a matter of hours.

So be it. I'll give the case to Marcel.

I knock back the last swallow of my orange-pineapple juice, and head for the shower.

Before my life can be allowed to unravel in dealings with my half-witted brother, there's the matter of my own law practice and clients awaiting me. The Hudson case beckons, for one.

Including one innocent Lamb, who needs all the help I can provide.

At noon, I am meeting Sue Ellen for lunch. We are going to discuss her offer to remove her alimony claws from my back for ninety grand. A bargain basement deal for a guy like me.

I'm only too anxious to meet her.

13

I'm back in court at nine o'clock on the Hudson case.

I'll be honest with you. Most lawyers my age would have given up trial practice five or ten years ago. It's a young man's game, and I'm no longer a member of that group. I'm not only not a member, but I also don't even want to be a member. The classroom for young lawyers is too rough and tumble, too physically and mentally exhausting for me ever to want to go there again. No, I've made most of the rookie mistakes, and I'm still standing and still have a law license—so I'm one of the lucky ones. The problem is, I have nothing set aside for the coming winter. And that coming winter portends to be a cold one.

Today I'm appearing in the United States District Court, Room 9089, in downtown Chicago. My client is Bill Hudson, the CEO of a large Midwestern chemical company, Organo. Hudson is accused of insider trading. Insider trading happens when someone with inside information about a company uses the information to profit from the stock

market. Hudson allegedly knocked down seventy-five
million dollars based on his company's upcoming merger
with Magnachem. The merger was a sweet deal for Organo.
It meant a four hundred percent increase in Organo's stock
value, of which Mr. Hudson owned a truckload by the time
the merger went public. His stock soared. Of course, the
SEC keeps tabs on employees whose stock sharply increases
in value where there's a change in how the company does
business. The SEC turned over what it knew to the FBI. The
FBI looked into it, indicted Mr. Hudson, and now he's
looking at twenty years in a federal prison. Twenty years of
despair and self-loathing, followed by the inability to make
a living even laying bricks, once he's branded with the C of
convict. It's my job to make sure this final act of his financial
Hamlet never appears onstage.

My client is sitting at our table trying to call out on his cell
phone. I leave him to it; it keeps me from answering the
same questions for the tenth time. Not that I mind, but I'm
tired today. My brother Arnie had a restless night and called
me at four a.m. After listening to his darkest hour, I couldn't
get back to sleep.

"I'm stepping out to the hallway to see if I can get reception,"
says Hudson.

"No, you're sitting in your seat. The judge will be here any
second now."

He sniffs and looks away.

We are awaiting the arrival of Francis Pennington, Jr. While
he is the alleged victim in the Lamb case, we have agreed
that my cases in his court will continue unabated as if the

other matter never existed. Lawyers and judges can actually pull off a balancing act like this; we do it all the time, it's part of our training. At last, he appears and ascends the bench and seats himself quickly. He glances at the Assistant U.S. Attorney, a dour man named Ingersoll McDermott. Then he fixes his eyes on me. Immediately I am nervous and full of regret. I should have asked for a different judge, and I kick myself for failing to do so.

"Mr. Gresham," he says, "I have read your motion. Why wasn't this worked out with the Assistant U.S. Attorney?" Not exactly a friendly reception. Maybe everything isn't as stitched off as I thought.

"Your Honor," I begin, "My client, Mr. Hudson, needs to leave the state of Illinois on company business. The government wouldn't agree."

"So you want me to enlarge the geography of conditions of release. Isn't this something a phone call could have settled between you and Mr. McDermott?"

I shake my head. "Tried and failed. Mr. McDermott voiced several reasons why he couldn't agree to Mr. Hudson leaving Illinois. His main reason is his belief my client has hidden fifty million dollars offshore. McDermott says Mr. Hudson is just looking to flee the country and beeline to the Bank of Cayman Islands. But there is no evidence that my client has transferred money out of the country. Which leaves me trying to prove a negative, which, we all know from our debate days, is impossible."

"Mr. McDermott, what say you?"

McDermott, a fit man in his late thirties—a marathon man,

I hear—shoots to his feet and exclaims, "The FBI believes we haven't uncovered all illegal profits taken by the defendant in his insider trading scheme. We believe huge sums are hidden offshore. Within forty-eight hours, I can come into court with documentary proof of this. I'm only asking that you delay this hearing for two days, Judge Pennington until I can get you that proof."

Beside me, I can sense William Hudson shaking his head in complete disagreement with the AUSA's representation to the court. "I can explain that," he whispers to me.

"One moment, please, Your Honor," I say, and bend to my client. "What?"

"The stock in the bogus account they traced back to me? Remember?"

"What about it?"

"I have all the brokerage invoices and receipts. One hundred percent. We can easily prove there is no other money."

I shake my head. "No, we can only prove what has been found. We can't prove a claim that there's no more. Besides, that's not our job. Hang loose." I squeeze his shoulder and return to my upright position at the lectern, standing there beside AUSA McDermott.

"Your Honor, my client is needed in Seattle and Portland over the next forty-eight hours. It would be a denial of due process to keep him from his business only because the government is chasing a will-o-the-wisp."

Judge Pennington rocks sideways in his chair. "A will-o-the-wisp? Haven't heard that term for a long time, Mr. Gresham. Okay, counsel, here's what I'm going to do. Mr. Hudson may travel to Seattle and Portland. Likewise, the FBI can send along an escort on the airline. While I doubt that escape is in Mr. Hudson's mind, the government can indeed follow him if it likes. There's no law against following him. Tagging along might be a better word. But after this trip, unless the government brings proof to me that Mr. Hudson indeed has funds squirreled away someplace, I'm going to enter a restraining order for the government to cease tailing the defendant." He raises his hand and continues, "No, hold on, Mr. McDermott. I know this will raise the ire of the Justice Department and that I'll probably get a call from the Attorney General, but we're not going to make a federal case out of it. I will enter that in my written order to follow later today. Thank you, gentlemen, you've been more than a little helpful this morning. By the way, give me your cell numbers in case there's a problem. Here's mine on these two Post-Its."

McDermott and I jot our numbers on a single sheet of paper, and I pass it up to him.

Judge Pennington studies the numbers and nods. "Dismissed, gentlemen."

McDermott, Hudson and I duck out to the hallway and McDermott puts a hand on my shoulder.

"Hold on, Michael," he says, "I need your guy's itinerary."

"What for?"

"We're going to tag along."

"I thought the FBI already had everyone's itinerary. I thought you guys already knew when and where I last peed."

"Funny man. Please email it over. You have my email."

"No, I'm not going to do the FBI's work for them. Besides, my client has no itinerary. He's taking the corporate jet to Seattle. In about thirty minutes."

McDermott's face purples with rage. "You should have told Judge Pennington about that!"

"You should have asked. Was there anything else?" I am moving toward the bank of elevators halfway down the hall, and Mr. Hudson is following along, a small smile playing at his mouth. He looks at his watch.

"I should be airborne in thirty, Michael. Thanks for your help."

I look at him. "That's what you paid me for, Bill. We've only just begun."

I look back. McDermott has disappeared, probably back inside the courtroom.

Rather than wait for the elevator and a frantic shout from the judge's clerk, I push Hudson through the door leading to the stairwell, and we descend two steps at a time. Three floors down, we bounce out and ride the elevator the rest of the way.

We step out on the sidewalk of Dearborn Street, and Hudson is swallowed up by a waiting Mercedes limo.

I head toward the corner, breathing in the sweet spring air of Chicago. My city is coming back to life after an eternity of snow and bluster and ice that lasted from late October to April 1.

At the corner my light is green, and I step down onto the crosswalk.

The green light is a sign my life is finally coming together, I tell myself.

The prevarications just never end.

14

Sue Ellen has selected a small, on the beaten path bistro at Jackson and Wacker, so I walk over, nice spring day that it is. Coming out of the Congress building, I first head right, go a hundred feet, then abruptly turn on my heel and head left. My eyes are playing across the traffic, intent on finding anyone who might be trying to turn somehow and follow me as I walk along. But traffic is heavy, and nothing clearly reveals itself. Mostly cabs and SUVs dropping people along the curbs, and UPS/FEDEX vans pulled alongside, blocking a lane with blinkers blasting, bringing us all our packages and picking up our boxes. A very busy noontime.

At the corner, I abruptly turn left and stop and flatten my back against the wall. Waiting to see if anyone is following on foot. If they are, they'll have to come around the corner and walk past me to escape my discovering them. No one comes; at least, no one comes who looks like anybody. Especially anybody Hispanic. MexTel people will be Hispanic, I'm thinking, but then I'm immediately chiding myself for such simplistic thinking. As rich as MexTel is, their under-cover people could be crown princes from Romania, for all I know. The bottom line is that I'm not one for skulking around trying to avoid people or find people who are attempting to stay hidden. I was never a cop and never a private investigator. Those people have their methods but, for the most part, I'm not privy to them. The notion that someone is following me is actually quite unnerving. I push away from the wall and continue my route to The Flame, Sue Ellen's eatery of choice.

There are three small, white iron tables on the sidewalk out front and, lo and behold, Sue Ellen has seized one. I walk up from her side and bend and kiss the top of her head. We're still pretty good to each other, all things considered. More than that, I still have a soft spot for her; hell, I probably still love her and maybe that never goes away. This is my first time through the divorce idiom, and I still don't have my bearings and really don't know how to expect I might wind up feeling about her. For now, this mild confusion of feel-ings will have to do. Only time is going to heal this wound. I've been around long enough to know that.

"Hey," she says up over her shoulder. "Glad you could make it, Michael."

I take the seat across from her and push my sunglasses up on my nose.

"Me, too. It's been a busy morning, but I always have time for my favorite lady."

"You're sweet. I always did like that about you."

"You too. A super woman with a huge heart. Maybe not a heart that includes me, but a huge one anyway."

"Oh no, Prince Charming, you're still snuggled up in there. I would never let that go, darling man!"

A waiter appears and takes our drink order. Sue Ellen orders a medium-priced wine, and I ask for iced tea with a slice of lemon on the side. I like to actually chew my lemon; it makes people around me gasp when they see me take a big bite. The total effect is heightened by acting like you think nothing about biting into the modern world's most bitter fruit. The best thing is, Sue Ellen has always hated the practice. How can I let up now when I am still angry at her for leaving me for a younger man? Is eating lemons in front of her all I have left to get back at her? Sadly, yes. Even more, I no longer want to get back at her. I only want her to...come home.

"So," she says, "Eddie saw your name in the *Tribune*. You got the case defending that famous judge killer. What's his name?"

"My guy is James Lamb."

"I mean this is about the judge whose wife was murdered by your client. Eddie showed me the article, and I read it. Very interesting."

"Oh, Eddie did, did he? He must be quite a study in things legal."

"Come on, Michael, lighten up. You know Eddie's not brilliant like you. I've told you that already. Give a bum a pass, okay?"

"Okay."

"Besides, I have two things I need to tell you. One of them can't wait."

Our drinks come. I do, in fact, take a chomp out of my lemon. Sue Ellen, without quite realizing what I just did, grimaces.

"What can't wait?" I ask, chewing my lemon and following it with a nip of iced tea.

"Arnie called me."

"When?"

"Last night."

"Did you get his number?"

"No. He said he was in a public transportation station."

"That's what he said, 'public transportation station'?"

"Yes. Odd, isn't it?"

"He's playing it close to the vest. He's thinking his phones are bugged. They probably are, knowing MexTel."

"Who's MexTel?"

"It's a long story. So why did he call you?"

"He asked me to beg you to leave Chicago. He said they—whoever they are—are after you now too. He said you'd be killed if you stayed in Chicago. Is he right, Michael? Are you in some kind of danger? What's it about?"

I brush her words away as if slapping gnats.

"That's just Arnie. His usual histrionic self. So, did he tell you how I can reach him?"

"He said to come to Cozumel. You'll receive further instructions there."

"Damn it all! Always with the 'come to Cozumel' thing. I can't just abandon my law practice like he can. I don't have partners to cover for me like he does. Damn him!"

"Well, you know Arnie. He does have his issues."

"You mean his psychoses? Goddamn, right he has issues. This time, he's going to wake up dead over them too, I'm afraid."

"Michael, no. Arnie's really in that much trouble?"

"Bet your ass he is. This is ridiculous. So he didn't leave any callback number?"

"No. He just wanted me to try to convince you. He was very serious and very pushy—unlike the Arnie I know who's usually gentle and sweet and never pushy."

"Damn."

"Well, if it makes you feel any better, he asked me to make you go. He said I should offer to go with you. So I'm offering if it will help change your mind and get you down there."

For a moment, it's as if everything around me has gone silent. Did she just say what I think she said? Is she actually offering to go to Cozumel with me?

"Would you need to bring Eddie along?" I ask and immediately hate myself for it. I don't want to look like I want to pry her apart from Eddie. Even though I do.

"No, silly, I don't need Eddie. Besides, he has to work. He's got a job."

"Doing what?"

"Working as a lifeguard at my tennis club. It's not outside, so the sun doesn't damage his skin. He's very fair, you know."

"You mean his complexion is very fair. He's not very fair. He took you away."

She laughs. It's a short, lilting laugh as if she's pleased to have been taken away by Eddie and considers it trivial. My face reddens. I shouldn't have gone there. What the hell am I doing?

"So you'll tag along to Cozumel. What if we're gone two or three days?"

"You mean will I sleep with you? Well, we were married once. I don't see—"

"Wait a minute. You're trying to get pregnant. What if I got you pregnant somehow—you've started with hormones or something?"

"I'd like your baby, Michael. Oh, here's the waiter back."

The young man takes our order. Sue Ellen is having the crab legs, and I think that sounds good, so I double down. With steamed asparagus, a rice pilaf, and freshly baked bread. I order as if from inside a fog: did she really just say she'd like my baby? Is that why I can't order beyond ordering whatever she's having?

It is. My brain is baked.

"You just said—"

The waiter is gone now.

"I know. I said I'd like your baby. Don't take it the wrong way, Michael, I'd like any baby."

"But you'd prefer if it were Eddie's baby?"

"True. I'm with Eddie now. But that's the second thing I needed to talk to you about. You know the ninety thousand dollar alimony thing?"

I pat my breast pocket. "Got your check right here. Just need you to sign an agreement first."

"Well, that's just it. I'm having second thoughts about the whole entire thing. I'm forty-five years old. I mean, what kind of mother do you get when she's forty-five? I'm not going to feel like PTA or building snowmen or going to the Shedd with the first graders. I'm too busy for that. I've got my friends—"

"Our friends—"

"Michael, you're not still bitter that they turned out to be my friends mostly?"

"Not really. I'm doing all right."

I don't add, "Alone every night since you quit organizing my social calendar."

"Well, you can still see Ralph Egerton. He asks about you every time I have everyone over."

"You have everyone over while Eddie's there?"

"They've all quite taken to Eddie. Except for Ralph. Eddie can be very charming in his disarming way. You know, no airs, no trying to be something he's not, no trying to prove he's more successful than others."

"Good for him. I'll bet that's a real turn-on for you, someone charming."

She reaches across the table and takes my hand. "Michael, Michael. I've hurt you so deeply. I'm so sorry."

I pull my hand away.

"Don't feel like you need to tend my wounds. I'm doing okay."

"Well, tell me about that. Are you seeing anyone?"

"Not really."

Translation: I can't find anyone who might be interested in a fifty-five-year-old man. Not that I've been actively looking, actually. It's just that I'm a little old—by thirty years—for the club scene, and there's really no other place I know to look. It was so easy back in college: everyone knew everyone, everyone was in everyone's age group. But now, it seems everyone is younger than me. They're all younger and probably looking for hardbodies. Something I definitely no longer possess.

"You should see someone. Hey, I hear Sandy Darnell and Edmund are splitting the sheets. What do you think of Sandy?"

"I think she drinks too much, and she comes across like she's on speed. She's probably driven poor Edmund away."

"Yes, I think you're right. But don't worry. I meet eligible women all the time. I'll start keeping my eyes open for you."

"God, thanks."

Until right now I didn't realize how low I'd actually sunk, with my ex-wife trying to solicit dates for me. Our food comes, and I give up feeling pathetic while I use the little pliers to crack open my first King Crab leg.

We chew in silence for several minutes. At one point, Sue Ellen removes her sunglasses and dabs at her eyes with her linen napkin. I wonder what that's all about, but I don't ask. Probably the hormones.

Then I dab my mouth with my napkin and ask, "So, do I tear up the ninety thousand dollar check in my pocket? Or do we still have a deal."

She stops, her mouth dropping open.

"You—you got the money?"

"I did. Line of credit on my house. So I can pay you."

"Oh. My. God. Well, that does it then. Full speed ahead, baby. Yes, I'll sign whatever you have for me to sign. Eddie is going to be thrilled!"

Eddie this, Eddie that.

I couldn't be happier.

The crab is rubbery, and the pilaf has no spice. In the center of the table is my plate with its lonely, half-eaten lemon.

And my ulcer is churning. Citrus can do that to me.

We finish up, promise to get documents signed and the check transferred to her, and we embrace and say how nice it's been, and we should do it again sometime.

Sometime.

Walking back to my office I try to count all the ways I hate that word: Sometime.

15

"I'm taking you shooting," Marcel says to me as we enter my building lobby. "You've got too many bad people after you, with the MexTel thing going on."

"You must have spoken to Mrs. Lingscheit."

"Yes, Evie clued me in," he says, using her first name. "Plus I've had my eye on you this morning. They followed you all the way down from Evanston. As we speak, they're across the street in a loading zone, eyes on you."

"Were they following me to lunch?"

"One of their thugs did. I'm pretty sure he's back across the street with the others."

"Good work, Marcel. This is like learning I have head lice."

"I wouldn't know about that," he laughs. "What do you say we lose them now?"

"I'm up for that. What do you have in mind?"

"I rode my bike today."

He's talking about his FXRT Harley, a beautiful old road bike with a very comfortable passenger ride.

"Sure, let's do it."

"We'll head outside, take a left, back around the corner, and I'm parked right across the street. We can rip out going north, and there's not much they can do to follow."

"After you, my friend."

We leave the Dirksen Building, turn left, and begin walking rapidly toward the light at the opposite end of the block. The light is green, and we hurry across, down fifty feet, there's Marcel's blue bike with the chromed-out engine and pipes and black leather seating. It even has hard shell saddlebags where Marcel often hides a gun. It wouldn't surprise me if he had one along today.

We climb aboard, and he guns it out into traffic. We stay in the left lane, up one block and then head left and zip down a few blocks then right. We go a dozen blocks toward the lake then head back toward the freeway, where we head into Indiana.

Across the state line, we pull into a gun range and Marcel parks the bike. We both climb off, and he sticks the key into the right saddlebag and twists. I was wrong. He doesn't have just one gun; he's brought two. He wasn't kidding about working on my shooting.

Inside we go, me bringing up the rear. We buy several hundred rounds and the woman behind the counter lends us two earmuffs. Hearing protection.

The range is down at the end of a hall, and it is deserted except for the two of us.

We go through field stripping the Glock 19 that I'll be shooting, and we go through loading, ejecting, checking the bore, inserting the magazine, chambering a round, sighting, and squeezing the trigger. I fire off maybe thirty or forty rounds. Marcel watches, moving my hands into a proper grip and kicking my legs into the new sideways stance intended to reduce one's silhouette in a combat shooting situation. Another forty rounds, during which I field strip and go through the whole loading/unloading routine several more times. Then the targets noisily re-position at the press of a button and they've suddenly gotten much smaller. But the Glock is a dream. It's one of those guns that, as Marcel puts it, shoots where you point it. After my first hundred rounds, I'm feeling proud, and my ears are ringing. I look at my hearing protection and Marcel shouts, "Ears ringing?"

I nod, and he tells me to unload my weapon and hand it over to him.

We check the weapons, holster them, and return to the lobby. There's a soft drink machine and a lounge at the other end.

"Let's grab a drink and have a talk. It's time."

"All right."

We buy our drinks, stack our guns in the center of a round table, and scrape back two wrought-iron chairs, black frames and red seats. Marcel crosses his leg over his knee and leans in toward me.

"These are bad guys following you around, Michael. Two of them are what they call *sicarios*, in Mexico."

"What in the world is a *sicario*?"

"Up here we call them hit men. Seriously, I don't like this at all. Your brother's chances of making it through this alive are slim to none if he doesn't stand and deliver their file."

I spread my hands. "He won't listen to reason, Marce. He's so manic without his meds that he's blowing every which way with any little breeze that comes along."

"And right now that young chick has his ear. What's her name again?"

"Esmeralda. She's definitely not the feel-good he needs right now. But that's Arnie—he substitutes one drug for another. Romance for medications. It's not the first time we've been down this road."

He takes a long pull at his orange crush. He wipes his mouth with the back of his huge hand.

"All right. What can I do to help?"

"Do you know where the Mexicans are staying?"

"Sure, Hyatt hotel on Wacker. Want their room number?"

"No room numbers, please. I just need to know how to get the MexTel guys to back off Arnie."

"You want me to bug their room? Probe for an opening?"

"Thought of that. But, as an attorney, I could never ask my investigator to burglarize a hotel room."

"Never mind. Don't ask."

"Do you still have those carbon monoxide detectors with the built-in video cam?"

"Yes, indeed. I'm thinking one right above their eating area. They'll be having drinks and talking right about there."

"Wait, have you already been inside their room?"

He smiles. "Don't ask and I won't tell."

"You're right. Is there something that I can do—"

"Tell me again about the missing file."

I take a drink of my Diet Coke. I wipe my hands on my suit pants. "Okay. Arnie was working with these guys from MexTel for the better part of three years. They're being sued for poisoning groundwater at various places in Mexico. People have died; people have contracted cancer and other horrible illnesses. MexTel has denied responsibility and Arnie was defending them, going along with their claims of innocence. Then he found a file that contained groundwater test results from in-house testing they'd done. Turns out the chemicals their infrastructure leached into the groundwater were highly carcinogenic. Cancer-causing stuff that is illegal to even produce in the U.S. But not so, Mexico. So MexTel orders Arnie to bury the file. Which he does. Until one day he quits taking his meds and decides to do the right thing and tell the citizens of Mexico their own communications cartel has been poisoning them. He takes off, but of course we don't have a clue where. MexTel is going to probably find him before I do and kill him. That's where you come in. If I can understand how to manipulate MexTel into leaving Arnie alone, I'm happy. That's about it."

"We need conversations, then. I'm on it."

"We need conversations. We can't tap their phone lines so—"

"So we'll do the next best thing. We'll bug their rooms." He stands. "Let's go. They might be meeting up while we're sitting here gabbing. Time's a-wasting."

I set aside my can of Diet Coke and stand. "How about letting me drive the bike on the way back?"

"In Chicago traffic? Are you out of your mind?"

"Just testing. Just wanted to see how far along you'd go with me."

He turns and pulls the ignition key off his belt chain.

"Not that far, Mikey boy. Far, but not that far."

16

Making my way across the crosswalk—Marcel has dropped me on the opposite side of the street from my building—I receive a call from the Cook County Jail. James Lamb needs to speak with me immediately. There has been a stabbing. That's all the caller can or will tell me. From the lobby of my building, I take the elevator down to the parking garage and jump into my SUV. I head for California Avenue.

Instead of the infirmary, this time, I head straight for the lockup. They review my ID and usher me right through. The detective squad, I am told, is in Conference Room III, alone with my client.

Just as I feared, it is two Chicago Police Department detectives. One is Anglo, and one is Asian-American. One is holding a notepad, and one is holding a smartphone. They have Lamb between them at the table, firing questions at him. Lamb is handcuffed to the table through a metal eyelet, and his head is hanging forward. When I walk into the room, he barely raises his eyes and doesn't speak to me.

I sit down at the table and wave at the detectives to back off.

"You realize this is my client, and I have previously told his jailers that he is exercising his right to remain silent?" I remind them.

The white guy smiles and moves closer.

"Not so fast. We're not talking to your man about the Pennington murders. We're here on a new beef."

"What might that be?"

"Your client stabbed an inmate to death."

"Really? Did you witness this?"

"No, of course not."

"Did anyone in the jail tell you they witnessed it?"

"No, it happened in the cafeteria. There were thirty guys at the table, and no one saw it. But according to a guard who was across the room, the victim was sitting across from Lamb, and he suddenly keels over. Your guy stands up and says, 'Piece of shit!' or some such. So he gets pulled in here, and they call us because we're the CPD investigators on Pennington. Hope he has the money you need because he's looking at his second murder indictment."

"All right, have you taken any statements from Mr. Lamb?"

The Asian-American laughs, a big horsey laugh. "He ain't talking, Gresham. You've got this guy sealed off better'n a cheap bottle of wine."

"No statements?"

"None."

Lamb shakes his head No.

"Then we're done here. You two guys are excused; please leave me alone with my client now."

The two cops look at each other.

Then the Anglo leans down and yells into Lamb's left ear, "We'll be back with papers for you, shithead! Don't run off!"

I stand and rap on the door. A pause, then it opens, and the jailer sticks her head in.

"We all done here?"

"They are. I'm not."

"How long for you?"

"Ten."

The two detectives slowly move out of the room. There are whispers between them, and one laughs a nasty, low laugh. Then the door closes, and I am alone with James Lamb.

"All right, buddy," I begin. "Let's have it."

"It was the guy who put me in the infirmary."

"How bad is he?"

"They said he was dead. I stuck a fork in his throat."

"Who witnessed this?"

"Everyone."

"Everyone? Who's everyone?"

"Everyone at the table. They were pissed because I hit an artery. There was fuckin' blood everywhere, man."

"But no one saw you do this other than the inmates?"

"Right."

"That explains why you haven't been hauled off to jail."

"Hey, shithead, I am in jail."

"I'm talking segregation. You still may be. And watch your mouth, James. People call me those kinds of names often find themselves alone at the next court session."

He eyes me bitterly. He bites his lower lip and drops his head. This is definitely a new, more aggressive and intelligent James Lamb than I knew existed.

"Can you get me uncuffed?"

"No. You're officially in custody on the murder case."

"So what can you do for me?"

"What can I do for you? I can cash your check for fifty thousand dollars when you pay me to defend you. Up until then, you're on your own. I've only been paid for the Pennington case, and that was just twenty-five hundred. Deal of the century, so don't start in on me with this what can I do for you bullshit!"

"Jesus, lighten up, Mr. Gresham. I was only asking."

"You know, you led me to believe you had a severe mental deficiency, James. But the more I see of you, the more time I spend with you, you're starting to come across to me as just another street hoodlum."

"Hey, you got that from my parole officer. I never told you mental stuff."

"No, but when I asked you before you went along with what she said. You played dumb."

"Well, I am. Kind of. I keep getting caught, don't I?"

"So what about the Pennington case? Did you kill the wife and you're not telling me?"

"What difference would it make?"

"Probably none. Maybe lots. I don't know."

"I didn't kill anyone that didn't have it coming, ever."

"So is that a yes or a no?"

"Did they have it coming?"

"No."

"Then it's a no. No, I didn't kill the lady. I'm not that kind of punk. I sell drugs, small time. Satisfied?"

"Not really. I don't believe you anymore, James. Not since you just stabbed a guy in the throat with a fork and killed him."

"Who said he was dead? You know that for a fact?"

"The deputy who brought me here said Mr. Jarinmosa died an hour after. They couldn't save him. He lost too much blood and went into shock. Someone is looking at a murder one charge. You'd better hope your lunch crowd keeps its mouth shut."

"Relax. None of them's talking."

"You know this how?"

"That's the Crips table, dude. I'm eating with my brothers."

"So how do you kill a brother Crip and no one gets upset?"

"Shit happens. Guys die."

"Did you give the cops anything?"

"I told them to stick it up their ass."

"We'll talk in the morning. So long, James. Remember, you don't talk."

"Shit, dude."

"Right, then."

~

ON MY WAY IN, Marcel calls me. He says he's onto something that can change the Pennington trial and bring it to a screeching halt. I get down to the office, park, and hurry upstairs.

"He's in your office, Marcel," Mrs. Lingscheit says.

"Morning to you, too."

In my office, his back to the door sits Marcel, the *Sun-Times* spread on my desk before him.

"Marcel."

"Hey. You ain't gonna believe this, Boss."

I plop down in my chair. Mrs. Lingscheit enters and makes a Keurig cup. She hands it to Marcel and asks if I'd like one. I wave her off.

"Try me. Let's see if I believe or not."

Marcel holds up his iPad. He clicks the PLAY arrow, and a

video takes form and rolls. I don't recognize the room, but I recognize the men. Same setting as an hour ago, different date and place. Fordyce and Burns are standing behind James Lamb, who's seated at a table in what I can only imagine is an interrogation room at the FBI installation.

"FBI office?" I say, pointing to the screen.

"Uh-huh. Just keep watching."

"Louder."

The sound comes up.

The two agents are telling Lamb they know he murdered the judge's wife. They are holding up a gun and saying it came from under his mattress. Lamb is cool, sitting back with his hands clasped behind his head, legs crossed, staring up at the ceiling and ignoring them.

Their questions start coming faster.

Lamb doesn't respond.

Their voices turn angry and they threaten him with every conceivable kind of criminal charge they can think of if he doesn't cooperate.

He still ignores them.

Then it is still for several minutes as the detectives step away from the Lamb.

Suddenly, without warning, Agent Burns drives his fist into the side of Lamb's head. The impact knocks him out of the chair onto the floor, where he rolls onto his back, holding his head. Then, in one sweeping motion, Burns produces a foot-long sap and, while Lamb is writhing on the ground, slaps him hard across the mouth with the lead embedded end of the hard leather sap. Lamb screams, a long crying scream of someone in great pain. The agents each grab an arm and jerk him back up to the table. A sheet of paper is pushed at him.

"Sign," says Fordyce, "or else I'm going to turn him loose on you again."

Without hesitation, Lamb takes the pen from Fordyce and scribbles across the paper.

"And put the date there, too."

The kid asks the date and Fordyce prompts him.

Then both cops turn to the lens of the corner camera and Burns mouths the words, "This thing on?"

The screen then goes black, and the video ends.

"Holy shit," I say. "Did you see how hard he hit that poor bastard?"

"Took four front teeth right off at the gum line. And no, I've never seen anyone sapped like that and live to tell about it."

"So it wasn't resisting arrest. Our kid really was beaten out of a confession."

"Yeppers. Trial's over, Hoss."

"Yes, this trial's over. The obvious question: where did you get this?"

"Don't know. Whoever sent it was clever. Couldn't trace it."

"So it came from some unknown friend of the court? It's got to be from the FBI."

"Our very own Deep Throat. Richard Nixon must be spinning in his grave."

"So I'll resuscitate my motion for directed verdict. Based on the fact the video confession should have been kept out, etc. The sanctions I'll be seeking will be complete dismissal with prejudice so they can't file again."

"I'd say you win on that one." He blows across his coffee cup and sips.

"Now get this. Lamb was questioned by the PD this morning. Someone got stabbed in the jail cafeteria."

Marcel groans and sits back. "You gotta be shitting me."

"Nope. Two detectives were there. Robbery-homicide dicks."

"Did he say anything?"

"No, the kid's a pro. Kept it zipped."

"Well, that's a win. Were there witnesses?"

"Dozens. All Crips."

"I *thought* that was a blue Crips rag I saw at his place."

"Remember the P.O. saying he couldn't qualify for his GED? I don't know where the hell his P.O. got that."

"I thought you said his IQ was eighty-something."

"Eighty. That's what his parole officer told me. They had him tested in prison and he was too damn dumb to get his GED. That had all the social workers crazy. I mean how do you rehabilitate someone who can't pass the GED?"

"Damned if I know. Give them their Crips rag back, I guess.

Spot them a hundred to buy a stash and get to pushing product."

"Or maybe give them a badge and call them 'detective.'"

"Don't say that too loud."

"Yes, well, I think the stash thing is more or less what's been happening. I mean we know he's dealing."

"Yeah. Small time."

"But we didn't know he was a killer until he stuck a fork in someone's carotid artery this morning."

"Guess not."

"So let's do this. Email me the video and I'll pass it along to Bob LaGuardia over at the U.S. Attorney's office. We might even have a voluntary dismissal in the next few hours."

"Roger that. On the way."

"Damn."

"I know."

"Damn."

—

17

❝ *Chicago Tribune, April 3*

In an almost incredible series of events, a video of the confession made by James Lamb was revealed today. The parties won't release the origin of the video, only saying that it came directly from a public agency.

The video depicts the beating of James Lamb by an FBI agent while his partner stands by. Following the beating, Lamb is seen confessing to the murder of Judge Francis Pennington's wife.

Keenan J. Harshman, Reporter

I file my renewed motion to direct a verdict and Judge Amberlos responds by calling us into chambers at one o'clock sharp. Marcel accompanies me to the court-house, and we talk about Lamb as we hit all traffic lights on green—a new record. We park in an off-street lot and walk up the sidewalk to the double doors. There's a fifteen-

minute delay while we go through security. Then up to
Judge Amberlos' chambers and in we go. Bob LaGuardia has
beat us there because his office is inside the Dirksen Building. He looks grim and shuffles his feet when we take up the
only remaining seats—one on either side of him.

"Where the hell did you get the video?" he half-whispers
to me.

"From my investigator."

"Where did he get it?"

"Email. Unknown who. They didn't exactly sign off on it."

"I'd like a copy of the email he received. We'll try to trace it."

"Uh-uh. Marcel says he tried tracing back to the mailing
address. The sender used an IP out of Argentina, it turns
out."

"No shit? Man, someone's in big trouble with me. You've got
to believe me, Michael, I had no idea this video even
existed."

I've known Bob LaGuardia for a long time. I probably
mentioned before that he's an honest, career prosecutor
who doesn't play games. I do believe he didn't know
anything about the video. He's as astonished as me at what
it shows.

"I don't believe you did know about it, Bob. I'm going on the
record with that."

He reaches into his manila file folder and hands me a single
sheet of paper bearing his signature. I glance over it and
look at him.

"You're dismissing with prejudice?"

"Hey, the judge is going to do that, so I beat him to it."

I know the politics behind the dismissal. The SA's office doesn't want to appear to be in bed with the FBI over this one. Someone over there has committed perjury, starting with Fordyce and Burns. This one has legs.

"So, what happens to the two dicks?" I ask.

"Powers greater than me are making that decision as we speak. Honestly, I have no idea. But I'm betting on criminal complaints before closing time. With a press conference featuring our U.S. Attorney himself, exonerating his office and explaining the dismissal. The video has already been leaked to the *Tribune* and *Sun-Times*. So we're ahead of the curve on it."

Our little talk is interrupted by the judge's chambers secretary, Marilyn Sweeney. She is a relaxed, calm force that rules the office with an iron-fist. "Go on in, people."

Marcel and I follow LaGuardia into the judge's wood-paneled sacristy. The air smells of bourbon, and I wonder how the man is still holding his calendar together. Of course, it's Marilyn, out front, who's the enabler. She's an accomplished enabler, too, from where I'm sitting, enabling his alcoholism to flourish and continue. But the rumors are rampant the JEC is about to pull rank and either jerk his ticket or send him to rehab in Wickenburg. Wouldn't be the worst thing.

"Gentlemen, and lady," says the judge in an almost morose tone. "We're on the record in *USA v. James J. Lamb*. The court reporter is here and taking this down. The court has, within the last hour, received a *Notice of Dismissal* from the U.S. Attorney's Office. The *Notice of Dismissal* is with prejudice so the charges can never be renewed. I would ask for your comments on the record. You first, Mr. LaGuardia, it's your *Notice*."

LaGuardia settles back in his chair and picks at his sock. Then he begins.

"Judge and Counsel, I just want to put on the record that no person in the U.S. Attorney's Office was aware of this video and no one was aware of the incident it has captured and portrays. It's easy to see that the so-called confession of Mr. Lamb was coerced—no—obtained with physical violence. Even as we sit here, the person or persons guilty of this violence and perjury are being addressed in our offices by the U.S. Attorney himself. I was directed to dismiss with prejudice, and I have done that. Thank you."

The judge turns his rheumy eyes on me.

"I can only report that my client is happy to be vindicated. He has told me all along that the so-called confession was obtained from him by his being beaten, and now we can all see he was telling the truth. It remains his position, too, that the gun that was reportedly found beneath his mattress was also a lie concocted by Special Agents Fordyce and Burns. The gun bore no fingerprints and will never be connected to my client by these two liars. This afternoon, after my client is released from jail, I intend to counsel fully on the need for him to retain civil counsel to sue the FBI for this horrible prosecution, for the mental anguish its brought to him. Thank you."

We then file into the courtroom and James Joseph Lamb is

brought in wearing handcuffs, a waist chain, and ankle chains. The judge has him brought up to the lectern, and he then explains what has happened. Lamb begins smiling, turns to me and winks and nods, and I return his look without blinking. The court instructs the Cook County Sheriff to immediately release without delay Mr. Lamb and return his personal effects to him.

Then we are in recess and Lamb is returned to the jail for processing out.

My representation of him is officially at an end, and I am glad. While it makes no difference in how I work, I've never totally trusted James Lamb and especially now, with a dead man investigation ongoing, my distrust appears justified.

Marcel leads as we exit the doors of the court building, and we hasten our return to the car.

"It will be good to get back to the office and put our feet up," I tell him.

"This has been a tough one, hasn't it?"

"Very. You can feel very helpless at times doing this work. Very helpless."

"So, who sent the video?"

"I have no idea. Somebody within the FBI. But why they would do that, I really don't know. Unless."

He is starting up my SUV and backing out when he turns to me and says, "Unless what?"

"Unless someone wanted him out of jail where they could get to him."

"Oh my God, you are a suspicious man."

I look at him and give him a tight smile.

"It comes with the territory, Marcel. Trust no one."

"Not even you?"

I grimace. "No one. The bottom line is the system is run by imperfect people. Do not trust it or them, ever."

"Not even you?" he repeats. I can see his smile out of the corner of my eye.

"The jury's still out on that one. Patience, Marcel."

"Well, I think you're someone I do trust. Until proven otherwise, at least."

"Fair enough."

18

Two weeks after the Lamb dismissal, I am behind my desk, reading the latest brochure on the Sundancer boat line. I'm thinking of getting a power boat for Lake Michigan. My doctor says it would be a great way for me to get away and wind down. So I've taken it into serious consideration. I'm thinking maybe thirty-five feet, sleeping four, all the latest electronic gear on the panel. I'm a sucker for electronics and will go for every last trinket they can stuff in front of me as I sit in the captain's seat and steer.

My phone buzzes and Mrs. Lingscheit says James Lamb wants to see me. He's in our outer office, no appointment, and he won't say what's up. I tell her to send him on in, and I fold the brochure and place it face-down on my desk.

Lamb comes in wearing his jeans dropped below his buttocks like all good gangbangers, a Crips blue rag on his head, and heavy, blackout sunglasses. He's also wearing a gold grill over his teeth. Totally ragged out.

Without being asked, he sits down across from me and exhales a huge sigh. Then he leans forward and places his smartphone on my desk.

I look at him, waiting for him to speak.

"I hate those bastards thinking they had the only good shit."

"You mean the video?"

"Yeah. I mean I've got my own pictures. Want to see what I didn't tell about?"

"Sure. Let's see."

"I'm emailing you my Instagram link."

"You have these pictures up on Instagram?"

"Relax, Mr. Gresham. You said they can't come after me no more. Prejudice or some such."

"You were dismissed with prejudice, right. And no, they can't come after you."

I check emails on my laptop and find his email with the link to his Instagram account. I click on his page, and it shows me the first picture. At first I'm shocked; there is lots of blood and a woman lying on her back. She is wearing a thin dressing gown. In the next picture, her gown has been opened. Three bullet holes in her chest are displayed. Both pictures are close-ups, faceless torso shots. I click again. I am stunned. The dead woman is Judge Pennington's wife. These are death photos from the murder scene. Photos that I have never seen before. And I've seen all the official photos. That much I know.

"Where did these come from?" I ask as I continue through

more shots and more, each one depicting the dead woman. My mind is careening down a long hallway that grows imminently darker the farther I go. "James, tell me."

"Shit, dude, I took 'em."

"You took these pictures?"

"Course, man. I capped that bitch and made my own photo album. I figure fuck, everyone else has a family album, I should have one too. I even wore my roommate's big shoes. Pretty fuckin smart?"

"I—I—" I cannot form the words I want to say. There are no words. Just the quickening realization that I have been a party to a hoax, to a murder that is never going to be prosecuted. I could send these photos to LaGuardia this very instant, and there would be nothing he could do.

"We got the last laugh, dude!"

"James, you need to leave. Now!"

He stands and begins backing away. I remember that I have a pistol in my drawer that I keep for self-protection. It's not the silver Colt that Marcel gave me, but it's a nine millimeter, and it would drop this piece of shit in a heartbeat.

But I don't go for the gun.

I allow him to leave and then and only then do I stand, pull my coat off its hook, and leave my office without a word.

Mrs. Lingscheit is ignored as she tries to get my itinerary for the afternoon.

I am downstairs, in my car, and gone.

19

Two weeks later I'm still tied up in knots. The better part of me wants to turn Lamb out of my mind and move on with my life. But another part of me wants to go gunning for him. I am plagued night and day with thoughts of this total asshole. I cannot sleep without awakening during the night two or three times with thoughts of the gold grill leering over the dead woman's body. I wrack my brain trying to think of ways the U.S. Attorney could prosecute him, and I'm a pretty damn good criminal lawyer, but I come up with nothing.

Marcel drops me at the Congress Building after court. It is nearing the end of April, and the air is warming up. Nights are still cool, but there is a hint of summertime humidity down here in the Lower Loop where I operate beside the Lake.

In the lobby downstairs there's a fairly decent restaurant or two, American and Chinese. I opt for the American and find myself all but alone in the rather large dining area. I check my watch. 11:15 a.m. Too early for the lunch bunch, but a good time for me to crawl off alone and steal a few minutes in which I just might consider my own life and time.

I call Mrs. Lingscheit to tell her I'm downstairs.

Immediately she asks, "Did you get a call from Judge Pennington?"

"No, but my phone's on vibrate. Let me check."

I check my calls. Sure enough, there's a 312 number that I didn't answer. Exactly eleven minutes ago.

"I think I've got it. I'm going to hang up and call him."

"Roger that, Michael. I'll see you by two?"

"Probably. I'm grabbing a sandwich and then returning his call."

Pennington's call is the call that no one ever expects. A person who once hated you now wants to talk? Maybe to tell me what a fool I am. Well, I deserve that. The thought of Judge Pennington causes Lamb's face to focus in my mind. There is a circular target drawn on his face and a bulls-eye right between his eyes. I force the image out of my mind and turn my attention to lunch.

I place my order for a roast beef sandwich, heavy on the Dijon, fat-free mayonnaise. Then I have second thoughts and switch to the Cobb salad. Healthier, I'm thinking. With coffee. The girl smiles, and I notice a large bruise on her upper arm. Plus one eye is drooping. I wonder if she's a victim—

My phone begins wildly vibrating. It's the 312 number again.

"Yes?" I say after punching to accept.

"Michael? This is Judge Pennington. I need to meet with you without delay."

"Is this about James Lamb? I honestly wasn't trying to—"

"No, this is about me personally. I've been arrested."

A chill etches its way down my spine. Where I spend my days, judges don't get arrested. This is highly improbable, but I do recognize the judge's voice and I know he's the last person on earth who would lie to me about such a thing.

"Where are you, Judge?"

"California Street."

"Talk to no one. I'm on my way."

"Of course. Hurry, Michael. This isn't looking good."

I toss a twenty on the table and sprint for the lobby entrance. I blast through the double doors on the right of the revolving doors and dash to the curb. A cab a half-block away sees me waving frantically and moves from the center lane to the right. I'm good.

"Twenty-Sixth and California," I shout over the seat.

The cabby nods and turns his head. "You going to jail?"

"I'm going to the jail. I'm not going to jail."

"Same difference," he shrugs.

"No," I say, adamant. "Not the same thing at all."

∾

AT THE JAIL, they run my briefcase through a scanner and then I step through the security ring. No beeps.

I wait for them to buzz the door and allow me inside.

Finally it buzzes and I pull the handle. Inside the airlock I wait for the second door. A voice comes over a loudspeaker above my head. "Please wait just inside the door," it instructs me. "We're very busy today. Someone will come for you."

I do as I'm told, holding up just on the other side of door two.

Ten minutes later, a deputy sheriff, female, comes up to me all out of breath and wiping a damp swatch of hair from her forehead. "You're Pennington?" she says.

"I am. I'm Michael Gresham, his attorney."

"Right. Mr. Gresham, would you mind meeting with Mr. Pennington in his cell? Our conference rooms are bursting at the seams."

"Not at all. He's single-celled, right?"

"He is. I've had him out twice to make phone calls. One time was to you."

"How would you know that?"

"I listened in on an extension. We always do that during the first forty-eight just to make sure someone's not going to hang himself with a shirt or something."

"I'll have to remember that."

"Lawyers are too smart to discuss stuff with their clients on jail lines anyway. Aren't you?"

"Sure. Never, no way, and I make sure my clients know it."

We access a long hallway with cells lining both walls. The hallway floor is gray cement, the walls are lime green cinderblock, and the only light is thrown down from parallel fluorescents that run the length of the hallway. We reach the end. She speaks into her shoulder mike, and moments later my client's cell door buzzes open. Electronic everything. I've only been inside California Avenue jail cells a couple of times, so it's a relatively new experience for me.

Judge Pennington looks up at me. He is seated on his cement "bed," which really is a six-foot slab raised up off the floor with a thin mattress loose along its top. A brushed stainless steel unit composed of a toilet and a wash basin complete the decor at the far end of the cell. I say "far end"; it actually is about eight feet deep by six feet wide. There are no radios, no TVs, no computers or laptops, no reading materials, nothing to while away the time for an active mind such as one belonging to a United States District Court Judge.

He waves weakly.

"Come, Michael," he says, "sit by me."

There's no other choice. I sit beside him and turn to my left.

I say, "Start at the beginning." He knows what I need to hear.

"All right. I got home from my Christmas golf outing, and there's a confidential letter waiting for me. It's from the Chicago field office of the FBI."

"Do you still have it?"

"Of course."

"What did it say?"

"It said that their computers had returned a hit."

"On?"

"On a conspiracy to murder James Joseph Lamb."

"How would the computers know something like that?"

"They said the decedent had appeared before me, that I had sentenced him to a term in prison, that he had done his time and that he had later on been on trial for murdering my wife. They said I had then conspired to purchase the murder of Lamb."

"What was the upshot?"

"The upshot was that they wanted to send an agent to speak with me. Just for the record. They made that very clear. I wasn't indicted yet or anything. They just wanted to be able to say they had made contact with me."

"What did you do?"

"I agreed to meet with them."

I am flabbergasted. I am dumbstruck that a sitting judge would agree to meet with the FBI on a case involving the potential death of the man who had killed the judge's wife. Dumbstruck is an understatement; I am rendered mute. I simply sit there, not knowing what to say next. And I am wondering how far the plan moved down the tracks: is Lamb still alive?

So the judge speaks up. "So, we met."

I recover enough to say, "And now you're in jail and don't know why?"

I am struggling to grasp what he is telling me. Early this morning, I appeared before this same judge, and he allowed my client to go to Seattle on business. The judge did ask for my cell number after court was over, but I thought nothing of it. I thought it had to do with the insider trading client. Wrong: he called me on that same cell number just as I was about to bite into my roast beef sandwich in the lobby restaurant of the Willis Tower. So he knew—or was afraid—something was coming, and he wanted my number. Which I consider a huge compliment, that he would select me to represent him out of the 60,000 lawyers in Chicago. This will be great for business and really may mean I eventually get to retire when news of my landing the biggest fish in Chicago hits the streets and back rooms where my client roster gathers and plots their crimes.

"I have the indictment. I'm just having trouble reading it all the way through. I've been charged with conspiracy to murder James Lamb. Now, I need a lawyer. How much do you need, Michael?"

"You're sure you want the guy who defended your wife's killer?"

"I have to have the best. How much?"

"Two hundred fifty."

"My CPA will send over your check. Two hundred and fifty thousand dollars."

"It could run more, if there's an extensive trial, if we need expert witnesses, or if there's an appeal. You would be responsible for all those things."

"I just don't want to lose my federal retirement. And of course, my freedom."

"Let's talk about this a little more. It was the FBI that arrested you?"

"Yes. The same agent I spoke with initially."

"Who is that?"

"Nathan Fordyce."

"He's still working for the FBI? After trying to frame my client with a coerced confession?"

The judge spreads his hands. "Strange things over there in FBI Land. I know better than to ask."

"He's after you now that Lamb walked free?"

"Evidently."

"He brought you here?"

"Two U.S. Marshals brought me here. Both have served in my courtroom at various times."

"May I see the charging documents?"

He passes his papers to me. He is charged with conspiracy to commit homicide, a charge being brought by the U.S. Attorney for the Northern District of Illinois. Pursuant to 18 U.S. Code §371, two types of conspiracies can be prosecuted. The first type lists a Conspiracy to Commit a Federal Crime, which requires that the underlying criminal activity be a crime that is outlawed by federal statutes. Murder is one of these, and this statute could be used against the judge. The second type of conspiracy listed in §371 is a Conspiracy to Defraud the United States. This kind of allegation does not require that the underlying criminal activity be a federal crime, although, as a practical matter, such a conspiracy charged in a federal court Indictment would often, if not likely, allege criminal conduct that is an offense against the federal criminal statutes.

"We're looking at a three-seventy-one case."

"Yes," he says. "So it appears."

"Have you discussed this idea of killing Lamb with anyone?"

"No one. They're saying it's cartel hoodlums in Tijuana I contacted."

"Have you been to Mexico in the last year?"

"No. I've been to Maine for skiing and Florida for golf. But Mexico is way off my beaten path."

"If you had been there, would anyone be able to trace that?"

"You mean, would I have been stupid enough to use credit cards? No, I wouldn't. But I didn't go anyway. You'll just have to believe me on that. Remember from this morning, when you said you couldn't prove a negative? Well, that's my exact same position right now. I can't prove I didn't go to Mexico, but neither can they prove I did."

"Understand. Now, I have to ask. Have you ever talked to anyone about getting revenge for the murder of your wife?"

"Never. Ridiculous."

He is flustered with me. "Please, Michael, don't reduce me to the status of a common defendant who might have done something that stupid. That's not at all how my mind works. *I* don't work that way."

"You know, I know that. But I'd be remiss if I didn't ask. You might hate me later if I missed something really obvious and you went down because of it. So bear with me."

He sits back, and his flip-flops fall to the floor. It is an awkward moment, a sitting federal judge barefoot in jail. Could I say it's unnerving? Yes, but more than that, it's surreal. That's it; this should never be happening, and I almost want to pinch myself. I bite my cheek instead. The pain reminds me that yes, I am here, and this is my life.

"Okay, now tell me about the hit on the FBI computer. The one they first contacted you about. What kind of hit was it?"

"The thing that stands out the most is the agent said I had had in my courtroom the son of a Tijuana drug lord. They said I gave him a break and in return he would kill James Lamb for me."

"Their computers made that connection?"

"FBI computers are capable of predicting the most remote connections that humans would never begin to dream of. It is artificial intelligence built on top of a very suspicious neighbor watching your every move out of her window. Have you wondered how they are able to track a terrorist living in Boise, Idaho, who goes to Pakistan and a year later shoots up a college in Maine? Did you know those connections would have been made at the time of the original trip and would have been assigned a numerical value of interest? Sixes and fives might be ignored for manpower reasons. Fours and threes would get reviewed. Twos and ones would have agents actively knocking on doors and asking questions."

"So you were a two or a one?"

"Well, I got the confidential letter, didn't I?"

"But this isn't a case of terrorism. Why would the FBI be concerned about the commission of what could just as easily be a state crime?"

"Because I am a federal judge. We're all subject to constant oversight. It comes with the territory."

"You and—"

"Me and every other judge, U.S. Attorney or assistant, congressmen, senators, administrative chiefs and their second level staff, cabinet members. Even the president is watched by the FBI."

"So we're not at all surprised your name went into a search string."

"Not at all. Happens every day."

"All right. Now about some housekeeping."

"Yes, time to talk about getting me out of here," he says. He wilts somewhat as he says this, knowing he's caught up in the federal system where he holds office, which means it will take days to find another federal judge to come to Chicago and hear a bail motion. Of course, there are statutory time limits, so there's always that.

"When I leave here, I'll go by the U.S. Attorney's Office and see what I can find out. There's probably another indictment on file, too, a co-conspirator. I'll round that up and come back tonight, and we can go over whatever I find out."

"Thank you, Michael. I knew I could count on you."

It is too much to hold in. I have to ask.

"Judge Pennington, why me?"

"Why not you, Michael? You have tried two jury trials before me and participated in dozens of discovery and procedural motions. You are unyielding, obtuse, and brilliant. You were my first choice and, well, here you are. Now go do your pick-ups, including your check, and let's talk again tonight. As of now, I'm single-celled because of the position I hold in the judiciary. I'm going to go back there and try to catch a nap. I'm sixty years old and tired."

"I know the feeling. I'm fifty-five."

"I know you are. Fifty-five, divorced, living alone and working horrendous hours, so you don't fall behind on your alimony."

I am stunned at his knowledge. "How—how—"

"I have a computer too, Michael. Remember?"

"Thanks, Judge," I say.

I never know whether new clients are guilty or not. I'm one of those lawyers who doesn't want to know, either. I don't wish to know because it makes no difference to me whether a client is guilty. If they have the money to hire me and if I agree to the job, I'm in, period.

So when Judge Pennington swore up and down that he is innocent, I told him what I just said. It makes no difference to me. Besides, my mind is much further down the road than simple questions of guilt or innocence. My mind is spending the money the judge has just promised to pay me for his defense. Two hundred and fifty thousand dollars, ninety thousand of which will buy my freedom from Sue Ellen. Who can say? Maybe she'll even make me the child's godfather.

"When do I get initialed?" he asks. The initial appearance is where the subject of conditions of release might first be brought before the magistrate judge. There are time limits involved, but Pennington is more familiar with the ins and outs of all this than most federal lawyers. I read the second page of his paperwork. There is an order setting his initial appearance for tomorrow. Evidently he couldn't stand to read the second page; he is asking when he is initialed.

"Tomorrow. There's a note here from an Assistant U.S. Attorney that you will be brought before a magistrate who's coming up from the Central District tomorrow. Plus a motion for detention."

"Who's the magistrate?"

"Doesn't say. Does it matter?"

"Not really. They're not going to allow bail anyway."

"Hopefully, that's not true. I want you out of here ASAP."

"You'll help me?"

"Of course, I will. That's what I do. But why me? I've been thinking you must hate my guts for taking the Lamb case."

"Naw, you were just earning your keep. Somebody had to do

it. Well, as it turned out, he was forced to confess anyway, so it turned out for the best when they dismissed it."

I can't tell him about the pictures Lamb led me to. This is neither the time nor the place.

"Well, I'm just glad there are no grudges against me. I really want to help you, Judge. Starting now. It's the least I can do."

"Good. Glad you're on my team, Michael."

He turns and leans back against the wall at the head of his bed. He is still in his orange jumpsuit and is wearing white socks with an indent between great toe and second toe where the thong of his sandals has forced its way in. I am struck with how far beneath this judge's dignity this whole setting is and I'm sure it must be totally surreal to him. I can't wait to spring him out of here.

I flip through his papers during a lull. He gives me several minutes to read.

Then he asks, "What do we know?"

"We know there are two co-defendants. An Emmanuel 'Emmie' Ramon, and a Raul Demad Ramon. They reside in Tijuana. Ring any bells?"

"No bells."

"Well, according to this, you met with Mr. Raul Ramon in Tijuana. And you also adjudicated the case of *USA v. Emmanuel Ramon* in your courtroom. Does that ring any bells?"

"None. Should it?"

"Maybe; maybe not. Okay, here's the twenty thousand foot

view. The indictment states that you conspired with the two other defendants to murder James Lamb."

"That's ridiculous!"

"It says you gave Emmie Ramon special treatment in your court and in return Emmie and Raul agreed to kill James Joseph Lamb."

"I only wish I had. That's a conspiracy I might seriously have considered involving myself in."

"So none of this rings a bell?"

He pushes air at me. "Of course not, Michael. If I was involved in any of these shenanigans, you'd be the first person I would tell. I know you must have the truth in order to defend me properly."

"That's right."

We both stare into space for a minute or more.

Then I need to move on it. "Let's talk about our theory of defense."

"I did nothing wrong. That's my defense."

"Well, unless they come up with some kind of evidence that you made a trip to Tijuana or San Diego, I think we go in and just deny any and all conversations between you and the Ramons. God only knows how close the FBI is to those two. If they've given them immunity in return for testifying against you, then that gives us even more ammunition against them. Otherwise, I say we just sandbag. One, you don't know them. Two, you've never met with them. Three, you've not been out to the West Coast in years. Four, there are no phone records showing calls to any area codes out there. And five, you have an alibi at or near the time they are saying any conspiracy was hatched."

"Sandbag them."

"Absolutely. You don't have to get down and play at their level. You're way above these losers, Judge."

"What else are we doing?"

"Well, we also need to get our discovery requests and motions on file. We need to know where any alleged meeting took place—Chicago or Tijuana? We also need to know what kind of payment was supposedly made by you in exchange for the hit. We also need to know what kind of evidence they have. Is it written or video? If they have hard evidence such as video, it will probably make their case. So then you've got to negotiate a deal. But without video or documents they lose nine times out of ten with a jury. This is about as much as I can tell you right now, Judge."

"They can't have written or video. I didn't do what they're saying."

"I understand. I'm just stating the possibilities, so we get a feel for your status in any case."

"You said there's a motion for detention?"

"There is. My guess is that they'll put a Special Agent on the stand to make the case about the weight of the evidence against you. You know the drill. So then I have to win on the other points. Such as whether you're a flight risk or a danger to the community. There will be conditions, but I'm hopeful we can spring you on bail."

"I would be surprised if they allowed me out. But I'm pulling for you, Michael."

"I'll talk to my investigator. He'll be working up your background data and he'll be my only witness. You, of course, won't testify."

That went without saying. We both look blankly at each other.

I say, "I'm sending him back along with a power of attorney. I need you to sign it so I can start gathering together copies of your credit card statements, cell phone records, and all the rest of what they might be looking at to make their case. I never trust them to turn all these things over to me in discovery; I get them on my own."

"I know you do. That's why I hired you, Michael."

I stand up and stretch, bending at the waist and touching my toes.

I come upright. "All right. My investigator will talk to you briefly in the morning when they bring you to court. Now, what assets do you have in case they set bail? How are we fixed?"

He sits back and flattens his spine against the wall.

"Paid for house. Probably one-point-two million. Federal retirement: nothing that can be cashed out or borrowed against. I had a five-hundred-thousand dollar life policy on my wife. That money is still at Fidelity in a low-yield mutual fund. I don't ever touch it. So there's that. Your payment will come from the sale of my holdings in Facebook stock. I was early in and once they learned how to monetize their website my stocks soared."

"About your bail, Judge. It sounds like all told we're talking about maybe one-point-seven or one-point-eight in money we can put our hands on."

"Yes."

"All right. We'll be putting together all the deeds, titles, and so forth to the unencumbered amounts available. We can take care of that in the morning. Now, part of the detention hearing is going to be taking a look at the weight of the evidence against you. That's going to be hearsay, of course. Like I said, expect to see a Special Agent on the stand lying his head off."

"Lying in a courtroom? Seriously?" His sense of sarcasm hasn't left him.

"I like to use the detention hearing more for discovery purposes than anything. I get to cross-examine their witness about all the facts of the case. So even if the magistrate allows the detention motion and you don't get out, all is not lost. We'll have their chief investigator's testimony nailed down, and that's a beginning as we build your defense and win this thing."

"Yes."

"Now, I have to ask you for the record: are there any crimes that I don't know about?"

He laughs; a scoff, actually. "Of course not, Michael. I couldn't continue my judgeship if there were."

"I know, but I have to ask. Forgive me."

"Forgiven."

I stand there and nod, allowing my eyes to break contact

with his for several moments, giving him time to collect his thoughts in case there's something I've left out or something he wants to tell me.

Then, "All right then," I say, slowly.

"All right. Thank you, Michael."

"Not necessary to thank me, Judge. But let me thank you for your trust. I won't let you down."

"I know you won't. You're the best of the best."

"Thanks for that."

~

BACK AT THE OFFICE, I am going through the day's mail when Mrs. Lingscheit knocks on my open door and walks inside.

"Oh, this came over by courier."

She lays a plain envelope before me. I slice it open with my letter opener and pull out a check.

It's from Judge Pennington's CPA. It's made out to me, and I have to study the zeroes.

$250,000.00 it says.

I hand it back to Mrs. Lingscheit.

"Please stamp this and deposit it. General account."

Without looking at it, she stuffs it back inside its envelope.

"Will do. Now you run along home, Michael."

"You first."

"I'm on my way," she says.

Ten minutes later, I'm alone in the office. The front door is locked. I checked it after she was gone.

I start moving the pieces around in my mind—Pennington, Ramon, Ramon, Fordyce, Lamb.

I told my new client I would be back tonight.

That is one promise I will definitely keep.

20

I live in a Tudor north of Chicago. My home is located on Lake Michigan. At seven o'clock it's time to head home because Maddie's cooking tonight.

I decide to drive home—rather than take the L train—since I'm coming back down to the jail anyway. I head over to Lake Shore Drive and slowly make my way north. At Sheridan, I continue north, putting the sun roof back on my SUV and letting the cool air off Lake Michigan blow through my hair. Looks-wise, I'm not much. Never turned many heads, although I've pretty much been able to go out with whatever women I chose—at least when I was younger. Sue Ellen and I were together so long that I'm not sure whether that would still be the case or not. The truth is, I haven't been on a date since we separated, and the divorce went through. It just isn't in my DNA to feel like I have to rush right out and make a connection. That's just not how I'm wired.

Coming north on Sheridan, I'm able to cut over to Lake Shore Boulevard and a few miles down I hit the garage door opener and pull into my garage. I'm a block over from a frontage road that parallels Lake Michigan. Houses in my area don't turn over that often, and I'm lucky to have this one. The previous owners went down in an airliner crash while they were visiting Austria. A probate lawyer friend of mine, who was settling up the estate for the heirs, remembered that I was newly separated and living out of a suitcase in the Palmer House. He called me up, gave me a key, and I took one look and had to have it. My banker balked at the price (excess of one million) but a mortgage company liked my $200,000 down, which came out of my SEP-IRA, and they financed me. The payments are less than what I pay Sue Ellen in alimony, but not by much.

Three nights a week Maddie Jefferson comes to my house and cooks dinner. She's an energetic black woman in her early thirties who's getting her Ph.D. in romance languages, and our paths crossed when I put an ad in the local paper looking for some help around the house. She needed the extra income while she wrote her dissertation, I needed meals, and it's worked great for both of us. Not to be stereotypical, but I've learned to love turnip greens, grits, old-time fried chicken (and lots of it), mashed potatoes and gravy, cornbread, fried okra, ribs, and the occasional ham and navy bean soup. Dishes like that. Maddie's mother was from Magnolia, Georgia and she passed along to Maddie what she knew about cooking. Maddie can do Yankee; it's just that I've come to prefer southern since she introduced me to it.

Friday nights there's a poker game that rotates between the homes of the six guys. One of our group is a circuit court judge, one is a computer programmer, three are lawyers and the sixth is either a psychologist or a parish priest, depending on who wants in. We have a few drinks, smoke enough cigars that we stink up the place, and gobble down KFC and Ben and Jerry's before we clear the table and spread the green velvet table cover. I bring the chips and the table cover and the beer; the other guys do the rest. Our usual game is straight poker, nothing wild, and, of course, Texas Hold 'Em. Once the deal is face down and the hole cards are dealt, then it's free-for-all check, bet/call, raise or fold until the wee hours of the morning. The most I've ever lost was a hundred and fifty dollars. The most I've ever won is seventy-five. Nobody gets hurt; nobody gets drunk, and nobody goes away mad.

That's about the extent of my social life.

But there is a particular woman who has been very friendly to me. She works as a trainer at my gym, and I've had a few training sessions with her. By now she's probably wondering why I keep hiring her, and yet my extra ten pounds isn't going away, no matter how fast she has me pound the treadmill or how many minutes I log on the elliptical. The weight remains and, in between sessions with her, I'm usually found relaxing in the steam room and the sauna, after I've skipped the workout, which is where I do my best thinking. Her name is Ann Horford, and I haven't noticed a ring but, come to think of it, she mostly wears gloves. She's very friendly, smiling and encouraging my pathetic efforts to please her as she moves me through the stations.

Tonight is a Maddie night, and as I come inside through the garage, I can smell the unique fragrance of ribs barbecuing on the Jenn-Aire mingled with the boiling collard greens and simmering green beans. The oven light is on, and I'm guessing cornbread. A sumptuous meal awaits, and I could kiss the cook.

Instead, I say my warmest hello.

"Maddie, it smells like heaven in here. And you're my special angel."

Maddie is early thirties, lithe and beautiful, a Halle Berry lookalike, and she turns from the stovetop and wipes her hands on her apron.

"Well, look who finally decided to come home. I've been treading water with all this food since you called and said you were on your way—an hour and a half ago. What happened?"

"You know what, I had some papers come in that needed to be looked at and I didn't get to leave when I said I was. Sorry about that."

"No problem. I just turned everything down and fired up my iPad and did some editing."

"Dissertation?"

"Uh-huh. Working on the bibliography."

"Ouch. That's all got to be APA format, am I right?"

"More or less."

"I hated that stuff in college."

"It's become another language to me. When I'm teaching full-time next fall, I'm going to need it lots."

I go to the refrigerator and open the door. Surveying the contents, I ask if there's any Diet Coke. She steps into the pantry where I have a second refrigerator and returns with an icy can.

"Ice?" she says.

"No. Straight out of the can. So what are you teaching?"

"Just signed my contract since I saw you. I'll be teaching freshman French and a literature course."

"French literature?"

"Yes."

"Books in French?"

"Yes."

"God. Don't know how you do that."

"Well, that makes two of us. Don't know how you do law."

I knock down a slug of Coke. "How's Jethro, by the way? Is he still taking care of your every need?"

We're old friends. I can talk to her like this.

"You know what? Jethro and I are no longer an item. He's going to run off to California and try to make it as a studio musician."

"What's wrong with Chicago?"

"I don't know. He says L.A is where it's happening for him."

"So, just like that?"

"Just like that. Gone, baby, gone."

"I thought you were engaged or something."

She steps past me and turns the ribs on the range.

"Or something," she says, but doesn't go into it, and I don't pry.

An idea suddenly hits me, but I ignore it. I'm far too old for her, and it's a stupid thing even to think.

"Okay, well, I'm gonna go in and change. Then I'll chow down and head back downtown. I've got a client waiting to see me yet tonight."

"My, we are keeping long hours!"

"He's in jail. It's the least I can do to let him know someone actually gives a damn about him."

"Love that about you," she says and laughs. But she gives me a look that's more than just a look if you know what I mean. It's more like an invitation to ask maybe a little more about what else she loves about me. But I turn away and head for my bedroom. I'd only make an ass out of myself, and I don't want to risk losing a cook where I don't know—forget it. Maddie's way too young for an oldster like me.

Just before eight o'clock, I'm headed south again.

Judge Pennington has called me. The reality of his being in jail is settling over him like a cloud. He sounds depressed. It always sets in in the first forty-eight hours of incarceration. My job right now is to give my client some hope, something to cling to, some reason to think things are going to get better.

The only thing is, I've got to make sure I'm not just blowing smoke.

I really do have to have a plan.

Which makes the judge a happy client, because I do. Have a plan, I mean.

A good one.

My cell phone chimes as I'm driving southbound on Sheridan. It's Maddie.

"Hey," I say, "I left your check by the phone."

"No, this isn't about that. Do you like jazz?"

"I do. Coltrane, Miles, B.B. King. Why?"

"I know a club on the South Side. We should hit it."

"We should? I'd like that." It blurts out before I can edit it.

"Saturday night. I'm coming by to get you. This isn't a date. Just a couple of single people—I didn't say lonely—going out to dig some tunes."

"I'm in."

"I'll pull in around eight. We'll take my car."

"Okay. Thanks, Maddie. This will be a blast."

"We can have some drinks and laughs. Oh, you don't drink. Well, I'll have some drinks. Maybe we should take your car."

"We'll take my car," I agree. "I'm the DD."

"See you then."

I hang up.

No matter how hard I try to repress it, a smile crosses my face.

I step on it. There's an anxious, very frightened member of

the federal judiciary waiting for me to come and help. It's a critical case both for the judge and—I'm embarrassed to say because it makes me seem so small—for my career. This could be the case that fills my office with new work, allows me to hire an associate attorney, and begin the long process of retiring from the law.

Then there's Maddie and jazz.

Now I can't stop smiling.

21

Hon. Mary Robles-Wanstedt peers down at me from her high bench in Courtroom 1109, Dirksen Building. She is the federal magistrate judge the all-knowing federal judiciary has run up from the Central District of Illinois to sit in judgment of one of its own, Francis Pennington Jr.

"Mr. Gresham, if I may interrupt your conversation with the man next to you, are you ready to proceed with the initial?"

I break off my last-minute preparations with Marcel, who I will call as the defense's only witness today. He has had the opportunity to load up on background information that he can impart to Her Honor when he takes the stand to tell-all about Judge Pennington. This is the Who, What, Why, Where, When stuff about his life that will, it is my intent, serve to prove to the court the man has deep ties to the community that would weigh heavily in favor of doing the right thing about appearing in court if the court should grant him bail. Marcel leans away, and we break it off. Seated at Marcel's left is Judge Pennington, and I spin my fingers to indicate they should trade. They do, and now the judge is next to me, where he belongs in the traditional scheme of taking-your-client-to-court.

"Your Honor," I reply hastily, "the defense is ready to proceed."

"Very well. Mr. Pennington, will you please approach the lectern with your counsel? Thank you."

We both step up and Judge Pennington stands directly behind the lectern while I am one step to his left. The AUSA remains sitting, and beside him is Special Agent Nathan Fordyce, who is, I am confident, primed and ready to go.

"Mr. Pennington," Judge Robles-Wanstedt begins, "Rule Ten provides that a plea will only be taken at arraignment and this hearing today is not your arraignment so be careful in speaking to me that you do not indicate whether you're pleading guilty or not guilty, fair enough?"

"I understand, Your Honor," says my client.

"Good. Now, there are certain things we must accomplish here this morning in your initial appearance. You have been charged with a felony—multiple felonies, actually. You have been accused of several counts of conspiracy and similar accusations to purchase the murder of a James Lamb of Chicago. The case is venued here in Chicago because the U.S. Attorney alleges in his information that the facts under-lying the indictment—the conspiracy portion—took place here in Chicago.

"You have the right to retain counsel, and you have exercised that right. Attorney Michael Gresham is appearing before

you today, and Mr. Gresham is a member of the trial bar of
the Northern District.

"You may secure pretrial release if certain conditions are
met. However, in this case, the government has filed a
Motion for Detention, which the court will hear this morning, and following that hearing conditions of release, if you
are released, will be ordered by me. Are you with me thus
far?"

"Yes, Your Honor."

"Very good. Pursuant to the Bail Reform Act of 1984, defendants will be released prior to trial without any special
conditions, unless the court concludes that you are likely to
flee or are a danger to others or the community.

"During this morning's detention hearing, the court can
determine that certain pretrial conditions could reduce the
likelihood that a defendant will flee or endanger others or
the community.

"In the event the court determines there are no conditions or
combination of conditions to ensure you would not flee or
endanger others or the community, the Court will order that
you be detained."

"Do you have any questions so far, Mr. Pennington?"

"No, Your Honor."

"Finally, you have no right to a preliminary hearing because
the government has indicted you. Mrs. San-Jish, are we
thinking amendments to the indictment?"

The AUSA, a mid-fortyish woman wearing a saffron dress
of Indian descent stands to her feet and addresses the

court. Her voice is small, courteous, and straight to the
point.

"We will be taking the case before the grand jury on
Wednesday, Your Honor. There may be additional counts."

"Mr. Pennington, you have the right not to make a statement.
I expect you will have discussed that aspect of the criminal
proceeding with your counsel, and you will act on his direction. Having said all that, the court has read the government's Motion to Detain and has studied the file, slight as it
is, and is ready to proceed with testimony to support the
government's position if, indeed, the government wishes to
offer testimony."

Again, the brown-skinned woman stands at the government
table.

"The government calls Nathan Fordyce to the stand."

The witness is sworn in and takes his seat on the witness
stand.

Preliminary questions and answers are passed back and
forth, and I am struck with the youthfulness of Nathan
Fordyce. From our previous confrontations in court and out,
I had thought him much older. If he's a day over thirty-five, I
would be surprised. However, as he responds to the AUSA's
questions, he answers with a maturity level far beyond his
age. This is a guy who has long proven that he knows his
way around a courtroom. Moreover, this is probably the
biggest case of his career—the prosecution of a sitting
federal judge—and he has dotted all i's and crossed all t's.
To put the capstone on the fact he is going to be an impres-
sive witness and opponent at whatever stage of the proceed-
ings he appears, he is handsome in a blond, crewcut way

with full Hollywood sideburns, blue eyes that are blessed with almost a surfeit of honesty, and a perfect smile.

The AUSA continues. "Now, Special Agent Fordyce, one of the questions the court must decide today is the weight of the evidence against the defendant."

"I understand."

"Please give us the factual basis for the charges that have been brought against Mr. Pennington."

The witness swallows hard, gathering himself. This is the moment of truth for him and his case. Too much detail and he's given me way too much to work with; too little and the judge quickly lets my client loose.

"Well, I was assigned this case by—"

"Please, let's skip the administrative portions and just tell Her Honor what the defendant did."

"From his cell phone while in Barrington, Illinois, the defendant made contact with a gentleman by the name of Raul Demad Ramon. This subject is the father of Emmanuel 'Emmie' Ramon. These two subjects are co-defendants of this defendant. These two subjects reside in Tijuana, Baja California."

"The government has alleged a criminal conspiracy between the three defendants. Please tell us about that."

"After Judge—Mr. Pennington—made contact with the senior Ramon, he held a hearing on the younger Ramon's case here in Chicago. The younger Ramon was a defendant in Judge Pennington's court at the time. He was facing drug charges, and there was a motion to suppress based on *Wong*

Sun v. United States, the fruit of the poisonous tree doctrine. Following a very short hearing, the judge found the search and seizure were illegal and dismissed the government's case against Mr. Ramon.

"Sometime after, a man named James Joseph Lamb was targeted for assassination in Chicago, Illinois."

"How is that, if at all, connected to Francis Pennington Jr.?"

"I have interviewed the father and son. They are on record saying the defendant traded the son's freedom and dismissal of his case for the murder of James Joseph Lamb."

"Is there a recording of that interview?"

"Video recording. I met with the father and son in Tijuana and arranged to have a video recording made of their statements."

"Why would they give you statements? That makes no sense."

"It was simple. We told the father and son that the charges against the son had been dismissed without prejudice and that we were going to refile and put the son in prison. Judge Pennington had slipped up and left a way for us to refile."

"Last question. Why would the judge want James Lamb dead?"

"Objection. Foundation," I say.

"Sustained."

There are no virgins here this morning; we all know why Judge Pennington would want the guy dead. None of us blames him, either. Deep down we can all put ourselves in his shoes. It wouldn't be a hard call to put the Mexican Mafia onto the guy who murdered your wife.

"That is all, thank you."

The young agent swings his gaze to meet mine. I stand and take my place at the lectern.

"Mr. Fordyce, isn't it true that you also obtained that alleged statement by promising immunity to both the father and son from prosecution for Lamb's murder?"

"I can't testify to their motive, sir."

"But it's true they've been given immunity?"

"Yes."

"And the son also has immunity from prosecution on the Chicago drug charges, correct?"

"Yes."

"Do you happen to have the phone numbers for these people?"

"I do."

"Would you provide them to me? I'd like to talk to these gentlemen myself."

He smiles. "Careful, counsel, this is an ongoing investigation. You want to be very careful about interfering with a federal investigation. You've been warned. On the record."

"Just call my office with their number, please."

"Yes, sir. I'll do that."

"But the bottom line is, you have completely insulated the

Ramon duo from prosecution in the United States in return for their testimony against Judge Pennington, correct?"

"You could say that, I suppose. Sounds more like argument to me."

"The witness will answer the question without editorializing," the judge interjects before I can object to the answer. Robles-Wanstedt has been around and isn't going to allow commentary during testimony.

So, I decide to push it.

"In fact, isn't it true—" I am fishing now, "that there are other crimes that have been committed by this Dynamic Duo in the United States, and that you and U.S. Attorneys in other jurisdictions have guaranteed there will be no prosecutions on those cases in return for helping you bag Judge Pennington in the biggest case in the office of the DOJ?"

"Object to Dynamic Duo. We don't believe they're all that dynamic, Judge," says San-Jish, proof that she too has a sense of sarcasm that she's willing to share with us.

"Sustained. Counsel will cease his own commentary."

I look at the witness. "Please answer the question."

"There are other investigations underway, particularly as to the father. I'm not at liberty to say what those are."

"Your Honor," I say, "please instruct the witness to answer my question whether he feels he has the liberty to or not."

"No, I don't think I need to," says the judge. "I've heard enough to get a pretty good feel for the weight of the evidence against the defendant and that's the standard that I am by law required to apply."

"Then I have no further questions for this witness," I say, and I sit down.

Judge Pennington is breathing heavily beside me. I am trying to breathe normally, but the testimony about the phone call made from Chicago to Mexico is hugely troubling. Scary, I'm sure the judge would agree. Who knows what all they've put together on him? Even worse, how do they have anything at all? He's promised me that he's guilty of nothing, and yet they claim he made a phone call? I shiver violently but am able to keep it inside my suit.

The government rests its portion of the hearing, and it's my turn.

I call Marcelino Rainford—Marcel—to the stand. He's sworn and takes his seat and looks around casually. Another pro of the courtroom wars.

After we have his name, education, and work history, I begin to narrow in on what I need. It's my job to produce evidence that Judge Pennington has close ties to the community that would keep him in our district and that he doesn't pose a threat to others or the community. I plunge ahead.

"Mr. Rainford, you've spoken to Judge Pennington?"

"I have. Just this morning."

"As a result of that conversation, do you have information concerning his ties to this community?"

"I do."

"Please elucidate."

"The judge is a lifetime resident of Chicago. Grew up in Forest Lawn, and has lived in a Chicago suburb for twenty years. He was married; wife now deceased; one living son. He has two sisters and two brothers living in Illinois; only one of those lives inside Cook County. He has served as an Assistant U.S. Attorney in the Northern District, ran unsuccessfully for State's Attorney, and was appointed for life to his current position on the federal bench in Chicago by President Clinton. He attends the Unitarian Universalist Church of Chicago, plays second flute in the BurbsPipes and serves two inner city kids as a Big Brother. Shall I go on?"

"What about his being a danger to the community or others?"

Marcel can't suppress a small smile.

"Really? Well, Judge Pennington's criminal record is non-existent. I checked. And I checked county and city records as well. Not even a speeding ticket. However, he does go to State Prison twice a month."

"State Prison? What for?"

"He speaks to Twelve Step groups there about legal resources for people imprisoned over addiction-caused issues. Drugs, drunk driving, prostitution, all of it."

I look up at Judge Robles-Wanstedt. After enough time spent in courtrooms you can read a judge's look. Right now she is telling me that she's heard enough. So I back off.

"Nothing further, Your Honor."

"You may cross-examine, Counsel."

"Mr. Rainford, how long have you known Francis Pennington Jr.?"

"Less than one hour."

"Do you think one hour is enough time to form an opinion about someone?"

"Counsel, I formed an opinion about you in the first two minutes I saw you."

San-Jish's head flies up from her notes, and her eyes blink rapidly.

"Well, I-I—"

"I decided you were a pretty fair prosecutor."

"That is—I think that's all we have, Your Honor."

"Very well. The witness may step down. Counsel, would you like to be heard?"

The upshot is, after we finish our arguments to the court, Judge Pennington is granted pre-trial release, subject to some very harsh conditions. Ankle bracelet, check. Surrender passport, check. Stay inside the Northern District of Illinois, check. Post a property bond in the amount of one million dollars, check. And there is more, much more. He will be a free man but he will wear an electronic hobble on his ankle, and he'll have no money with which to flee. He'll continue to receive his salary from the federal government; it turns out he has voluntarily recused himself from all pending cases and will accept no new assignments from the Chief Judge until the case is resolved. That's not a requirement from this morning, but it did surface during discussions of conditions. The judge, on the record, voluntarily recused himself.

Now it's up to me to make the property posting and work up the rest of the conditions.

Judge Pennington can hardly restrain himself.

He pumps my hand and thanks me over and over. Tears come into his eyes, and he blinks them away. Marcel shakes his hand and then the judge turns back to me and spreads his arms. He wants to hug. I jerk my head toward the hallway and begin marching up the aisle.

Courtrooms are no place for judges and lawyers to be seen hugging.

Particularly a courtroom jammed with members of the media.

Which that one was.

The case will be all over the local, state, and national news all weekend. CNN will carry it every day and do three-minute updates like it does with significant developments in government affairs. Plus, the major networks had previously done the very sad and tragic story when the judge's wife was murdered. You might imagine they won't let go now that the judge's murderer has been targeted.

We won't find an unbiased juror in the entire state when the case comes up for trial.

Maybe that's not such a bad thing, all things considered. The judge's wife was killed by the guy the judge now stands accused of plotting to kill.

Lots of people call that an eye for an eye.

I know I do.

What about the fact he may have lied to me, telling me he's uninvolved? These thoughts process in my mind as I open the door and begin walking the hallway toward the elevators. So what if he's involved? Now that I've had a chance to see how the government is pulling out all the stops to nail my client, I'm outraged. Making all kinds of deals with Mexican drug lords in order to put a federal judge in prison? How is that fair when those witnesses have killed thousands of people with their drugs and murdered thousands more who they had disputes with? Give them all a pass for one federal judge whose wife was murdered?

I find myself just that much more alarmed at the lengths to which the government will go to make itself look good.

But this time, that's not going to happen.

This time, the whole truth is going to come out.

Because my entire thinking has changed. Sandbag the case? Hell, why not claim temporary insanity. I know I would be temporarily insane if someone slaughtered my wife.

Perhaps the judge was insane too.

It's worth a look, I decide.

I step into the elevator and plunge toward the lobby.

Marcel is ahead of me, waiting just outside my elevator. Good, now I can discuss Arnie with him.

Arnie, who's about to get himself murdered.

Arnie, my beloved brother.

22

Marcel drops me in front of the Congress building then swings back into traffic and roars off. They are installing a new security system at my home, and Marcel wants to be there.

In the lobby is a Fox and Hound, a charbroiled burger/charbroiled steak and seafood place, which people in my building heavily support as the food is the best. So, I stop in at the Fox and place an order for a charburger with mushrooms, onion rings, and milk. My ulcer is rumbling in my lower right gut, so I will lay off the soft drinks and caffeine for the rest of the day. When my food comes, I dig a ten out of my wallet and pay the guy, who's so busy balancing new orders and checking customers through the long line that he's unable to stop and even thank me for my patronage. Which is all right; the place is the best around, and I'll be back.

The elevator is slow today. It is jammed, and several people look at my bag of food and smile. I open the bag of onion rings and hold it out, and everyone looks away. It has occurred to me that onions might not be the best influence on my ulcer right now, especially deep-fried, but there are no takers. I can't even give them away. Oh well, I'll have just one. Maybe three, but that's it.

"Hello, Mrs. Lingscheit!" I call out on my way through the outer office.

She looks up from her computer monitor, speaking into her clear telephone headset as she nods at me and raises one finger.

I pause. She usually follows me into my office. This must be significant.

Her call clears and she reads a note she's made.

"Sue Ellen has called and called. She just has to see you again."

"We just met. Tell her to come here."

"No, not here. She wants to meet you for lunch again tomorrow."

"I'll call her tonight and find out what's changed in the past two hours."

"Okay, here's the breaking news. The AUSA has filed an emergency motion in the Hudson case. Seems William Francis Hudson, III hasn't returned from Seattle, and poor Mr. McDermott is worried he's fled and isn't coming back. He wants Hudson's bail revoked and a warrant issued for Hudson's arrest."

"You put the motion up on the server?"

"Of course, Michael. When haven't I?"

"All right. What time's the motion?"

"Two o'clock. New judge since Pennington's off."

"Who?"

"Israel Benachem. The guy from Sanderson Royal and Hague."

"Sounds like the U.N. All right. I don't know much about Benachem. Why don't you call around and see what you can find out? Is he defense oriented or is he out of the U.S. Attorney's judge mill?"

"Will do. One other thing. I got the judge's check deposited and guess what? It cleared. We've now got almost three hundred thousand in the general account."

"Cut a check for ninety thousand to Sue Ellen, please. I'll take it along with me to lunch tomorrow."

"Are you sure, Michael?"

"Mrs. Lingscheit, why don't you believe me when I tell you things? Just once I'd like you to trust that I'm telling you the truth."

"It's just that it's so much money. You have your retirement you should be funding."

"Getting rid of this alimony payment by giving her a lump sum is the first step in retirement planning. That's seventy-five hundred a month I can get out of it. Cut the check, please."

"Yes, sir. All right. Your desk is all organized, and Hudson's file is pulled. Have an excellent lunch."

"Thanks, Mrs. Lingscheit."

She's already peering at her flat screen and tapping her keyboard. The conversation has apparently come to an end.

I go into my office and close the door behind me. Tearing off a paper towel from the roll on my sink, I lay down a grease barrier on my desk for the sandwich bag and paper-wrapped food inside. The bag flies apart in my greedy hands, and the first bite of charburger is heaven. Ketchup packets. None. Under my sink is a mini-fridge. I search it for ketchup and find a half dozen ketchup packets in the door. They will do just fine. Back at my desk, I squeeze ketchup onto the sandwich paper and dip an onion ring. Three onion rings just won't be enough; I can already tell, although I have limited myself to just three of any such deli-cacies. Food is my weakness. In the basement of my house is a treadmill. I try to hit it at least, four times a week for an hour. There is also an elliptical machine and I try to do it at least three times—good for flexibility in the low back and legs. Up in my bedroom is a recumbent bike and it's good for a half an hour just about every morning, just to get the blood flowing. So I'm pretty good with cardio stuff, and that helps keep me reasonably trim. So...I eat two more onion rings before diving back into the charburger.

The burger's half-gone when my desk phone buzzes.

"Yeah?" I say over a mouthful of charburger and rings.

"Michael, there's an Esmeralda Settles on the line for you. It's about Arnold."

I punch line two.

"This is Michael. Is this Esmeralda?"

Crying gushes through the receiver and drums against my

ear. Visions of my brother in a gutter with a bullet hole in the back of his head—it all comes racing in my mind.

"Mr. Gresham, it's Esme. Esmeralda. Arnie's gone."

"Okay, let's settle down. Esmeralda, where are you?"

"I'm in Hermosillo."

"Mexico."

"Yes. He was supposed to meet me here and then we were going to cross the border at Tucson."

"Why Tucson?"

"We were coming back to Chicago. Arnie said he had an idea. He was coming to see you."

"But he didn't make it?"

"We took two flights so they couldn't follow us both. I went first; then he was supposed to be right behind me on the ten o'clock. But he's not here, and I'm scared, Mr. Gresham!"

Crying breaks out again. I'm somewhat stupefied. The notion that a teenage prostitute who probably hasn't known my brother more than six weeks suddenly crying for him and being this upset just baffles me.

"Esmeralda, why are you so upset? It's not like you and my brother are married."

I stop. Cold. All stop.

I continue. "You're not married, are you?"

"How did you know? We got married in Cozumel, and we're trying to get pregnant."

"Pregnant after one night? Seriously?"

"No, I've been with Arnie for a month now. We stopped using birth control after the first week. Arnie said it was time he had a love child with me."

"A love child."

"He doesn't have any kids, you know?"

So he must have told her. Arnie actually has two kids by his first marriage and three more by his third marriage. All five are out of college and launched. Well, giving him the benefit of the doubt—I have to give him that at this point—maybe none of those was an actual love child. How does one even know these things?

"He told you he doesn't have any kids, and he wanted a love child? That sure sounds like Arnie, all right. So, listen now. I want you to come on ahead and come to Chicago. Let me know when you get here and I'll pick you up at the airport, okay?"

I don't have a clue what I'm saying or why. I have absolutely no idea what I'll do with her once I pick her up at O'Hare. I'm making it up as I go. That's what I'm usually doing when I'm dealing with one of Arnie's messes—making it up as I go. And, frankly, I'm exhausted with it. I've spent my whole life following my brother and sweeping up the shit. Now I'm beat down.

"You think I should leave Hermosillo?"

"Definitely. You need to get to Chicago and let me pick you up. Then we can decide what to do about the pregnancy."

Dead still calm quiet.

"What do you mean, do about the pregnancy? I'm going to have the pregnancy. Have his baby. What else were you thinking about?"

"Esmeralda, my brother, in case you haven't noticed, is a good half-a-bubble off level. You really don't want to have a baby with him. And I can almost tell you the Mexican marriage is invalid here. Arnie doesn't have the necessary state of mind to give legal consent to the wedding. It won't hold up, and it shouldn't hold up."

Crying again. "He warned me about you, Mr. Gresham. He said you never have supported his best things."

"His best things? Like marrying a teenager when he's sixty years old and getting her pregnant?"

"Age means nothing. This is about love. I've been looking for a man like Arnie forever."

"You mean a father figure. No, a grandfather figure would be more like it. Did you miss out on having a grandfather, Esmeralda?"

As soon as I say it, I regret it. It's catty and mean, and I don't mean it.

"I'm sorry. I'm just upset. This is all taking its toll on me, Esmeralda."

I wait for her to reply. And wait.

I swing around and look at the desk phone. The line is dead.

That crack about the grandfather did it. I frantically do a callback, but there's no answer and I am reasonably confident she called from a payphone in the airport.

Never mind, my intercom buzzes again. I pick up. Maybe she's thought better of hanging up.

"Michael, Ms. LaGrande is back to see you. She doesn't have an appointment, but she was wondering if you got a chance to read her resume."

I hold the phone away from my ear and look at it. Is this really happening? Did someone leave their resume with me? But even as I think it, a new thought takes hold. I'm flush. For the first time in thirty years, I'm flush as a lawyer. If I want to, I can actually hire an attorney—maybe part-time at first—and get out from under the double-calendar appearances that are showing up more and more often. That's when I'm supposed to be in two different courts at once. Criminal calendars are difficult to manage because so much of criminal procedure is statutory, set forth by law, and various court events are required by law to be done a certain number of days after the initial appearance. This is done to protect defendants' rights, so we no longer see people languish in jail for a year without ever seeing a judge. But what it does to a sole practitioner like me is make my calendar tough to manage. Then there are the emergency motions, such as the one this afternoon filed by McDermott. Those crop up all over, and they're like weeds trying to stamp them out. So there's a young woman out front—it's coming back to me—who graduated from St. Louis University School of Law and is desperately beating the streets, handing out resumes, trying to land something —anything—with some lawyer or firm. My mind is made up for me by my calendar problem.

"Give me five and send her in," I tell Mrs. Lingscheit.

"You're sure? You've got that emergency hearing—"

"Please, Mrs. Lingscheit. If you can't believe me, then humor me. I'm really sure I want to talk to her. Five minutes."

Five minutes later, in she comes, visitor striding confidently through the doorway, a happy-to-see-you smile on her face and her hand extended to shake.

She is older than I remembered. I guess early forties. Wearing a gray knit suit with a white silk shirt and pointed collar held together by a gold clasp. Her hair is probably ear length and brushed back on the sides, brushed over on top, dark blond. She has a lamplight flush of color in her cheeks that I am sure is natural and when she wants to shake my hand I know I'm in the company of a solid personality. She says that with her eyes, firm handshake, and her carriage. This is no child and no flighty, overnight law school stamp-out.

"Please, have a seat, Ms. LaGrande."

"Danny, please. It's Dania, but everyone calls me Danny."

"All right, Danny it is. So, you've left me a resume. Let me apologize right up front, I can't put my hands on it."

She nods and immediately two-fingers another document from her shoulder bag.

"There," she says, and passes it across the desk to me. "My resume. As you can see, I've been working out of my dining room trying to scare up clients. But it's very hard in this town to get any kind of traction."

"It is," I say, glancing over her paperwork. "Chicago law practice can be brutal. Where are you located?"

"I'm in Mount Pleasant. Lots of blue collars there, so I was tacking up my card where workers might shop or stop for coffee--anywhere there's a cork board. I've tried going to church and making friends. I've tried joining Rotary and—"

"Got it," I interrupt her. "How much court time do you have?"

"Next to none. I did have one drunk driving case that I got dismissed. But that was city court."

"Now you must have a past life somewhere that I should probably ask about. What made you go to law school?"

"I was a kindergarten teacher. Fifteen years, but I always wanted my own condo and after all that time I still hadn't been able to save a down payment. So, I changed horses midstream and went to law school."

"Are you from Saint Louis?"

"East Alton. I crossed the river every day to attend class. A little bit of a commute, but what the hey. Can I just say that I read in the paper you were defending that judge? I knew you'd be swamped and need help with it. Or help with the other cases. So I decided to come see you."

"Good timing. In fact, I do need some help. I was hoping for someone with a year or two around the criminal courts, however."

She leans forward and raises her hands. "Please. Let me follow you around for one week, go to court with you, get to know some files, at no charge. I won't ask for a penny until you feel I'm ready to earn a salary. I'm even willing to start part-time."

Bingo. Exactly what I had in mind. And no down payment?

What's not to like? If it works out, she's worth her weight in gold to me, and she'll be well-paid. So I plunge ahead.

"When can you begin?"

"Right now."

"Done. We have a two o'clock court appearance. So you go on back to the waiting room and start reading the rules of criminal procedure, federal. Federal court is where you'll be starting. I will stay here and finish my sandwich and onion rings."

"Yes, it looks like I interrupted. But it smells good, though."

She smiles, and her side of the desk lights up. I like that. And I like that she's able to carry on such a natural conversational tone with me although she's only just met me.

Now, why can't Arnie find someone like this to woo? Hell, why can't I?

This just might work. In more than one way, I'm thinking, but then I pull myself up short.

Stop, I excoriate myself. Leave. It. Alone.

23

Following the two o'clock court call, as we stroll back to the Congress building office, I assign Danny's next task to her. First I explain the case against Judge Pennington. We're still talking as we ascend in the elevator.

"Come on in, and we'll give you some details, and then I'll show you your office."

"Excellent," she says, "let me hit the ladies' room and I'll be right there."

I go into my office, Mrs. Lingscheit hot on my heels, and plop down in my chair.

"Well," she says, "haven't we had an exciting couple of days?"

"I mean, can you even believe this?" I say. "Judge Pennington?"

"And don't forget your ex. She only wants ninety grand."

"Did you cut the check to her?"

She grimaces, standing before me with a legal pad hugged to her chest under her crossed arms.

"I did. It was damn hard, Michael, but I followed your instructions."

All because of me, a new baby will be born.

It sidetracks my one-track mind for just a moment, and I am glad.

Babies can do that.

24

At mid-morning I'm returning from the County Clerk's office where I've been checking through old criminal records. Anything I can find on James Joseph Lamb I have pulled and read. The juvie files are all sealed, of course, but there's the natural progression of less serious to more serious in adult court.

The cab deposits me in front of my building on LaSalle, and I step up onto the sidewalk. My attention is on my briefcase, and I don't see the two men approach me.

Then Agents Fordyce and Burns each have an arm, and they're guiding me toward a tan, late model sedan. I struggle and push to the left and to the right, but they are young, burly, and resist my efforts without much exertion.

"Just relax," says Fordyce, the larger of the two. "We just want to talk. Give us five minutes, okay?"

I am surprised at his understated request. Then I feel his hip holster through my blazer.

Agent Burns releases my right arm and opens the back door of the sedan. It's parked in front of Bank of America on LaSalle, right down from my entrance. Fordyce, hanging off my left arm, places his hand on top of my head and steers me down and into the backseat. A real cop move, I'm thinking, and I relax just a little. Then he slides in beside me, pushing me on over.

He removes his Ray-Bans and turns to me in the seat.

"Good to see you, Mr. Gresham. Thanks for agreeing to meet with us on such short notice."

"So why am I being held against my will? Do you know there's a crime for that? Something like false imprisonment? Kidnapping?"

"Please, don't start," says Agent Fordyce. "We only want to talk. We didn't go to your office and wait there because most defense attorneys don't want FBI agents flashing their ID in their waiting room."

"You're doing me a favor? I get it now."

"No need for sarcasm, either. We can be friends here. Or maybe no, after you hear what we have to say to you."

"Four minutes," I tell him.

Burns slaps the steering wheel and looks out the window. "Lawyers," I hear him say as if it's a bad taste in his mouth.

"You are talking to our friend Judge Pennington. That's all well and good. But know this: the book isn't closed on the right Honorable Judge Pennington, yet. Meaning, our investigation is ongoing. If it should turn out that we find you are helping him cover up in any way the chain of events that he has been indicted for, we're more than happy to bring charges against you too, Mr. Gresham."

"What?" I exclaim. "You're threatening me for defending Pennington while he's exercising his Constitutional right to an attorney? What a load of crap! Let me out! Move it!"

"Don't go all postal," Burns says. "We're just explaining our boundaries. You're still free to make any moves you think you need to make."

"I'll do that. Are we done here?"

"Just watch your step. We aren't done rounding up bad guys yet."

"Speaking of that, how come *you* haven't been rounded up yet? Seems to me you and Burns would be right at the top of the *FBI's Most Wanted* list after the way you beat the hell out of James Lamb and then lied about it."

Fordyce smiles. Burns, in the rearview, joins him.

"Need-to-know-basis, counselor. You're not on that list of who gets to know these things, it appears."

"I'll just bet not. Okay, let me out."

He opens the door and gets out. "Come ahead, sir."

I step out onto the sidewalk.

"Do I copy you on my letter to the U.S. Attorney where I'm seeking obstruction of justice charges?"

Fordyce grins a real, big grin.

"We thought you might try something like that. We're here at the request of the U.S. Attorney. One step ahead of you, counselor. Sorry about that."

"You might want to tell your U.S. Attorney this. Tell her I'm not about to back down or back off or even backtrack. I'm here, I'm on the case, and I'm going to win a not guilty verdict for my client. He didn't do what you're claiming, and I'm going to prove it."

Empty words, coming from me. I have nothing to back them up with, but I'm saying them anyway. At this point, I have absolutely no clue about the pros and cons of Judge Pennington's case. But I do know this: these people are in for a fight. I've been waiting all my career to land a case with as much visibility upside as this one. I don't plan on allowing a conviction. The fact is, I'm way down the road on that. Even if it turns out my guy did what they claim, they don't have him on video or tape soliciting the hit. In cases like this, it's one guy's word against another guy's word. Whoever they fish out of the sewers down in Mexico to testify, my guy's side of the street is cleaner.

So I return Fordyce's grin with an even bigger one of my own.

"You fellows have yourselves a nice day, now. I know I am."

Then I turn and enter my building. There's no looking back over my shoulder. They're watching, I know it. But I'm not giving them points for intimidation by looking back.

Score it 1-0, my favor.

Why? Because my defense is already in place and I haven't

even seen the entire case yet. I've been defending people for thirty years, and I'm an impossible adversary in the courtroom.

I tell myself this over and over as door closes behind me.

25

M rs. Lingscheit nails me at the door when I walk in.

"Michael, the U.S. Attorney wants to talk to you. They have a meeting they would like you to attend at two o'clock."

I check my watch. 12:15.

"Any idea what's up? Did they say anything?"

"Mrs. San-Jish—I think that's her name—said it was about your client Judge Pennington. Do you have a witness interview or something you're trying to get?"

"Nope. This is all new to me."

I decide to head on over to 219 S. Dearborn where the USA is officed. I'll stop along the way, pick up a Starbucks and sit in on one of the criminal courts while I'm waiting for two o'clock. The educational process never ends, and I always learn something watching other attorneys navigating the slippery slope of federal criminal court. It is an art form, practicing successfully in those rooms, especially given the horrendously complicated maze of rules governing federal sentencing. Practitioners like me also know that when the feds go after someone, they're usually going to be successful. Cases are worked up months in advance of indictments coming down, by the FBI, the greatest collection of criminal investigators the world has ever known. I know there's a lot of downsizing of the brilliance and smarts of these federal agents in film and fiction, but the average citizen and the most gifted lawyer is wise to disregard such naive commentary. These men and women are the best in the world, and they'll get you if it falls under the U.S. Code as a violation of one of the thousands of federal crimes scattered hither and yon through the books. A slippery slope, indeed.

Coming up Dearborn I pop into my favorite Starbucks where the baristas (the female ones) are head and shoulders above any other coffee bar in town. I can't tell you why it is; it just is. It's fun to go window-shopping at my age. Just remembering what once was and never will be again. Well, damn, that sounds tragic, and I don't mean for it to be. Actually, I'm quite okay with my bachelorhood right now. I just need to figure out how to make it work for me, so I'm not so dumbstruck lonely all the time. Maybe a dog's the answer, who knows?

Venti in hand, I proceed toward the court. There will be no taking my drink inside, so I ordered an iced latte and will have it mostly down by the time I reach my destination.

The city is getting less friendly traffic-wise as I near the federal enclave. Both sides of the street are lined with pillars and posts and contraptions of all manner, shape and size designed to prevent vehicles from standing or pulling over or parking along there with the idea of bringing a bomb close up and detonating it. Cops are everywhere, and I'm sure there are armed men around whose job it is to watch the traffic go by and make sure it keeps moving and to return fire immediately if shooting breaks out. It's only a matter of time before someone tries to storm one of these buildings and take out a floor of district court judges. I am hoping they are stopped before any part of that plan is pulled off and so, going inside and passing through the long security lines, I'm not put off by the wait. Whatever it takes is fine by me. Seriously fine.

Finally, I make it to the fifth floor and find the office where I'm expected. I come up to the glassed-in receptionist's window in the sealed airlock, and she asks if I have an appointment. I explain I was called over and she buzzes the door, allowing me into a small waiting room with a small love seat and two side chairs. There is a table, no magazines, and a picture of the President on the wall. He is smiling as if to tell me all is well in Department of Justice land. He looks happy and confident; I feel nervous and just a little unhinged. I've never been summoned to a U.S. Attorney's office, and it's not conducive to restful thinking. In fact, my mind is racing, wondering whether I have crossed some imaginary federal line and done something I'm going to regret greatly in about seven minutes when the clock says two o'clock. Yes, I'm nervous. This is the Big Leagues, the feds, and above all else I've always gone out of my way to avoid crossing them. That's not to say I won't zealously represent my federal clients; I will. But careful is as careful does. And careful I do.

Several minutes later, the inside office door snaps open, and there stands AUSA San-Jish, dressed in saffron, this wrap being stitched together in very bright orange and yellow hues. She extends her hand and greets me warmly. A part of me is put at ease, but the overseeing part says, "Not so fast. This is neither the time nor the place to feel at ease. This is the DMZ."

"Thank you for coming, Mr. Gresham. Please follow me."

We pass through a short hallway and then turn right, into her office. Special Agent Nathan Fordyce is already there. He half-smiles when he sees me. Ms. San-Jish takes her place in her high-back chair and waves at me to sit down.

I sit, and Fordyce reaches across and we shake hands without words. I wonder if San-Jish is aware of the confrontation. I decide she is not.

"Mr. Gresham, you represent Judge Francis Pennington Junior."

"I do."

"He is charged with two counts of conspiracy to commit murder, which involves the man who killed the judge's wife and walked away free. That man, James Joseph Lamb, was released on a coerced confession. We have evidence that your client visited San Diego and met with a gentleman in Tijuana who has now confessed to being hired to kill Mr. Lamb."

"I assume this so-called gentleman has also been given immunity to say these things."

"Yes," she says, "he has. As well as his son. He's been given immunity too, because he was to be the actual trigger man."

"I didn't know that. But let me ask you this. Independent of what this Tijuana Dynamic Duo tell you the judge did or didn't do, what corroborating evidence is there that my guy was even involved? Is it all hearsay, or do you actually have a case?"

"We have commercial records placing your man in San Diego within thirty days of the homicide. And we have video."

I am stunned. "Video? Video of what?"

"Video of your man filling up his gas tank one block away from the hotel where we found his registration. He paid in cash and our agents then did a review of all video shot within a one-mile radius of that same hotel, hoping to turn up pictures of your client, and, lo and behold, they found him gassing up his car, a 2014 Volvo sedan."

For several moments, I am speechless. This can't actually be happening! Judge Pennington assured me—promised me—that he had nothing to do with any plot to murder James Joseph Lamb. Now this? The feds actually have something? Plus, they went out into the streets and hunted down video of my guy in the area within thirty days of the conspiracy? I sit back in my chair and try to appear relaxed as if I expected these items to be turned up and as if they can easily be explained away with a flick of the wrist. This is the defense attorney's best reaction at such moments: to try to minimize the importance of what he's just been told. With all my acting ability summoned, I attempt to evince a look and posture that minimizes their hearsay, their hotel registry, and their video.

But it doesn't work.

"This evidence puts this case to bed for us," says Agent

Fordyce. "Except for one minor thing. Our investigation was just about concluded until we intercepted a letter from your client written to the Tijuana Dynamic Duo, as you call them."

"A letter?"

"A letter," says Ms. San-Jish.

"What does the letter say?"

"You'll be receiving a copy of all discovery before you leave here today, so you can read it for yourself. But let me just summarize. The Judge, in writing to the Ramons in Tijuana, says, buried in the middle of the letter, that you were complicit in setting up the hit on Mr. Lamb."

Now I am stunned. A line has been crossed against me that has never been crossed before. Warning lights and bells are going off all over my body: I am no longer regarded by my hosts as some reasonable defense attorney out to do his job: now I am the enemy. And the hounds of hell are headed my way. It is time to seek counsel of my own, to shut up and say no more, to take the Fifth.

I gather myself and ask, innocently, "He uses my name?"

"He uses your name if you are Michael Gresham of Evanston, Illinois."

"And the letter—how do you get around the federal law that prohibits anyone interfering with the U.S. Mail?"

"He was out on bail. Part of the conditions of his release was that he commit no other crimes. We received a tip that he was sending the letter and we intercepted it because the attempt to influence a witness in a federal investigation is obstruction of justice and witness tampering. Added to the underlying conspiracy to commit murder charges and you've suddenly got yourself a client who is going away for a very long time. My intention is to make sure he loses track of all time, never sees the sunlight again, and knows the month only from what others tell him."

It's Fordyce's turn. "Which brings us to you, Mr. Gresham. I would like to interview you about the contents of that letter and the things being said about you. Can we set up a time to meet at my office?"

"I—I—no. No, I won't be meeting with you."

Fordyce smiles, and I realize what a great, handsome, attractive witness he is going to make in the case against me.

"You won't meet with us?"

"No. I'll be seeking counsel as soon as I leave here. I'm sure she won't want me speaking to you."

"She?"

"She will identify herself to you just as soon as I have her retained. That should be by Monday."

"We're sorry it has come to this," says the AUSA. "We never like to see defense attorneys get bitten by the hand that feeds them.

I wonder what sage U.S. Attorney aphorism that has descended from.

She passes me a thick Redrope expanding folder. It is packed with documents and, at least, two CD's (videos). They really do have video.

And they really do have a letter that involves me in this crime.

I want to pinch myself. I have just been admitted to the dark world of conspirators in a federal murder case. If this inquiry proceeds, I will be facing the same charges that Judge Pennington is facing.

"One last thing," Ms. San-Jish says with a huge smile. "Let me hand you this." She turns around a document on her glass desktop and hands it across to me.

My hand shakes as I accept the document. I am almost too frightened to look because I almost know what it's going to be.

It is. An indictment. A formal criminal charge.

With my name on it. "Michael Gresham," it says in large print in the caption, "Defendant."

I find myself on my feet and lurching for my door.

"We're not going to have you arrested, Mr. Gresham. Just be sure to appear for your initial appearance at nine Monday morning before Judge Howard Staunton. We won't oppose unsecured conditions of release."

What a relief.

They're not taking me directly to jail.

At least not yet.

26

In a daze, I walk back to my office. I am utterly sick at heart, and as soon as I come inside my little safe haven I find I have a walk-in. Mrs. Lingscheit whispers that the girl sitting in our waiting room is someone involved with James Lamb, and she must see me immediately. Still dazed, I hang up my coat and motion to bring her in. Mrs. Lingscheit leads her into my office and stands to the side. I am greeted by a sickly young woman—maybe twenty-five, if that—with sleeve tattoos on both arms. She is wearing a navy T-shirt and baggy khaki pants held up by a belt that looks like a piece of rope with buckle. Sunglasses are perched on her forehead; her reddish hair looks like she hasn't run a brush through it in a week, but there's a low light in her eyes that is reaching out to me, earnestly reaching out even before she says a word. So I give her a smile, and she sits down.

We introduce ourselves. Her name is Sylvia Manes, and she's James Lamb's girlfriend. She has lived with him off-

and-on for six years, and she tells me he is a difficult person to be around.

Well, I want to say, duh. But I don't, of course. She deserves a fair listen.

"So what brings you here, Sylvia? How can I help you?"

She purses her lips and fiddles with her sunglasses, taking them off and then putting them back on, this time on top of her head.

"He's got my baby and won't give her to me. He threw me out and said he was gonna sell her."

"What? Are you serious? Is this his child too?"

"He says not, but she has to be. I was loyal to him."

"He's going to sell the baby? Do you believe him?"

"James will do it. 'Course I believe him. He said he was gonna get back at the judge who sent him to prison first time around, and he did. Didn't he? Knocked off the man's wife. James will sell my baby and never think twice, Mr. Gresham."

"Why would he do this? Is it about money?"

"He's been having to lay low. Cops follow him everywhere. He can't make a dollar on the streets. So he thinks selling my baby he can get at least five thousand, and he can move. Maybe Los Angeles, maybe Phoenix. He don't know for sure."

"Well, where is the baby now?"

"James won't tell me. I went over there with the po-lice and

The Lawyer   223

he played all dumb and shit. Said he didn't even know I had a kid. Played like we didn't ever live together. Just all kinds of James shit, you know? You know him, Mr. Gresham. He's probably sold her already."

"So what do you want me to do?"

"Call him up and tell him to give her back. Tell him I'm dying for my child. Please, Mr. Gresham, you gotta help me."

"I can try calling him. I'll try right now."

I've still got James on my cell phone. I punch his name and the calls rings, but there's no answer on the first three rings. Then it goes to voice mail.

"Sorry, but he's not answering. Let me call again, I'll leave a message."

"Threaten his ass or somethin."

I don't threaten him; I ask him to call me before he does anything with Sylvia's baby.

I take down her number and tell her I'll call when I know something. She takes one of my business cards and puts it inside her pants pocket. She breaks down and cries for several minutes and I buzz Mrs. Lingscheit, who comes in and helps her out of my office.

"You are trouble," I say to Lamb under my breath.

Three hours later I receive a call from a Chicago police officer. He's a patrolman, and he says he found a badly beaten young woman behind a 7-Eleven store in South Chicago, a block from the old Cabrini-Green projects. Is she all right? I ask. She is dead; he tells me.

And she was carrying my business card. Inside the right-hand pocket of her pants.

27

Her name is Valentine Quinones, and she is the top federal criminal lawyer in Illinois.

I can't afford her out of current cash, but I hire her anyway. It takes only an hour and one phone call to get the HELOC on my house. First State Bank of Chicago had the first mortgage, which I paid off with the proceeds from an accident case something like twenty-five years early. They are only too happy to open a homeowner's line of credit for me now.

Valentine has made room for me on her calendar since I have court Monday morning. And since I told her I could pay her asking price.

Truth be told, I've had a very terrible two hours since leaving the AUSA's office. I've sat in my own office, eyes closed, trying to think how and why Judge Pennington would implicate me in his case as a co-conspirator. I want to call him, desperately, but the lawyer within tells me not to act until after I have spoken with my own attorney. I will do what she says at all turns in the road. When it comes to being on the wrong end of a criminal charge, we are our own worst enemies. In fact, half the time the prosecutors wouldn't get convictions if the defendant hadn't just had to tell their story in an effort to "straighten things out" when they're first confronted by the police. Damn, people, shut the hell up! Otherwise, when you tell your story, you're actually testifying against yourself. It never fails to be just that. So I sit in my office with my eyes closed, trying not to panic.

Consider this. I've been a practicing attorney thirty years, ages twenty-five to fifty-five. In all that time of hanging out with criminals and fighting with police and prosecutors, I have never been charged with the commission of a crime. It's never even been mentioned. There was one guy who got himself convicted because he wouldn't listen to me. He turned me into the State Bar, and I had to defend my license to practice law. But that's the closest I've ever come to being accused of anything (leaving out Sue Ellen, who forever was accusing me of being downright boring). The bar complaint was the closest I've ever come to the sharp blade of the justice system. No charges were ever filed against me by the bar, and the whole thing died a quick death.

But now I'm just another civilian with an indictment setting his whole world on fire. Criminal charges are never fun, but criminal charges instituted by the feds are plain old hell. As I mentioned before, these people don't just tap dance around the edges of a criminal case. They will have the entire case made up front.

So, I'm scared to death.

At 4:55 I pull into the parking garage just down from the Monadnock Building. The Monadnock is a skyscraper located at 53 West Jackson Boulevard in the south Loop area of Chicago. The building sits almost directly across the street from the Dirksen federal courts—a smart, convenient location for Valentine's boutique criminal defense practice.

The elevator opens and a rush-hour crowd of workers circles around me as they flee their building. Once the elevator has cleared out, I am on my way upstairs.

In the hallways, the wainscoting is blond wood and the skylights overhead let in brilliant, spring light. The place gives me a good feeling, and my hopes rise. Not much, but some.

The receptionist smiles at me and offers water, juice, or coffee. Nothing, I tell her. I'm already wired and don't need more coffee. Five minutes later, she's showing me into the office of Valentine Quinones.

Ms. Quinones turns from her credenza to the front of her desk as I enter and I am struck by her raw beauty. Here is a woman who could put the cosmetics companies out of business because she doesn't need them. Dark, black eyebrows and hair, dark skin—her name is Latino—purple eyes with long, un-enhanced lashes, and full lips that break into a welcoming smile as I saunter up to her desk, trying to appear cool about everything even though I know she knows I'm in full-on panic mode.

"Michael," she says. "I'm so sorry about what's happened to you. Let's see if we can just make it go away. Here, sit down."

"Thanks."

"Do you need tissues?" she says, moving a box toward me. "It's okay to cry in here."

"Cry? I'm ready to shoot a particular federal judge."

She smiles again. "Well, let's limit that kind of talk to just my office, shall we?"

"You know what I mean."

"I do, I do. Now, I've read over the indictment your secretary faxed over. Like I told you in our brief talk, it's a very serious set of charges they've brought against you. I also told you that my fee to defend a federal murder case is five hundred thousand. Did you bring a check?"

I open the flap on my shoulder case and produce the check. She holds out her hand, and I pass it to her.

"Good," she says, "I'll deposit this on the way home."

"It's out of my HELOC, so it's good."

"Fine, fine. Now, you were told your initial appearance is set for nine Monday?"

"Right, nine a.m."

"Now, let's talk about the substantive part of the case for just a few minutes. Are you up to that?"

"Yes. They told me I was implicated by Judge Pennington in a letter he wrote to Raul Demad Ramon in Tijuana."

"The kingpin *narcotraficante* in the country of my birth."

"You were born in Mexico? I wondered."

"I'm from Baja. I know all about your Mr. Ramon. So what discovery do we have so far?"

"They gave me this Redrope folder earlier. They said it

contains a letter written by Judge Pennington to the Tijuana killers that implicates me in the murder. This file was to be my discovery as the defense attorney for Judge Pennington. But that's not going to happen now that he's implicated me, so I'm just turning it over to you. I don't even want to look at it."

"You'll have to at some point, but not today. We'll set up a time maybe next week when we can go over these items."

"All right."

"Now, back to the letter. Have you seen what Judge Pennington wrote to Raul Ramon?"

"No."

"Well, whatever it was, it was enough to get you indicted. Have you ever spoken with the Tijuana family?"

"Well, yes and no."

"What about James Joseph Lamb? You defended him."

"James Joseph Lamb? Yes, I did."

"What did you learn about Mr. Lamb?"

"I defended him in the case that he wound up going to prison over. This would be the first case where Judge Pennington sent him to prison."

"Then he came out after that prison time and killed the judge's wife?"

"Exactly."

"Did your defense of Mr. Lamb have anything to do with the charges brought against Judge Pennington? I'm asking whether you knew of Lamb's vulnerabilities, say, as his attorney and maybe you tipped off the judge."

"Not for a second. I would never do that." She has set me to thinking, though and I go back over the past several years since Lamb first went to prison. I didn't handle his appeal. The federal appellate defender did that. "No, I was finished with the guy after the trial court sentenced him. I might have filed the notice of appeal, but that would be common, as you know, for defense counsel to get that done in order to bridge the gap between the trial court notice of appeal and when the federal appellate defender takes over. So that's a possibility."

"What about this: what if Judge Pennington thinks you in some way conspired to get Lamb out of prison early so he could come and murder his wife? What if Judge Pennington has been playing you all along?"

I can't even swallow. That has never occurred to me. Would never have occurred to me. But then I instantly realize she is right. I have been played by this man. He has hated me forever and now he's out to take me to prison with him. Or worse. Federal prisoners sometimes even get the death sentence. I can feel my bowels straining to relax and dump all over the chair. I have never been so afraid in all of my life as I am right this minute.

"Oh, my God," I breathe. It is like a prayer.

"But you never discussed Lamb's case with Judge Pennington after you defended him in the first instance?"

"No."

"And you said yes and no when I asked if you'd spoken to the Tijuana family?"

"I called them, yes."

"When was that?"

"After the judge retained me to defend him. The call I made would be shortly after I found out they were turning government witnesses. Probably the same day."

"What was said during those conversations?"

"Nothing, actually. They were trying to locate Angelo somebody, a guy who spoke English and could translate for them."

"Would that have been their attorney, Angelo Juan Martinez in TJ?"

"Possibly, I don't know."

"Could they have been telling you to call Angelo Juan Martinez, their attorney, and talk to him?"

"Possibly. I honestly don't know. It was very confusing."

"Did you tell your client you had called the Ramons?"

"No need. He was sitting right there with me."

"In your office?"

"In my office."

"Both times?"

"Yes. We were going to have him listen in. Speakerphone."

"Did you ever speak with the Ramons where you discussed the case against Judge Pennington?"

"No, like I said, no English. I left a message, but did we talk back and forth? The answer is no."

"All right."

She folds her hands on the desk in front of her. She checks her wristwatch.

"As you know, Michael, we'll need to review the discovery in the case against you before we can even know what it is they say you've done. Can you be patient while I put those things together for us?"

"I'll have to be."

"And in the meantime, I am going to instruct you to with-draw from Judge Pennington's case. And give him back his files. No, bring his files here and let me return them. That will keep you out of the middle."

"Can I bring them Monday?"

"Yes, please do. Now, what about bail?"

"They said they would have no objection to no detention."

"Well, big hearts there! Of course, you're not going anywhere anyway, and they know that. You've got an office full of clients. You can't go."

"They know that, yes."

"So for now, let's cool our jets over the weekend. No need to meet and discuss. Monday we'll meet just before nine across the street at Dirksen. That will be Judge Staunton; I'm guessing?"

"So they said."

"We'll meet outside his courtroom and check the calendar. Does that work for you?"

"It does."

"And Michael. Please don't discuss this case. Not with anyone. Not even your office staff. In talking to them about your case, that wouldn't be privileged. They could be called to testify against you."

"All right."

"Okay. Shake my hand and get on home. Don't worry if you're followed. They love to harass and intimidate. They think it will force some kind of plea."

"That's it, Ms. Quinones—"

"Valentine, please."

"Okay, Valentine. I was just going to say there won't be a plea. I've done nothing wrong."

"I hear that, and it's duly noted. Good night now, Michael."

"Good night."

28

After I leave Quinone's office, I am in shock. I have been played. I, who have played the system all these thirty-some years: I have now been played by Judge Pennington. My hands shake and I have trouble putting one foot in front of the other as I make my way to my car. Can I even pull myself together enough to drive through this rush-hour traffic north to Evanston? Do I have any choice? I can't just sit in my car parked in some garage on Jackson. I turn the key and the radio blares. It's immediately shut off by slapping the volume knob.

I turn and roll up the ramp and pay the ticket.

I have been played; I want to tell somebody.

Then I think of Marcel. Marcel, my investigator. He will be someone I can confide in, and he will know what to do. I would typically turn to Arnie, as well. Arnie is the smartest lawyer in America. He would surely know what I should do. But Arnie is gone. And I've done nothing to help him except stay in Chicago and pray he's okay. I have let him down when he's really needed me. Worse, I have let me down.

I call Mrs. Lingscheit and tell her to stop payment on Sue Ellen's check. The fee will be returned to Pennington, and I don't have the money to cover her check. I tell Mrs. Lingscheit also to call Sue Ellen and tell her. Tell her the check's no good.

Thirty minutes later, I'm rolling north on Lake Shore Drive when my cell phone chimes. I pull it out of my pocket. Sue Ellen. That's great; this won't be fun.

"Hello?"

"Michael, what the hell!"

"Yeah. I had to stop payment."

"But why? What the hell, Michael, was this all a gag?"

"No. I was paying you with money I had just earned. Then the case fell through, and I had to return the fee."

"It must have been one helluva fee!"

"It was. A quarter million bucks. Gone."

"I'm sorry for you, but what about me?"

"I'll work something out. I really want you to have the baby. Things happen."

"You're not just saying that? This wouldn't just be a jealousy ploy by you? That's the first thing Eddie said."

"Well tell Eddie I said to go—"

"No need, Michael. When I told Eddie about the money

getting stopped, he took off. He was furious and said he had to get out."

"Where would he go? Back to the swimming pool to drown himself?"

"C'mon, Michael. Don't be like that. I'm apprehensive right now. My abandonment issues are kicking in."

"Come over to my place for dinner. I won't abandon you."

"You wouldn't, would you?"

"Did I ever?"

"No, you always stood in the gap for me."

I'm coming up on a line of bicyclists in the bike lane. They are hanging half into the traffic lane, and I have to squeeze by them. In between doing that and balancing my phone, my hands are full. I hear Sue Ellen say she's got another call, that she'll call me back.

I put the phone back up to my ear, but she's gone.

Then the phone rings back just two minutes later. Her again. At that exact moment, I think I've spotted someone following me. But in a long line of northbound traffic, it's just too hard to tell. I force it out of my mind. Whatever. If MexTel or the FBI wants to know what I do on Friday nights, tell them to come ahead.

Her crying into the phone brings me back.

"Michael, it's Eddie. He's moving out."

She's sobbing in heaving gasps and exhalations.

"That's pretty childish. You can't get money, so he leaves you? Come on, what kind of relationship is that, Sue Ellen?"

She's crying quite violently right now. I'm not even sure she's still listening to me.

Then she pulls herself together long enough to say, "He's met another girl. She's a lifeguard too, and she goes to U of I where she's studying physical therapy. She wants to have a baby before she goes for the advanced degree. That's what he said. She wants her family spaced out correctly, she told him. She asked him if he'd be her sperm donor! What the hell, Michael!"

"Sue Ellen, you knew he was younger when you got together. Surely it occurred to you that he might want a family one day."

"I didn't think he'd throw me over to get one! He said I was the perfect sexual match for him. He said—"

"Whoa, you know, I don't want to hear this stuff right now. I'm hungry, and I'm angry, and I'm lonely, and I'm tired. That spells HALT. I'm going to halt and get something to eat and drive slowly the rest of the way and try to forget all about today. It's going to be a quiet Friday night for me. Bill Maher is on at nine then I think I'm going to bed early and start over again tomorrow. Your sex thing with Eddie is really TMI right now. You guys work that out."

"That's it? Us guys should work it out? Is there any room in there for me, Michael?"

I'm coming up on a red light that's backed up for a good two blocks. I might as well keep talking.

"Any room in where for you?"

"In your Friday night."

"What? Do you want to come over, is that it?"

"I might. It sounds cozy and sane. These younger men are very unstable sometimes."

"Sue Ellen, for years you complained because I was too stable. You called me boring. You want excitement, remember? Well, you've got excitement now. Maybe not the kind you wanted, but it's exciting, waiting to see whether your lover is coming or going."

"Damn you, Michael! I'm coming over, and you can just feed me too. I happen to like Bill Maher, too. Or have you forgotten?"

My head slumps. My chin is on my chest, and I'm moving from side to side in the seat like someone held in restraints against their will.

"No, I haven't forgotten," I finally say in a whisper. "Come on over if you want. I'll stop and pick up some Mexican food. Do you still like the *chile rellenos*?"

"Yes. And a beef taco. *Carne asada*."

Her choices seem pretty particular to me. And the crazy is gone from her voice. In fact, she sounds pretty sane right now. Did I just get set up?

"I'll get you all of that, and I have some of your wine coolers from last summer. But I'm going to bed at ten o'clock. So plan on getting home and dealing with Eddie yet tonight."

"Of course. Eddie and I just have some things we need to work on. I'm sure it will be all right."

I hold the phone away and stare at it. This is an entirely different person, suddenly, talking to me. She's level and low-key. What the hell?

"Sue Ellen, why did you call me?"

"I called you because you stopped payment on my check."

"Truth time. Did you already know you wanted to come over tonight?"

"Well, I did sort of push Eddie out the door. Just a tiny bit. Forgive me! He started talking about the baby thing, and I'm thinking mani and pedi and hair color—for me, not for some infant. Besides, I don't want stretch marks. I couldn't stand to look at stretch marks."

"Okay, see you there in about an hour, I'd guess."

Without another word, she has hung up.

The line surges ahead, and I make it across the main light between Chicago and Evanston with only two changes. That's a new record for this time of day.

Some days the low hanging fruit is all picked and missing. On those days, you settle for a fast traffic light and call it your big win. Then I remember Maddie. We're going to the jazz club tomorrow night. Sue Ellen will definitely not be spending the weekend with me; I don't care how many sperm-stalking lifeguards come on to Eddie.

Now I can laugh. What's the worst that can happen? Easy. I go to prison for something I didn't do, and Sue Ellen is the only one who'll come on visiting days for the next twenty years and each time it's about Eddie. Now that's cruel and unusual punishment in violation of the Eighth Amendment.

I'm glad I haven't lost my sense of humor. I'm going to need it.

29

Saturday morning I'm up early. It's still half-dark outside, and I pat the bed beside me. Yes, I'm alone. I sent Sue Ellen home just after the news at ten. It was a mutually agreed parting: time for her to go face Eddie if, in fact, Eddie had come home. She didn't call and try to involve me in her soap opera again so I can only assume they're working things out.

I pull on my cycling pants and a gray sweatshirt, white running shoes and a cap that says FBI above the bill and make a quick cup of Keurig's, which I pour into my bike's plastic bottle. It is a moment of perfection when I back my bike out of the garage, lower the door, and ride off down the street. I head to the lakefront where I can follow Lake Michigan for several miles and pretty much avoid automobile traffic. Plus, it's early, and the soccer moms aren't doing their carpools yet.

As I ride along, I notice my white fingers extending out the half-gloves. I like those white fingers, I'm thinking, and I like the rest of the package. I don't want to see it have to go through a criminal trial, but I don't know how to escape it, either. My head is clear after all the chaos of yesterday, and I'm in a pretty positive frame of mind as I recall my conversation with Valentine and how she said, "Let's see if we can make this go away." I liked that, and I liked her relaxed manner. A no-drama kind of lawyer. At least in her own office. In court, she's known for being a head-knocker, a hard-hitting, knowledgeable litigator with little use for prosecutors with thin cases. Which is how I hope she thinks of mine: thin.

At Irving and Cross, I turn right and head into a small alcove where I can park my bike and walk ten yards and be at the edge of the water. For several minutes I throw rocks across the lapping waters, skimming two and sometimes three times. One was even a four.

All right, I'll admit it. Despite my calm exterior and Saturday morning ritual, I'm hopelessly lost.

For the first time, I'm beginning to understand my own clients. Their irrational fear has become my own: irrational in the sense they oftentimes refuse to allow me to take over and carry them when they're unable to carry themselves. Maybe I need just to sit back and let Valentine take it from here.

Ten minutes later I'm on my way back home.

It's time to call Marcel.

Time to turn my attention outward.

∾

MARCEL WILL BE at my house at noon. He has some video to show me from the hotel room of the MexTel CEO. Evidently the deposition continued until yesterday, and evidently it's going to continue even until Monday. Marcel told me the CEO is now being represented by Sam Shaw himself since Arnie disappeared.

Marcel pulls into my driveway in a shiny Ram pickup, black. It has lights on the roof and dark tinted windows. They look illegal to me, but what do I know?

"Come on in," I say, and we do a fist bump.

"Hey, brother, I heard the news from Evie—Mrs. Lingscheit. What the hell, man?"

"I know. I'm still in shock."

We go into my office and take a seat on either side of my conference table.

"Well, how can I help with your case?" Marcel asks. "Do I need to go to Mexico and take down the Tijuana cartel?"

"That might help. But no, I've hired Valentine Quinones to defend me."

"She's the best, boss—after you, I mean." He smiles and drums his fingers on the table.

"So what do you have for me?"

He pulls a Macbook from his scarred leather satchel, a survivor of the wars Marcel and I have fought together.

"Got this," he says and opens the laptop. It fires right up, revealing a downshot of a typical hotel dining table.

"Carbon monoxide warning device. They never even look up."

"Is it still there?"

"You bet. Still there and still taking names and kicking ass. It's motion-activated, and the battery lasts a long time. It'll still be recording on Monday when they head back to the depo. I've got some places marked on here. Let me fast forward to the first one. Yes, here we are. The guy at the top of the screen is the MexTel CEO, Juan Carlos Munoz Perez. He's wearing the dark glasses and chewing on the cigar. Next to him, your right as you're looking at the screen is the MexTel chief legal counsel—"

"Roberto Aguilar. I remember that pushy so-and-so from my office."

"The other two guys, I don't get their names. Someone calls one of them Hermano or something like that. The other one might be Jakarta. It's fuzzy."

"'Hermano' is 'brother'. Maybe he's someone's brother? Or just a common term or reference?"

"Don't know, boss. Now listen to what Perez is saying here. It's in Mexican but Maddie helped me translate, and I did the captions you'll be able to follow."

"Maddie did this? Since last night?"

Marcel smiles. "She loves you, Boss. That girl would do anything to help you."

Yes, and I'm going to go hear jazz with her tonight. Maybe what he says is true.

The video rolls and I watch the captions:

"So this snake, you say he's outside Cozumel?"

"We think so. We can geo-locate his phone off our cell towers."

"Can you put eyes on him?"

"Not yet. He's very sly about getting located. He makes a call one place and an hour later he makes a call twenty miles away."

"So he's driving to avoid being chased down. That shouldn't stop your men from finding him and taking him out."

"I've passed along what you said. If he is found, it is the end of him."

"Good. Now, what about his brother, Michael Gresham? Can we put pressure on him?"

The man lights his cigar and looks from man to man while they hesitate. Then Aguilar picks it up.

"He is under surveillance from the U.S. already. It must be about that judge he's defending."

"You didn't answer my question, friend. Can we put enough pressure on him to bring Arnold Gresham back to us?"

"We could kidnap him and call his brother and let them talk. Maybe that would flush the rabbit."

"Kidnap Michael Gresham? How does that work, with the feds watching him every minute? Do you really think they're going to let us take him right out from under their nose?"

Perez reaches over and slaps Aguilar on the back of the head, emphasizing his point and his employee's wrong thinking. "*Stupido*!" he cries.

Aguilar pulls away. "Boss, boss. No need for that. We're on the same team here. What do you want us to do?"

"First, I want you to find this Arnold Gresham and shut him up. Second, I want my file back. Last, I want another law firm in this case. Sam Shaw knows there's a missing file, and he's already making noise like we're violating rules by not turning something over. I don't like this man. Don't trust him one inch."

Marcel interrupts at that moment and fast forwards ahead to his next location.

"Here's the best part. They're talking about you, Michael."

"Our legal department called me this afternoon late." It is Aguilar talking, the chief counsel to MexTel. "They tell me that a new criminal charge was filed today in the judge's case. It is against Michael Gresham himself."

"What?" CEO Perez asks, incredulous. "Gresham, you say?"

"Indeed. He tried to get Ramon in Tijuana to change his testimony in the judge's case."

"We can—we can make that case go away, no? What if we offer to Gresham to flush that case down the toilet? Will that gain his cooperation?"

Aguilar folds his hands and begins tapping the table. "Maybe. It might be just the thing if we get our friends to tell the FBI they won't cooperate."

"How do they do that? I'm sure the FBI has other plans for them if they don't cooperate."

"We have their entire business on our servers."

"The scrambled phone lines."

"Yes, we have recorded all conversations with Ramon for twenty months now. We know everything."

"But he will kill us all if we threaten."

"Yes, but—"

Marcel says, "Then the room service arrives, and they don't talk about any of this again. Perez spends the rest of the time until dinner on the phone to Mexico. Running MexTel from his hotel room in downtown Chicago."

"All right. So what do we know? One, we know they will kill Arnie on sight."

"Afraid so, Boss."

"Two, we know they would grab me if the FBI wasn't already surveilling me around-the-clock."

"And that could stop any minute. Now that you're indicted they might just back off."

"You're right. Which makes me an attractive target for MexTel."

"I should put a couple of guys on you. Get our first string on this."

"Yes, that would be a good idea. Have them keep a high profile, so MexTel thinks twice about grabbing me."

"You should hang around home this weekend, Boss. You're easier to guard that way."

"Will do. Except tonight when I go out with Maddie for dinner and drinks. Some jazz club."

"I don't like that. Can you change those plans?"

I push away from the table and look out the large bank of windows that open onto my manicured backyard.

"No, I won't change those plans. I'm not willing to become a prisoner because of something my brother did. I've been his prisoner too many times to do it again. I'm going out tonight with Maddie. We'll be in her car. Tell your guys to stay close."

"Will do. I would prefer you home, but if you're going where the Mexicans can't set up first, I think you'll be okay."

"You think?"

He spreads his hands. "Hey, if I had my druthers, you'd be staying in tonight and tomorrow night until the Mexicans leave town. I've told you how I want it played."

"Fair enough, Marce. Fair enough."

"You want to go to the range and put some more rounds through that Glock?"

"I don't think so. I think this afternoon I'll catch up with some cases that need motions and filings. Get that done while I can."

"All right. Tell you what. I'll go in the living room, make some calls, and hang out here until my guys show. Does that work for you?"

"Yes. Thanks, Marcel."

He reaches over and squeezes my shoulder.

"Think nothing of it, Boss. We're going to just hang in there and make this all go away."

Make it all go away. The second time in two days I've heard that.

It is hard, giving up control. But I'm going to do that now.

What choice do I have?

30

S aturday evening rolls around. I have been despondent all day, thinking about the young mother that Lamb —who else would it be?—has murdered and left behind a 7-Eleven. I am kicking myself for helping turn that animal loose on the streets. A review of my professional life is underway. In my home office, seated behind my desk, I am wearing boxer shorts and drinking a Diet Coke. There is no joy today in Mudville; the great Gresham has struck out.

Maddie arrives at seven-thirty sharp. By prior arrangement, she has one of my garage door openers and comes right into the garage. The door closes down behind her. She comes inside the house, and we have drinks: one-half of one of Sue Ellen's wine coolers for Maddie; an iced latte for me.

We finish our drinks and "catching up" conversation and load into her Highlander. She backs out of the garage while I lie flat in the backseat.

We pull down the street, and I wait for the sweep of headlights behind us to see if we're being followed. So far, so good, because it is all dark behind us, no telltale lights bearing down, no cautious lights hanging back.

Maddie announces we're at Lake Shore Drive, and now she turns right and I come upright.

"Well," she says enthusiastically, "I think that actually worked, Michael."

She swerves into a 7-Eleven, pulls around back, and I step out and climb into the front seat. Then we're off again, southbound on Lake Shore.

There's lots of traffic on LSD tonight, but there's always lots of traffic on Lake Shore Drive on a Saturday night. Everyone seems headed downtown; Maddie and I are breezing along with the mob, the windows rolled down, the sweet sounds of John Coltrane coming at us through eight speakers, and no cares.

"So who's the greatest guitarist?" she says.

"Mark Knopfler."

"Why do you say that."

"The songs. The bridges. The purity of expression. Even Chet Atkins was knocked on his ass when Mark played."

"But he's not jazz."

"Believe me. If he wanted to be, he would be."

She smiles, thinking.

She says, "Who's the greatest on the black and whites?"

"Art Tatum. The most virtuosic pianist in the history of jazz. Tremendous technique and could play at dizzying speeds."

"I'm thinking *Tiger Rag*."

"Exactly. Insanely fast, the 1933 recording of *Tiger Rag*."

"Not Thelonius?"

"Nope. Tatum. Number one in my book. How about you?"

She laughs. "Art Tatum."

"See?"

"I know."

We continue southbound and finally enter the Chicago city limits. I am trying not to keep watching behind but, in truth, I am a rank amateur and can't keep looking to see if we're being followed. Marcel has told me he'll have eyes on us tonight so even if I did spot something suspicious it could just as easily be Marcel's guys as MexTel. I have a quiet talk with myself and commit to just enjoying the evening. No more swiveling around in my seat.

We continue south, passing through the University of Chicago, and take Lake Shore Drive to Ellis Avenue then northwest of 59th near UC. House of Jazz appears on our right and Maddie starts looking for parking. We pull up closer and find valet parking.

"Out of the way?" I tease. "With valet parking? I guess."

"I've got a surprise for you, Mr. Worrywart. Let's get inside."

She hands the keys over to a college kid and we duck inside and are immediately greeted with the sweet sounds of a three piece jazz ensemble passing the tune around. Maddie waves off the hostess and says to her, "I see our table. It's being saved."

We move toward the front of the club and seem to be heading to a table populated by a man with a beard who's wearing a black beret, and a college-age girl.

We come up beside them, and I am stunned.

It's Arnie. And Esmeralda.

"Sit down and don't act surprised," Arnie murmurs out of the corner of his mouth.

Maddie and I place ourselves on either side of Arnie. Esmeralda is across from him.

"How—"

"He called me," Maddie says. "He didn't trust your phone line."

"I called her last night from an OXXO. They sold me a phone card and I remembered Maddie's number and called her."

"God, man, I am so glad to see you!" I say under my breath. I want to wrap my arms around him and bearhug him for five minutes. But I don't.

Maddie reaches and takes Esmeralda's hand. "How are you, sweetheart?"

Her eyes light up. "I'm pregnant. The stick turned blue this morning when we got back across the border."

"Congratulations!" Maddie says and squeezes the young girl's hand.

"Yes," I say, as I'm becoming resigned to whatever this is. "Congratulations. Let's order an appetizer to celebrate."

The waitress has arrived, and she takes our drink orders, and I ask for the sautéed mushroom appetizer.

Arnie's beard is glue-on, I see from up close.

"Nice," I say, stroking my imaginary beard.

"Found a costume shop in Cozumel. I'm thinking of adding the real thing. Before I forget, here's something I want you to have. Plug it into your computer only if something happens to me."

He takes my hand under the table and drops a USB computer memory stick onto my palm. He closes my fingers around the present.

"Jeez, man, don't say that. That's a real downer," I complain, little brother to big brother. "What is it?"

He puts a finger to his lips. "You're on a need to know basis. But it's the file everyone's going ga-ga over."

"MexTel?"

"Uh-huh."

I shove it into my jeans pocket and look nonchalantly around. No one in the immediate vicinity seems to give a damn, so the exchange is made, unexpected—and even unwanted—as it is.

"Not too much conversation," Arnie says to us.

"You've become an expert in this dark world of evading people," Maddie says with a giggle.

"Girl," Arnie says, "did you hear me?"

"What, laughing is out? Move off it, Arnie. We're having a night out. People laugh on a night out."

I'm not looking at him when I ask, behind my casually placed hand, "MexTel is after you. I think they're after me. Why don't we just turn the file over to them and go on with our lives? You're going to be a father; I've already got some bad stuff on my plate. Why don't we just skip all the drama and skip off down the street?"

"Can't do that," Arnie says. "I'm committed to the people of Mexico."

He sounds like he's back on his meds. So I ask. "Are you taking your Risperidone again?"

"As of last night. I needed to bring it down a notch for the move."

"I see. Well, that's a relief."

"It's only temporary. My thoughts are confused already. None of that startling clarity as I get when I'm sans meds."

"Oh, that's a loss," I say sarcastically. It isn't lost on Arnie.

"You'll see. We're talking huge headlines in the next week."

"In Chicago?"

"Mexico City. All of Mexico."

"Arnie, tell me you're not getting ready to turn the file over to the Mexican press?"

"That little drive I just gave you? That's got everything on it, in case something happens to me. Michael. Make sure it gets out if they get me."

"Come on, Arnie, lay off that negativity, huh? I almost liked you better off the meds." I realize it's the wrong thing to say because he'll take it literally.

"I definitely do like me better off the meds. It's just a matter of time."

Our mushrooms arrive with our drinks. The ensemble takes a break, and the noise volume increases as respect for the band dissipates and everyone's talking at once. Esmeralda excuses herself and heads off to the bathroom. Maddie goes with her: moral support; I can only guess.

"Listen, Michael," Arnie says confidentially, "that's my baby inside that woman. Please take care of it like it was your own if—"

"If something happens to you. Got it. Arnie, have you stopped to consider you're forty years older than the mother of your child?"

"What does age have to do with anything? We're both happier than we've been in years. Happy is all that counts, Michael. Are you ever going to get ahold of that truism?"

I remember the indictment. My happy meter plunges.

"I got myself indicted with the Judge Pennington case," I tell him.

"Who's Judge Pennington? You mean federal Judge Pennington?"

"I'm defending him. I made the mistake of trusting a client, and I made a call to a witness. The USA indicted me for it."

"Obstruction of justice?"

"Uh-huh. And conspiracy."

"Jesus. I'm going to have to get you out of that, I suppose."

"Not necessary. I hired Valentine Quinones."

"Val is the best. Second only to me, probably."

You know, he's right. My brother probably is the best when he's in town. I don't comment.

Just then, two Hispanic men enter the room. It's a half-light atmosphere, but I think—I can, I can make out their faces. It's the same two guys that accompanied Perez and Aguilar to my office.

"Don't look, Arnie. The goon squad just came in. I wonder if there's a back entrance. We need to leave, now."

Arnie, for once, listens to me and doesn't turn to look. They either haven't spotted me or are doing a damn good job of acting like they haven't spotted me. In an instant I realize it's the latter; why else would they be here? Latinos are not known for being jazz buffs—excuse the stereotype.

"Who is it?" Arnie asks.

"Two nasty-looking thugs. They came to my office with your client and his lawyer."

"Perez came to your office? With Aguilar?"

"Uh-huh. They're hot on your trail, brother."

"Oh, hell. I'm going to go over and confront them," Arnie says.

I seize his arm and keep him seated.

"Are you nuts? Look, you head back toward the restrooms. The kitchen has an outside entrance. Go take it and gather up the girls when you go by. I'll wait here, so they don't follow you."

"No way I'm leaving you."

"Arnie, this isn't open for discussion. Go. Now!"

For once in his life, Arnie actually listens to his younger brother. He tosses down the rest of his scotch and heads toward the restrooms. I purposely look directly at the two hit-men. They return my look, and their eyes sweep right on by. They're good. But...they stay in their seats. So far it's working. I remember the thumb drive in my jeans pocket. It wouldn't go well for me if these thugs laid hands on me and found me holding the drive. I have no doubt they'd kill me: after they had relieved me of the drive, that is. My eyes dart around the room while the two are avoiding making eye contact. I can't come up with anyplace to stash the drive.

Five minutes pass by. Seven. Then, out of the corner of my eye, I see one of the two men, the big guy, casually stand, stretch his arms and inhale mightily, and saunter toward the restrooms. He doesn't look at me as he passes me by. Cool Hand Luke, I'm thinking. In my imagination, I see his route: into the hallway and down to the men's room. Looking inside, no one there. At least, Arnie's not there. Back across to the ladies'. Pushes inside, shrieks of women in various stages of undress, ignoring them, realizes the women, too, are missing. Then a quick dance down to the hall to the kitchen doors and he's inside the kitchen, his eyes on fire, and looking at the back door, open to the alley and the cool night air.

He returns and almost runs past me. They don't go to the back as I'm predicting. Instead, they're out the front entrance in a flash, and I am suddenly off their radar. It's clearly Arnie they're interested in now that they've probably realized who the guy with the beard was. Arnie, not me.

So I lay two twenties on the table and head for the back door. By this time, I am sure Maddie and Arnie and Esmeralda have made their getaway, and now it's my turn.

The alley is dark, and two men are coming toward me from the near end. I turn and start walking as fast as I can walk in the opposite direction. I hear steps behind me that are the sound of running, not walking. I break into a run and make the corner and head back left, along the side of the House of Jazz, and then left again, heading toward the valet parking stand.

The twosome closes on me as I stand as close as possible to the valet stand. They boldly walk up and seize me by the arms and move me off.

A van pulls up just then, and the door slides open. I am pushed and dragged and forced inside and the door slams shut. My heart is pounding. My breath is coming in short gasps. I am thrown onto the floor, and someone straddles me, pinning my arms to the floor with their knees. A cloth bag is pulled down over my head and at the same time I am flipped over and my hands are handcuffed behind my back. Then the same person is straddling me again, sitting on my arms and hands. It hurts.

"Hey," I cry out, "please! You're killing my arms."

"*Cállate estúpido!*" someone growls at me.

My face is pressed to the floor, sideways, and I am hyperventilating. I try to slow my breathing by closing my eyes and forcing myself to breathe through my nose. Somehow I manage to slow down, and the dizziness begins subsiding. Whoever is upon my back rolls off and strong arms pull me up into a sitting position.

"*Puta*, where is our file?"

"I don't know where your file is!"

Hands jam down into my jeans pockets. The USB thumb drive is found and ripped out.

"*Aqui, Martino*! This pig had this in its pocket!"

"Plug it in the laptop," an Anglo voice responds.

I shout, "Arnie! Are you in here?" and someone backhands me across the mouth. It splits my bottom lip, and I can taste blood. Not a lot, so I'm not worried. Best of all, Arnie didn't answer. I'm hoping my three partners made it out of the alley and located Maddie's SUV in valet parking. As for me, we're rolling along, slowing at stop signs somewhere in the vicinity of the University of Chicago where there are lots of stop signs. Then I lose all sense of direction and lose any inner map of where we are. I am lost.

"*Puta*, you had our file!" the Latino voice exclaims again, and again I'm punched in the mouth. This time, there's lots of blood, and I'm swallowing it down and feeling my teeth with my tongue. My teeth feel intact, and I cringe, finding a seat with my back, hoping they don't hit me again.

"Michael Gresham," the Anglo voice says, "please tell us where you got this thumb drive."

"I don't remember," I say.

This time, I am kicked. Kicked in the side of the head with such force that I black out. When I regain consciousness, I realize someone is pressing a burning cigarette against my forearm. I scream, and the van squeals around a corner.

"What!" I shout and cry at the same time. "What is it you want?"

"We want to know where you got this thumb drive from. Did your brother give it to you?"

"My brother? I haven't seen—"

Again I am kicked. This time, I lose consciousness and am out for I don't know how long.

~

WHEN I FINALLY COME AROUND, I find myself sitting on something hard and cold—concrete, probably, and I hear voices around me. The hood is still over my head, and the voices resonating make me think we're in some kind of large room, maybe a warehouse. I am covered with something wet. I shiver and cry out when I smell gasoline. I have been doused with gasoline!

The Latino voice surfaces through my haze. "Señor Gresham, we are taking a moment before lighting you on fire. One chance remains to tell us where you got the thumb drive?"

I am beaten down, and I am terrified. No one can ever claim I would be a good candidate to stand up against threats of being burned alive when I'm covered in gasoline. I spill the beans. "My brother gave it to me."

"Aha! Smart man, Señor Gresham. Now tell me. Where does your brother keep our files?"

I shake my head violently. "That is something I don't know. I hadn't seen my brother for several days. Tonight in the jazz place was the first time. We never got a chance to talk. Please, tell the people at MexTel that I'll do everything I can to get their files returned. Please, tell them I've been trying to do that already."

"But your brother just won't listen to you, is that it, Michael?" It is the Anglo voice again. I realize I almost recognize the voice, but I'm unsure. For a moment, I think it's Special Agent Nathan Fordyce. But it can't be. It can't be MexTel and the FBI. Totally makes no sense.

Or does it? Is MexTel involved with the FBI in getting the Tijuana Ramons to testify against Judge Pennington and me? How would that even work?

"Agent Fordyce, is that you?"

I hear laughter—several voices around me are laughing. Then one says, "Wait! Don't toss the cigarette on him yet. This is too much fun!"

I'm beginning to have hope when suddenly someone sloshes another dose of gasoline over me. It hits my face and blinds me, and I am left sputtering and choking. The hood has become a toxic death mask tight against my face. I try to breathe without inhaling its fumes, and that is quite impossible.

Without another word, someone tosses a burning cigarette

against me. My clothes instantly are ablaze, and the mask on my face shoots flames up my face and over my head. I am blacking out just as I hear the loud squall of a fire extinguisher—I can taste the foam—suddenly covering my body, face, and head.

The pain is excruciating. The last thing I remember is wetting myself.

Then I am out.

31

I am trying to remember.

My eyes open. It is all pain. Dressings cover my body everywhere I can see: chest to toes.

I look side to side. My arms are swathed in white strips too.

I move my mouth to speak. It feels like my lips are missing. I try to bring the fingers of my right hand to my mouth to explore the loss of sensation, but the arm won't bend as I tell it.

And the pain. I am on fire.

Eyes closed, I am gone again.

~

HER NAME IS NANCY KELLY, and she's a student nurse. She is bringing flowers into my room and arranging them on the stand at the foot of my bed when my eyes open.

"How long?" I ask.

"You've been coming and going for about five days. Before that, they kept you in a coma for ten days."

I am astonished.

"You're telling me I've been out for over two weeks?"

"Yes, Mr. Gresham. You've been very sick."

"How did I get here?"

"Well," she says, "according to your chart someone pushed you out of a moving van under the ER port. You hit the ground pretty hard, so the doctors have done several brain scans while you've been unconscious."

"My God."

I can remember my name. I'm a lawyer, and I live in Evanston.

"My brother—any news about my brother Arnold?"

"I'm afraid I don't have any news about your brother. I'll ask out at the nurse's station."

"Good."

The pain is surreal. It starts inside, at the bone, and spreads outward as if my flesh has been cooked in a 350° oven. The worst part is, there's no escaping it. I can't turn it off. Over the next several days I study my pain and realize that the opiate painkiller doesn't relieve the pain so much as it just renders me unconscious. When I'm unconscious, I don't feel. So I'm grateful for the large dose they're administering.

Finally, I can touch my lips. What's left of them. They are encrusted with salves and scabs, and I am told that's because I inhaled the flames. Which is also why my voice is guttural and holds no volume even when I try to shout. The cilia in my lungs—partially burned away from the inhalation, will regenerate, the respiratory therapist tells me. Eyelashes and eyebrows will grow back. Probably I'll always be deaf in my left ear where my ear drum literally exploded and burned away when I jerked away from the flame flash and that side of my head caught the most of it.

A week into conscious recovery, Nurse Nancy provides a mirror. It is a small one, designed so the burn patient can only see portions of the face at a time.

I am horrified. With no hair on my face and bright red flesh sticking through where once there was skin, I look like the main character in a horror film. For one crushing moment, I realize no jury will ever again look at me like they used to. Now it will be with a large measure of revulsion and pity—both of which I cannot countenance. One thing I've never been able to endure is someone's pity for me. About anything.

They have told me about Arnie and Maddie and Esmeralda. Their SUV was northbound on Lake Shore Drive when a large white cube truck ran up behind it and slammed into it at a high rate of speed. Their SUV was thrown down a steep embankment and Maddie, who was behind the wheel, was thrown free just as the SUV rolled, her door flew open, and she was killed instantly when her forward momentum of 70 MPH was stopped by a large maple tree. Arnie is still in ICU with a fractured spine and multiple spiral fractures of his right arm and right leg. There is a question whether he will ever walk again. Esmeralda—where is Esmeralda? I'm wondering. She hasn't been around, and she was the one who came through without a scratch. The detectives have told me she was found hanging upside down in the backseat of the SUV, and it's probably because she was belted and asleep that the impact affected her very little. She hasn't lost the baby, and she's somewhere in the city, but no one knows exactly where. She was treated at the ER, the baby's well-being confirmed, and released. She was seen by the charge nurse waiting outside the ER at a bus stop.

I am so sad about Maddie that I can't stop crying. Feelings bubble up, and I no longer have a filter capable of restraining them. They just come bursting out, and I am crying one minute and laughing at my face in the mirror the next. It is not a good time, and I am very lonely.

Sue Ellen comes by with Eddie in tow.

"I'm taking the hormone injections," she announces. Eddie smiles stupidly.

"Oh, yes," I tell her and give them both a wave of my hand. "Sit."

"Got you this," Eddie says. He holds out a baseball. It is signed by people whose names I cannot read because my eyes will not yet focus. "It's the Cubs' pitching staff."

"That's very thoughtful," I say. I haven't watched a baseball game since I was in my twenties, but I'm not about to tell Eddie that. This is truly a gift of love, and I can feel how much it means to him to give this to me. "I will treasure this. Have it put under glass—you know."

"I've seen 'em like that," he says. "Good thinking."

Sue Ellen brushes him away.

"I heard about your indictment," she says. "Mrs. Lingscheit told me."

"That's private. She shouldn't have told you that."

"Actually, the detectives told me first, and then she confirmed. The detectives were around twice to see me. They wanted to know if I thought the incineration had anything to do with your criminal charges. I told them hell if I know."

"Unconnected, I think." But then I remember hearing what sounded like Agent Fordyce's voice inside the warehouse, and I'm not positive there isn't some connection. I will find out.

～

MRS. LINGSCHEIT SWINGS by and isn't there five minutes before she's pulling out a list of cases and asking me for instructions. I do the best I can. She says she called the judges herself and everyone continued everything for eight weeks. That's how long my doctors told her I would be unavailable. The State Bar is providing temporary counsel on some things that have fuses burning and couldn't wait, but that only includes four of my seventy-some cases.

From her purse, she pulls out a sandwich wrapped in wax paper. "Jimmy John's Italian sub," she tells me. She lays it on the small table beside my head and looks around the room.

"How have you been?" I ask her.

Tears come into her eyes. "Worried! Petrified for you, Michael!"

"Well, just continue paying yourself out of the general fund and we'll get by. I'm not finished yet."

"You will be coming back?"

"Oh, yes. I don't break this easily."

I am feeling better now. Every now and again there's even a moment when I feel some anger at whoever did this to me. Those moments are few and far between, however.

Valentine Quinones stops by one Friday night on her way home from work. Her chauffeured Mercedes is waiting in the visitors' lot, she breathlessly shares, so she can't stay but a minute.

"How are you, Michael?"

By now many of many dressings have been shed like a snake shedding its skin. I am coming back.

"Much better. I should be out of here sometime next week."

"How about an initial appearance the next week. Will you be up to it?"

"Yes, in fact, have you heard any more?"

"Yes, but we don't need to go into all that now. You just rest and get well and then we'll talk."

"Okay."

❧

I HAVE two sets of physical therapists, one for morning, one for the afternoon. They circle around me endlessly, like hawks pushing their young out of lofty nests to make them fly. Except with me, it's only turning on my butt and getting my feet flat on the floor that they're trying to get me to do. Then it's standing with a walker. Not walking, just standing. I look down at my hands gripping the walker's arms, and I see my angry red knuckles and hands and I am alarmed. Do I look like steamed crab all over? So far, only the small mirror has been allowed. But one day, they hold me by the PT belt and walk me down to the PT room and I at last get a look at myself in the floor-to-ceiling mirror of physical therapy.

Alarming is an understatement.

At first, I cry—unfiltered and full-tilt crying. I am crimson from head to toe. Across portions of my chest and upper arms are plastered dressings that still haven't fallen away. Blood still appears to be making them adhere to whatever lies beneath. It is alarming and much more. It is like seeing your favorite thing in the world damaged beyond recovery.

"Is this-is this—"

"Is this permanent?" says the physical therapist, a young man of about thirty. "No, it isn't permanent. The color will fade with time. The skin will slowly build and shed, build and shed, and one day you will look almost normal again.

Almost normal.

He holds my belt as I climb a set of three stairsteps and then descend the other side, also three stairsteps. It is excruciating to do this, as I must bend at the waist and behind my knees and the skin and tendons there cry out in pain. But we do it again and again and again.

At last, they return me to my room and my dressings are changed and lotions and salves applied. They are familiar smells, the creams, and ointments they use now. I feel like I once did when my grandmother would come near, and I could smell her ointments for arthritis. A friendly, warm smell.

Yes, the odors of burn rehab are now my friends.

~

SEVERAL DAYS later Arnie comes to see me. At first, I don't recognize him. He is now on forearm crutches and looks like an old, wrinkled man. The hospital stay and the accident and aftermath have not been good to him. We talk, and he tells me he's "laying low," as he puts it.

"What is your plan?" I ask him. "Are you back at work? Do you even dare show your face in public? What's happening?"

"Marcel came to see me. He found me this efficiency apartment and put it in a name nobody could trace. Esmeralda and I are hanging out there until our next move becomes clear."

"What about the MexTel file? Do you still have that?"

"I have access to it."

"What does that mean, access to it?"

"The file in digital form is on a server. But don't worry. MexTel will never find it."

"How so?"

"It's on their own server on their own computers in Mexico City."

"How do you know about this?"

Arnie smiles. "Because I put it there."

"You put their missing file on their own server?"

"Yep. It's password protected, and its filename is a dummy. They would never look there; it looks like a system file."

"How did you know to do this?"

"Michael, I've been a propeller head since the first PC was sold by IBM. Remember back when I was learning DOS and everyone thought I'd gone off the deep end? Well, it was a short jump from there to winding up working as lead counsel for MexTel in all its litigation cases. Last I heard, I had more access to their server farm and AWS storage than anyone in the entire company. It was necessary to give me universal access because I needed division files constantly and my having access cut through the company red tape. Aguilar and Perez both signed off on it."

"So now you've just hidden some of their files on their own servers."

"Exactly."

"Who else knows about this?"

"Just you. Is this your cell phone?" he says and picks up my new iPhone, courtesy of Mrs. Lingscheit since my own disappeared.

"It is. There's nothing on there, though. No contacts."

"Well, I'm putting in a new contact. The name is Michael Gresham."

"Me?"

"Yes. I'm putting in the web address where the MexTel secret files are hidden by me. And I'm putting in a simple command line you can enter when you go to that place."

"And this command. What does it do?"

"It off-loads the data to another service and then mails a copy of the smoking gun file to every subscriber in Mexico and Latin America."

"That must be twenty million people? More?"

Arnie smiles and hands me my phone.

"Imagine that," he says. "Sounds like everyone."

"And if they get the file—"

"If everyone gets the file it's all over for MexTel. The lawsuit will blossom and grow into the hundreds of thousands— maybe millions—of people making claims for toxic injuries."

"Well, Arnie, you always were thorough."

"Michael, if they get me, you enter the order. I want the files sent universally."

"Okay."

"Will you do that for me?"

"I will."

"Promise?"

"Of course."

"Good. I want to reach out of my grave and flip them off. A final screw you."

"This should do it, Arnie."

32

Colleen O'Connell, Psy.D., is the psychologist the hospital brings into my room the final week of my stay. The University of Chicago Hospital—my current home—prides itself on its holistic approach, so I get mental health clearance too before I'm released back into the world. Dr. O'Connell is a large woman, but friendly and —for want of a better term—feisty. She's always up for dueling wits with me.

"So who do you want to kill today?" she asks on my third session, the third in three days.

"Only the people who did this to me."

"What about the judge that did something—what was it?"

"Judge Pennington? Only got me indicted. Naw, I couldn't hold that against him."

"Bet me. He's on your hit list too, I take it."

"Actually, he's number two."

"And number one?"

"MexTel. A corporation that evidently thinks nothing of killing people."

"Can we talk about healthy ways of dealing with this anger or rage?"

"Rage."

"For example, there's always the old standby, physical work-outs. I'd like you to get a gym membership and workout every day. Especially with the body bag. Remember me telling you how healthy it would be for you to work out on the body bag? Just be sure and wear boxing gloves because there's a lot of anger inside of you to be worked through."

"All right."

"Then there's the courthouse stuff. What do you do about Judge Penningford?"

"Pennington. I kind of think I know why he would want to involve me. It's actually not personal with him."

"Why would he want to hurt you?"

"Because at one time, I defended the man who murdered his wife. In some obtuse way, that has made him hate me. In fact, when he retained me to defend him he did it with the ulterior motive of involving me in his crime. He's very twisted, our dear federal judge."

"Can you prove that?"

"Can I or will I?"

"Either."

"Yes to both. I haven't even started yet," I say. The words lend me strength. The words draw me along much more than silence. Hating in silence, without words, without action, is futile.

"By the way, Michael, did I ever tell you it's okay to hate the people who did this to you?"

"Yes, you did."

"Hate is what preachers try to talk us out of on Sunday mornings. Hate is what I try to get my victims to use the other six days of the week. Hatred innervates; it can bring strength and focus where without it we might only know self-pity or anger. Hate moves us toward a goal of freedom from rage. Keep this close to your heart."

"Wow, I've never thought of hate as therapeutic."

"It's the new thinking. Take it in and try it out. Let me know what you think."

～

I AM RELEASED the next morning, and it's Marcel who comes to take me home. We've spoken only once since the night I was immolated and Maddie was murdered, and that was just a drop-in to my hospital room. He's wearing washed out jeans and a green Lauren shirt with a vest over, and a cap worn low on the head, his eyes hidden behind purple shades.

He has come to get me in my own Mercedes 550, and I am glad to let him drive. It is still awkward for me to slide across the seat and turn my legs as it requires drawing my knees up toward my chest and that is very painful. I am told the scar tissue will loosen with time, but right now it's very tight and painful when forced, especially on my knees and elbows and fingers.

We leave UC Hospital and head for Lake Shore Drive. Marcel is quiet tonight, not his usual jocular self.

"So," he finally says as we head north on LSD, "have you heard any more from the dicks?"

"They think we were all four the victims of the same group."

"Any names getting thrown out there yet?"

"Not really. They keep saying they've got several leads, but they won't cut me in on the details. I keep telling them to look at MexTel and any of its security people that were in the U.S. when it happened. I don't know if they are."

He nods and checks the rearview.

"Well, I haven't told anyone this, I was waiting until you got out."

"What's that?"

"You remember we were following Maddie's Toyota that night? You had put us on it?"

"Yes. And we still need to talk about where your guys disappeared to. Following one vehicle shouldn't have been that difficult to do."

"Actually, I was in the car that got cut off by the truck that rear-ended them."

"You were? Did you tell this to the police?"

"No, I didn't."

"Why not, Marcel? Damn it to hell, man that's information they're dying to know. They keep telling me nobody stopped when Maddie was forced off the road. Nobody stopped."

"I called nine-one-one, but I also stayed on the trail of the white cube truck."

"Tell me about it."

"Well, it went north up to North Avenue then over to the ninety-four and the south back to the city. It came back down to Adams and then took back streets to a pay lot where it was left. Two guys got out, walked east a block, and disappeared inside a warehouse. The sign on the place was old and faded, but evidently they used to make chocolate there."

"Did you follow them? Confront them?"

"Nope. I parked in the alley, turned my lights off, and waited. It was half-past nine by now and very deserted. Plus, I was alone. I wasn't about to storm the place by myself. So I pulled out my Nikon, put on my night gear, and took some pictures."

He reaches inside his vest and pulls out a half-dozen pictures.

"Recognize these assholes?"

I flip through the photographs, unsure about anything or anyone, until the fourth one down. Immediately I recognize the face of the man walking toward the camera. He's about one hundred feet away, and he is grasping the arms of a body. With his back to the camera, another man has the legs. The face of the man I can see is one of the guys from the video Marcel made of the four men sitting in the MexTel

CEO's hotel room at the Hyatt. The photo is very clear, and the man has a deer-in-the-headlights look on his face, although in truth he wouldn't have seen Marcel taking pictures from that distance and in that lighting, such as it was.

"Holy hell," I say, "that's MexTel's guy."

"Yeah. And you know who they're carrying?"

"Who?"

"That, my friend, would be you. Your shirt is burned off, that's it, next photograph, when they turn you sideways to put you in the backseat of the Cherokee. There you are suspended between those two assholes, your clothes missing."

I can't breathe. My air catches in my throat and won't pass through. My throat is closing out of reaction to the poor burned up soul in the picture. It is a sympathetic reaction, and I know it will pass. It does, and I take in a huge lungful of air.

"You okay?" Marcel asks.

"Who—who—who are the other two guys in these first shots."

"Believe it or not, the guy in the suit of clothes is Aguilar."

"Chief counsel of MexTel."

"That's right. The other guy—I can't make his face out, but I'm willing to bet it's someone we know."

"Perez? The CEO? He wouldn't be in on this kind of dirty work."

"Neither would the lawyer. But there he is."

"How—why would they?"

"I think it shows how fearful they are of that file ever surfacing in Mexico. I think their jobs, their holdings, even their freedom depends on getting that file away from Arnie."

"They took the thumb drive from me."

"What thumb drive?"

"The one Arnie gave me that night. I felt them tear into my pocket and rip it out. I'm sure that's what it was because they plugged it in a computer and confirmed it."

"Assholes."

"So let me ask you one thing. Did you know that was me?"

"Michael, look at the picture. I know it's grainy, but can you make out any features on that guy's face, the one that's actually you? It's all black and burned up. There was no way I was going to recognize you."

"So what happened after they loaded me into the Cherokee?"

"Evidently they took you to the hospital at UC."

"Didn't you follow?"

"No. I waited until they were gone, and then I went back inside the warehouse."

"Did you find anything."

"Nope. But it wasn't for lack of trying. I took my light in with me and searched both floors of that place. There was a black spot where they had burned something, and there was the smell of gasoline hanging in the air, but I didn't link that to anything."

"And you haven't told any of this to the cops?"

"Nope?"

"Why not?"

"Because I knew you would want first shot at them."

We ride on in silence for a mile or more. I roll the entire scene around in my head. But then my anger begins surfacing. I want the guys that burned me.

"How's Arnie doing in his place you got for him?"

"Arnie is fine. He doesn't ever go out except to buy groceries at the local market and to take Esmeralda to the doctor for her checkups."

"So I take it she's still expecting?"

"Last I heard, Michael, that doesn't just go away by itself. Yes, she's still expecting."

"What I meant was, the accident didn't hurt the baby?"

"Like I told you before, she came through without a scratch."

"How's Arnie with the crutches by now?"

"He's down to a single cane now. He's going to have a pretty bad limp."

"But he's still alive. A miracle there."

"And Maddie's family? Did they ever try to contact anyone?"

"Her mother sent you a card. It came to your house. No one opened it. It's waiting for you."

"How do you know it's a card then?"

"You have gotten very suspicious of everything, Michael. You have definitely changed."

"Yes, I have definitely changed."

"So. When are we going after these guys?" he asks me, watching my reaction out of the corner of his eye as he drives us along.

I feel a twinge of pain in both hips. I'm cramping from sitting in the car.

"We are going soon. We are going to find the people who did this to me."

"And then what? We're going to sue them?"

"No, I was thinking of bypassing the court system this time."

I look out the window and flex my hands. The knuckles are sore and I realize I've been clenching my hands since getting into the car.

"What's that mean?"

"It means I need to talk to Arnie. Let's go there first."

"No, I haven't told you this yet, Boss. Your lawyer wants to see you ASAP."

"Valentine Quinones wants to see me? Why didn't you tell me this, Marcel?"

"You were in the hospital. Your docs would have killed me if I had upset you."

"Well, what's she thinking?"

"She didn't say. She called Evie—Mrs. Lingscheit—and Evie called me. You've got an appointment with Ms. Quinones at nine o'clock on the dot in the morning."

I feel my pulse quicken. My mouth is suddenly dry and not from the loss of half of my salivary glands from the fire I inhaled. No, this rapid racing pulse and dry mouth are related to only one thing: my freedom.

I do not want to lose my freedom for some imaginary federal crime I did not commit.

"I'll be ready for you to drive me downtown at eight," I say weakly.

Marcel stares straight ahead. But he nods. He'll be there.

33

Ms. Quinones is wearing a navy leather suit that looks incredibly soft and is tailored to fit her without a wrinkle or pull. Her hair is pulled back, and her face is without makeup—again—as makeup would be a step down for her beauty. She is at her desk when I am shown in, and she doesn't stand to greet me.

"Sit down, Michael, let me have a look."

I sit, and she leans forward in her chair and studies my face.

"Son of a bastard," she mutters. "They really did torch you, didn't they?"

The scarring on my face is pronounced. I am going to require surgery to revise some of it. It was all discussed and scheduled with the team that did the first two go-arounds.

"They did torch me."

"Enlighten me, please. I want to see if we can make a connection here."

"Well, the MexTel guys grabbed me outside a jazz club. Who they were really after was my brother, but he got away. So they used me to set an example for him once they discovered I'd been given a copy of the file they were after."

"What file is that?"

"What I call the smoking gun file. MexTel is being sued in toxic tort litigation. Thousands of penniless people are claiming they have lost loved ones and been made sick themselves by some of MexTel's groundwater practices where they have communications emplacements. MexTel denies this and the suit is pending in the U.S. because many of those injured are U.S. citizens living in certain enclaves in Mexico where the groundwater has been ruined."

"Go on."

"Well, the guys that grabbed me know that Arnie, my brother—"

"I know Arnold Gresham. Everyone does."

"They know Arnie has their file, and they were sending him a warning. Plus using me to convince him that his resistance to turning back their property just isn't worth it."

"So they burned you to set an example?"

"That and the fact I was found in possession of their file. They don't like people who have their secret files."

"And you had the file because Arnie was afraid for himself?"

"Exactly. I was to turn the file over to the plaintiffs in the lawsuit if anything should happen to Arnie."

"Did you?

"No. That would be the end of both of us if that happened. They would stop at nothing to get revenge."

"So does any of this fit with our Tijuana cartel problem?"

She leans back and takes a sip of her coffee. It is contained in a 16-ounce cup that says Starbucks in vertical lettering. She's a fan, and I like her for that as I am too.

"I'm not seeing a connection at this point. But let me think about that. I'll get back to you."

"Fine."

"Here's where we're at, Michael. While you were recuperating, I've received the discovery documents and copies of video and letters from the U.S. Attorney. For openers, the case is being worked up by Nathan Fordyce. He's a premier fifteen year veteran of the FBI. He's their go-to guy when they absolutely have to have a conviction on a case. He was originally selected because it was a federal judge. Unfortunately for you, now that the case has expanded to include you, he is now your lion tamer too."

"How fortunate for me," I say, my post-hospital sarcasm surfacing again. The injury and the painful treatment has made me very paranoid, very suspicious of everyone and their motives, and very angry about those who would torture me further. It looks like Nathan Fordyce is one of those and I do not view him with anything but pure hatred right now. "If he had a single cell of honesty in his body he'd see right through Judge Pennington's flimsy attempt to include me in his goddamn scheme against James Lamb and the prosecution he's facing. He'd be the first to admit I was only doing my job when I contacted the Tijuana guys and asked them to do the right thing when they testify. But no, he's used my involvement to widen his net and maybe catch another big fish—a defense lawyer. The guy is an utter asshole. Excuse my language."

"I understand. You're hurt, and you're bitter. I get that. But I also get that part of what he's working with is of your own doing. Have you seen the transcript of the message you left on Raul Ramon's phone? I have it here, if you didn't read through it before you turned your file over to me."

"No, I didn't read it. I was afraid to, I guess."

"Well, let me read it to you. Ready?"

"Let her rip."

"Instead of me reading it, let me give you the print-out. Here you are."

I begin reading:

> "Hello, Raul Ramon? Michael Gresham here. I'm calling you from Chicago?"
>
> "Si?"
>
> "Mr. Ramon, your name has come up in a very important legal matter. The U.S. Attorney in Chicago says you're going to testify against Judge Pennington. Can you talk to me about that?"
>
> "Si? No hable ingles, Señor."
>
> "Okay, then. Just take this down. What if Judge Pennington asked you to tell the truth instead? What if he said you called him about your son, who was appearing in your court and

that's all you ever talked to him about. Would
he be lying, Sir?"

"Una momento, Señor, quiere un—"

"Do you follow me? "

I hear it and I am horrified. I read it through again.

"I cannot believe I left myself open like that," I tell Ms.
Quinones. "No one who knows me would believe it. What
the hell was I even thinking?" I want to slap the side of my
head out of self-anger and frustration at my naiveté but I
don't. It would just hurt too damn much.

"Michael, you have made their case for them. They have you
soliciting a witness to change his story. That's enough to get
to a jury. In my opinion, this letter will get you convicted if
this case goes to trial."

This sudden change in direction alarms me. What does she
mean, if this case goes to trial? Of course, this case is going
to trial. I'm innocent, damn it all!

"I don't like the tenor of what you just said," I tell her. "Of
course, this case is going to trial. Why wouldn't it?"

"I cannot in good faith take this to trial. You would have to
change your story from what's recorded by you. You would
be telling a lie if you tried to change. That would be an
ethical violation for me to help you tell something else.
Which actually is a very small part of my thinking as it's not
for certain the facts would break that way. But what is
certain—at least in my opinion from trying hundreds of
federal jury trials—is that you will be convicted if you go to

trial. For that reason, I must decline your representation if you insist on taking this case to trial."

"What? I thought you have agreed to defend me! I've paid you five hundred thousand dollars, Ms. Quinones!"

She takes up an envelope and passes it across the desk to me.

"Your full refund," she says. "I won't take this case to trial."

"Tell the truth. Is it because you're worried about your public trial record? Is that it, you can't stand to have a black mark on your record?"

She nods slowly. "Yes, that's part of it. You and I know that our trial records are our pedigree. I've never lost a case in federal court. Not in the past ten years. I can't afford a loss now. The practice of law in Chicago is enormously competitive, as I'm sure you know. Our trial records are really all we have to recommend us."

"Okay. Say I agree to plead guilty. Do you see me doing any jail time?"

She leans back, her eyes wide. "Are you serious? On a conspiracy to commit murder case? Of course, there would be imprisonment. Ten years minimum, I'm thinking."

"No way. I'd be sixty-five and penniless and without a law license. That's not an option."

"Well, Michael, going to trial with me sitting in the chair next to you is not an option, either. So we'll just have to agree to disagree. It's best we part company now, before you waste any more time with me."

"Could I run one more thing by you before I leave?"

She checks her watch. "Sure. But I need to get ready—"

"Two minutes. Right before they threw gasoline on me and lit me on fire, I thought I could hear the voice of Special Agent Fordyce with the MexTel thugs. Does that even begin to make any sense in any of this, that he would be involved in MexTel kidnapping me?"

"Not for a second. No, I imagine it was someone else, and your mind just told you it was him. Well, I'd best get ready for my next client, Michael. If you need a reference for other attorneys who might be willing to take you to trial, let me know, and I'll get a list together."

"That won't be necessary. I've already found my new attorney."

Her eyebrows immediately arch upward as she hands me my file. "You have? Who?"

"Me," I tell her and take back my file.

We shake hands, and we are done here.

Marcel is waiting for me in the waiting room. I didn't go into the meeting with a file, but I have one now.

"You're taking your file back," he says in the elevator.

I shrug. "She fired me."

"Seriously?"

"She didn't want to go to trial. I don't blame her. It's one she could lose and she doesn't want a blemish on her record."

"Well, that's pure bullshit!"

"Actually, I'm glad she told me. My lawyer has to be a hundred percent certain about me."

"Who's going to be that?"

I pull my file up under my arm.

"Me."

Once we're in the car, I call Mrs. Lingscheit and ask her to let Danny know we're going to all meet at ten-thirty. It's time to clear the air I tell her.

And time to buckle down. We have a conspiracy case to defend.

34

I t's almost ten-twenty when Marcel and I step off the elevator on our floor.

"Hello, Mrs. Lingscheit," I call to her as Marcel and I pass by. She's on the phone, of course, and only nods and raises one finger.

She punches a button on her phone and says to me, "Danny's in her office. She has really been wanting to see you, so get ready."

I stick my head into Danny's office. "Hey, you got a few?" I ask.

Her face brightens up. "Oh, I am so glad to see you. I came once while you were in the hospital, but I doubt if you remember. You were pretty out of it."

"Tell the truth, I don't remember much. Especially at first. Now you know, Marcel, right?"

"Oh yes," says Marcel from beside me. "We've talked about a few cases while you're been on the rest cure. Hiya, Danny."

"Hello, Marcel. Happy to see you too."

"Come y'all," I say in a sunny southern drawl, trying to put everyone at ease. There's a definite tension in the air. And why wouldn't there be if your boss were under indictment? It's time to speak to everyone.

We three traipse into my office, and everyone gets comfortable. Marcel goes to the Keurig and makes a cup, which he then holds up to me and raises his eyebrows. I nod affirmatively. "Cream?" he says. "Half and half," I say, nodding at the under-counter refrigerator. Danny has brought along a stack of yellow pads and appears anxious to discuss. I think she probably keeps a pad inside each file folder as she's learned by now I like to do. One yellow tablet per file, with all notes, questions, etc. Written down so, like as happened here, if someone comes down ill or gets run over then the next lawyer to come along will have the previous one's thoughts and notes, etc. Most law firms do that on their case management software today; I still prefer the old legal pads. I can also pull them out during a trial and check witness questions and answers against my notes.

"Danny," I say as Marcel hands me a cup, "you know I've been indicted."

"Hold it," says Mrs. Lingscheit, hustling in to join us. "Phones are on hold. I want you to start from the top, please."

I nod and take a sip of Marcel's brew. Fine.

"I've been indicted. I was indicted because I did a foolish thing. I called a witness in a federal criminal case, and the FBI found out about it."

"How did they find out?" asks Marcel.

"The witness called the FBI. Rather, the witness's lawyer called the FBI. Turned me in. The transcript of what I said is inside this file," I say, directing this to Danny in particular. "You, Danny, will be working on this case with me. Start with the transcript of my call, please."

"Why will I be on it?" Danny asks. "You have Valentine Quinones, don't you?"

I smile. "As of about one hour ago, no, I don't. She fired me. Or I fired her, I'm not certain. What I am sure about is that she recommended I enter into plea negotiations and when I told her there wouldn't be a plea she said she wouldn't take the case to trial. Too risky for her reputation."

"Good heavens!" Danny exclaims.

"That's what happens when you get too popular," says Marcel. "You can't afford to lose. So you start refusing cases all over if they look like losers. Sorry, Michael, I didn't mean yours looks like a loser."

"Tell the truth," says Mrs. Lingscheit, "I'm glad she's out of the picture. Michael is ten times the lawyer the rest of these people are. Good work, Mr. Gresham."

"Thanks, Mrs. L. Anyway, Danny and I will take the case to trial."

Danny is beaming now. She apparently hasn't expected to hit the courtroom so soon. And on a case that promises to gain much media attention, since there's a judge and a semi-high-profile member of the federal defense bar on trial.

"So here's my plan. First, Danny I want you to give me a brief on Seventh Circuit witness tampering cases. Obstruction of justice where witnesses were involved, too. Do it more in the form of a motion for directed verdict, since we'll be needing just that when the government rests its case after it has called all of its witnesses."

"I'm on it. What kind of priority?"

"This is a one."

She nods.

"Marcel, I need you to try to talk to these jerks in Tijuana. I don't want to put you in danger, so I'm hoping you can arrange something in broad daylight, in a public place, and take an interpreter with you and one of your own guys for backup. In fact, take two of your own guys for backup."

"What's my goal line?"

"Your goal line is a statement from them to the effect that they didn't take my phone call as an attempt to get them to tell anything but the truth. That they didn't think I was asking them to lie. If we can get that, then we can begin formulating a case where the government says the words mean one thing, but the people who heard them thought they meant something else. We're going to take the approach that my call was harmless."

"You said something in the car about Judge Pennington turning on you."

"Not exactly how I said it."

Marcel shrugs. "Okay, so you said he was trying to fuck you."

Mrs. Lingscheit waves her hand like she's brushing off flies. "My goodness. How the hospital has affected our language. Did they talk like that over there, Mr. Gresham?"

My turn to shrug. "Worse. They talked much worse."

"When do you want me to go?" Marcel asks.

"Now. Yesterday. And try to get it on tape."

"They're going to be very leery and probably won't agree to talk."

"That's all right. I can then put you on the stand and let the jury know they were uncooperative and that the U.S. Attorney was probably instructing them not to speak to me. Juries don't like prosecutors who clam up their witnesses. They think it's very unfair and judge accordingly."

"Can I say something?" Danny asks.

I open my hands. Go ahead.

"Well, I'm just thinking outside the box for a minute. I'm thinking about your brother and his troubles with MexTel."

"Mrs. Lingscheit has been sharing with you."

"She has. Your brother has a very powerful group of Mexican businessmen after him. You have a very powerful group of Mexican businessmen after you. Is there any chance those two are connected?"

She has hit a raw nerve with me. I tell them about thinking I heard Special Agent Fordyce's voice just before they set me on fire. I tell them I've been wondering why—if at all— Fordyce would be having anything at all to do with a case that involved the MexTel communications group when his own case was a thousand miles away in Tijuana. What could they possibly have in common?"

"Easy," says Danny. "Don't you see it?"

"No," says Marcel.

"I don't see any connection," says Mrs. Lingscheit.

"Not yet I don't," I tell her. "Please enlighten me."

"Well. Cartels do all their business by cell phone. The FBI and Mexican government intercept cell phone calls and that's how they prosecute cartels. My guess is that MexTel has probably provided some kind of protected cell phone service to the cartels."

"In exchange for? What do the cartels give them back?"

"Protection. Like in your brother's case. Those weren't MexTel guys who grabbed you. Those were cartel guys. That explains why Fordyce would be with them."

"You're saying the cartel was doing the bidding of MexTel by grabbing me to get its secret file back?"

"Of course. Mexican communication companies don't burn people up. Cartels do."

I look at Marcel. At Mrs. Lingscheit.

"Thoughts?"

"It makes sense, Michael, if it was Fordyce you heard."

"I'm sure it was Fordyce. My ears were on high alert at that moment."

"Then she's probably right. It's probably the cartel that grabbed you and that killed Maddie and tried to kill Arnie."

"Then those would be cartel hitmen who came to the office with Arnie's client," says Mrs. Lingscheit. The two thug-looking men."

"Yes," says Danny. "I believe that would be right."

"How do I make this connection between the two companies," I ask Danny. "And what effect does this have on the case against me?"

"I'll have to think about that," she says. "Give me a day or three."

"Fine. You've got it. I don't think your theory changes how we work up my defense, does it?"

"I don't think so," Danny says.

"Not that I can see," Marcel adds.

"Then, Danny, here's a twist. One more job for you. I want you to put together a federal lawsuit against MexTel. We're filing a civil suit."

"Who's the plaintiff?"

"Me."

"What's the theory of the cause of action?"

"Personal injury. They or their agents set me on fire."

"Does this help keep you out of jail?"

"What do you think?"

"I think it gives you the right to take depositions and get documents. Is that where you're headed?"

"That is exactly where I am headed. Without a civil suit pending, I don't have any vehicle for getting inside MexTel because on paper they've got nothing to do with the criminal case. But now that you've made that connection, we need to sue them and get inside their computers and their protected cell phone setup. We just might blow the living hell out of this thing. And there's one other thing, a pressure point."

She looks at me and waits.

"Sure," I say, "what if we invent some way to subpoena their secret file? They'll tell us there is no such thing, knowing we have it, and then they'll have to settle the case to keep us from blowing the lid off. Maybe, if they're connected to the cartel, we get rid of the cartel good ole boys at the same time. Everybody goes down."

"Including Agent Fordyce."

"I'm working on that," I tell her.

"Keep going. This is brilliant."

"I love this," Danny says, her voice full of excitement. "I'm so glad they didn't kill you!"

Marcel and Mrs. Lingscheit look at me and burst out laughing. "Me, too!" says Mrs. Lingscheit. "I'm too old to have to train someone else!"

We laugh but then it turns serious again.

"We need to go see Arnie," I suddenly say to Marcel. "We need his input on Danny's theory."

"I'm ready. I'm yours today, Boss."

"Then let's go. Thanks, everyone."

Marcel and I leave the office and ride the elevator to the basement.

"Let's take my truck," he says, "in case they're following your car."

We arrived in my car that morning. Now we will leave in Marcel's truck. It makes perfect sense. "Lead on, sir."

We walk down two levels, giving us a chance to make sure no one is following us, and giving me a chance to get some exercise. By the time we reach his truck I am glad it's been downhill.

We drive south toward Interstate 90, and I am surprised when, instead of turning west into Illinois, he takes the junction with 94 and goes southeast toward Indiana. Twenty minutes later we're across the border and shooting up and down neighborhood streets, making sure we're not followed. The city limits sign says Hammond, Indiana, but it's my first time here, and I'm completely lost.

"They'd never think to come down here," Marcel says.

I can only agree.

"So you've hidden him in Hammond?"

"Yeppers. Right down here behind the courthouse. Lots of cops around here. He's one of the good guys, so I wanted him just behind the courthouse parking lot."

He's right. The U.S. District Court in Hammond can be seen one block away from the duplex where we've pulled up. Smart man, Marcel, I've got to give him credit yet again.

"Follow me."

I do, and he leads me inside the right door of the double front doors and we begin climbing upstairs.

Without speaking or calling out, Arnie appears at the top of the landing, and he's wearing a pistol on his hip. He hasn't drawn the gun; I'm sure he watched us walk up from the street.

"Gentlemen," he says casually. "So nice to see you."

"Cut the bullshit, Arnie," I say in half-feigned anger, "if it weren't for you we wouldn't be here in Hooterville, Indiana."

"Hammond, little brother."

"Hooterville to me," I say. "Bumpkinville."

"Who's that, honey?" I hear Esmeralda's young voice call.

"Nobody," says Arnie, and he laughs. "C'mon up, boys!"

35

We spoke twice in the hospital, Arnie and me, but we've never spoken about the events of that terrible night. But that's why I've come here, and I know he senses it.

He shows us inside his upper half of the duplex, and I am first struck by how clean the place is. Evidently Esmeralda is something of a homemaker, and she has made the place their own. New curtains are in place—you can tell by how they hang away from the wall, and nice, relaxing furniture has probably replaced the original, century-old stuff that came with the place. On the kitchen table—which stands between us and the kitchen—is a collection of cell phones and notepads.

Esmeralda comes to the table from the kitchen and greets us, hands extended, and I respond in kind. She is a sincere woman, from all I have gleaned about her, and I'm growing fond of her. I want to tell her that but now isn't the time.

"C'mon in," she says, make yourselves comfortable. Michael,

you take the overstuffed chair; Marcel, take the couch. It sinks in more so let's let Michael have the good support there. Arnie, why don't you sit over here by Marcel and I'll go make some coffee."

"Honey," says Arnie, "first tell them your joke."

He looks at his young—girlfriend? wife?—and she pauses and turns around to us. "Okay, but you have to promise you'll laugh."

"Promise," says Marcel, holding up his Scout's salute.

"Me, too."

"All right. Dr. Epstein was a renowned physician who earned his medical degree in his hometown and then left for Manhattan.

"Soon he was invited to give a speech in his hometown. As he placed his papers on the lectern they slid off onto the floor and when he bent over to retrieve them, at precisely the wrong instant, he farted, and the microphone amplified it throughout the room. He was embarrassed but regained his composure to deliver his paper. As he concluded, he raced out the stage door, never to be seen in his hometown again.

"Decades later, when his elderly mother was ill, he returned to visit her. He reserved a hotel room under a false name, Solomon Levy, and arrived under cover of darkness. The desk clerk asked him, 'Is this your first visit to our city, Mr. Levy?'"

"Dr. Epstein replied, 'Well, young man, no, it isn't. I grew up here but then I moved away.'"

"'Why haven't you visited?' asked the desk clerk."

"'I did visit once, many years ago, but an embarrassing thing happened and since then I've been too ashamed to return.'"

"The clerk consoled him. 'Sir, while I don't have your life experience, one thing I have learned is that often what seems embarrassing to me isn't even remembered by others. I bet that's true of your incident too.'"

"Dr. Epstein replied, 'Son, I doubt that's the case with my incident.'"

"'Was it a long time ago?'"

"'Yes, many years.'"

"The clerk asked, 'Was it before or after the Epstein Fart?'"

We explode in laughter.

Esmeralda is quick on the uptake. "You gents even want coffee?"

"I'm in," I say.

"Me too," says Marcel.

"Pass," says Arnie. "I'm jittery enough."

"Worried, Arnie?" I ask.

"Who wouldn't be? Those are some mean people after me. Look what they've already done."

"What are you thinking?" I ask.

He looks at me quizzically. "Thinking about what?"

"About how we're going to hit back and with what?"

"Let me ask about that. Did they get the thumb drive away from you that night?"

"Yep. In the garage or warehouse, whatever it was."

"Thought so."

"But it's still on my cell phone. The Internet address and the command."

"Good. I say we bomb them with the file. Turn it loose on all telephone customers in Latin America."

"I've thought about that. But you know what? I'm going to sue MexTel. And I want to save that bomb. I want to bring them down and make a ton of money while we do it. They've hurt us both bad; they should have to pay us for the pain and suffering and for our permanent disfigurement. So let me ask you, Arnie. Are you in?"

"In?"

"Do you want in on my lawsuit?"

His smile beams at me. "Do I? You bet your ass I do. In fact, I'd like to first-chair the trial."

"Well, you're the civil litigator. I wouldn't have any objection. But what about your conflict? You've previously represented them."

"You're right. Okay, I'll just be a party. They owe me for this," he indicates his legs with a smack across his thighs with his cane.

"Agree."

"And your face. I'm sorry, Michael, you don't look much like my brother anymore."

That is the most disheartening thing I've heard in weeks. My immediate response is to feel bad, to feel sorry for myself. But I check my feelings and say Wait a minute! The time for feeling sorry is past. Let's think about feeling angry, about taking that hate and striking back! Dr. O'Connell at the psychology department at UC Hospital would be proud to see me thinking down this path. If I'm going to be disfigured and unattractive to anyone then by god I'm going to be paid for it. They've probably sentenced me to a life alone because, I might as well admit it; no woman is ever going to want to kiss this face again. The red, tight lips, the plastic face, the stunted eyelashes and eyebrows.

"I don't know that I ever will," I tell Arnie. "The jury's still out on my face because the doctors aren't done yet."

He forces a laugh. "Don't get me wrong. You weren't exactly Antonio Banderas before."

"But at least I looked like me. The worst thing is looking into a mirror and seeing a stranger. That's the killer."

Marcel shifts his weight on his end of the couch.

"I had a lot of friends come home from Iraq with bad burns," he says. "Their wives took them in and loved them maybe more than ever."

"But Michael doesn't have a wife to do that for him, remember?" Arnie says.

At just that moment Esmeralda reappears holding three mugs of coffee in her fingers.

"Michael needs a wife?" she says. "I've got lots of friends who would love to date Michael. Young ones, too."

"Well, I'm not in the market for a wife," I tell the gathering. "In fact, my most recent one, last time I saw her, tried to invite herself to stay overnight with me."

"Did you let her?" Esmeralda says.

"Hell, no. She's run off with some young stud who's trying to get her pregnant. She was toxic on hormones and ready to conceive. Or I was afraid she was."

"I know a girl named Lucinda Larrapol who would be just right for you, Michael," says Esmeralda. "Let me give her a call. You can date her, and if you like her, you can start going out with her and see if it's a fit. One drawback is she has twin boys about two. I don't know how you would feel about that."

"Not right," I say with all the smile I can generate. "But thanks for the mention. No, I think I'll let some time go past, let the surgeons carve on my face, and then see where I am."

Marcel wonders if we should see what Arnie thinks of Danny's theory. I explain to Arnie what Danny has come up with, meaning the possible relationship between MexTel and the Tijuana cartel, where the one keeps things on the down low, and the other does the dirty work. Arnie is thinking. He leans back on the couch, drawing his right knee up inside his interlocking fingers. But the strain is too much, and he releases his grip. The pain is evident on his face, and I curse under my breath.

"Let me put it this way," he finally says. "I represented MexTel in its litigation as outside counsel for over twenty years, three years on the groundwater case alone. I know a lot about that company. I know a lot of things I'm not supposed to know, too. But to be honest, I've never come across any connection between MexTel and any of the cartels. I'm not saying it doesn't happen. I'm just saying I can't give you names and dates and places where it did. Sorry, gentlemen."

Marcel looks at me and shrugs. "So now what?"

"Easy," I tell him with a smile. "Act as if."

"As if?"

"Act as if there is a relationship. When I heard Nathan Fordyce's voice in that warehouse that night, it etched in my mind. The FBI and the Tijuana bad boys are in bed together. I don't know how or why, but I'm almost a hundred percent sure of it. I know I heard his voice there, and I know it was two crazy looking Mexican hitmen who dragged me into that van and took me there. Nothing will ever change my mind about that. You know what else? I also think the FBI has access to MexTel's scrambled phone lines. I believe they know everything about the cartels, thanks to MexTel."

"So why are so many drugs getting smuggled in if the FBI knows all and sees all?"

"I don't know. But there's a connection there. I'll probably never be able to prove it, and that's okay. That's a case for another day. Thanks to you, Arnie, I have a smoking gun that belongs to MexTel. Thanks to you I'm going to ruin them with that. Or at least cost them enough in damages to several hundred thousand of their fellow citizens that it hurts real bad. Not to mention the ten or twenty million I plan to drag off for me and you, Arnie."

Esmeralda returns and takes a seat beside Arnie. She begins rubbing his knee. He looks at her and their eyes meet. They both smile. In that moment, I know that I am not going to say the rest of what I came here to say. That is no longer any of my business. If my brother wants to destroy his life with a teenage hooker, so be it.

"So, Arnie, what's the plan for your life," I say, choosing my words carefully. "I'm talking professionally. Are you going back to your old firm?"

"You mean once this is all over and they're not looking for me?"

"Yes. Yes, that's what I mean."

"I don't know. I've got a bank vault full of money I've saved over the past thirty-five years, so I don't really have to work anymore."

"I'm voting we return to Cozumel when it's safe," Esmeralda says. "Me and Arnie and our baby."

"So...it's official? There's a baby on the way?"

Arnie shrugs and turns to Esmeralda. She grins and tosses her head back. Girlish laughter erupts, and she kicks her legs.

"The wand turned blue this morning!"

"You did the piss test?" Marcel says, ever the savant.

"Yes. It turned blue. I'm pregnant. We're pregnant!"

"Congratulations, Arnie, and Esmeralda," I say. Arnie's eyes well up. He never expected me to support him in this. "Let's celebrate with another cup of coffee, Esme'—can I call you Esme?"

"My folks call me Esme. Yes, you can call me that too."

Marcel stands and crosses the room. He draws aside a curtain and looks down at the street.

"I hate to break up a good thing," he says, "but weren't you going to take your mom to lunch, Michael?"

He's right. I had told him I wanted to be back in time for that. It's been a long time since I've been able to see her.

We say our goodbyes, telling Esme to cancel the coffee refills. She returns, wiping her hands on an honest-to-god apron, and leans up to kiss me. I turn my cheek. "Uh-uh," she says, "I want to be the first woman to try out those new lips."

She kisses me fully on the mouth.

"You pass the first test," she says with a laugh.

I turn away and head for the stairs, gripping the railing, so I don't trip and stumble. It's the tears in my eyes that might cause a fall. Lots of tears.

36

James Lamb called my office and made an appointment. Real appointment; not a walk-in. I told Mrs. Lingscheit to go ahead and put him in the book; if he admits anything about the death of Sylvia to me, I will go straight to the police and nail his ass.

He comes in again wearing a grill, this one silver with fake diamonds—they have to be fake, there's no way he could afford this many diamonds. His eyes are hidden behind silverized sunglass lenses, and I make him take them off if he wants to talk. Then I see why he's wearing them: his pupils are huge, and he's making wide, erratic swings in his greetings to me when he arrives. First I'm the hot-dog, and then I'm the great guy, and now I'm the courtroom chump. He is insulting, evil, and I wish I could shoot him myself on the spot. Or I wish that someone else would.

"Dude, what happened to your face?" he asks me. "I mean it's all like fucked up and sick, Dude."

I ignore him. He hasn't seen me since I was burned and not

only have my looks changed but I've changed too. I'm fighting down the urge to take out my gun and rid the world of this goddamn animal. But I don't.

"All right, James. Why are you here?"

"I need help with a baby."

My antennae go up.

"What kind of help? What baby?"

"It's my baby, Dude. But I can't afford to keep it. I want to adopt it out."

"Adopt it out to who?"

"There's a couple in Lafayette, Louisiana. Detembre and Anna Blake. They want to adopt. Here's their name and digits." He writes their name and phone number on the back of one of my cards and passes it to me.

"Well, James, the adoption should be held in Louisiana, and their own lawyer should do the work. Why would you need me? What would I do?"

"Well, that's just it. They're also paying me a fee for the baby."

"A fee? James, exactly what the fuck are you talking about here?"

"You know. Twenty grand and I give up all my rights. I'll cut you in for a third if you'll talk to their lawyer and get it done like they want."

"You're asking me to help you sell your baby?"

"Not sell it. Adopt it out, Dude. I can still see it if I want."

"You'll be going from Chicago to Louisiana how many times a year to see this child? And tell me something. Why did you kill Sylvia?"

"Who told you that! She was selling her ass behind a seven-eleven, and somebody knocked her around. Bitch fuckin' died and left me with her kid. That's why I'm selling it."

This is wrong in so many different ways I don't even know where to begin.

"I can't help you with this, and I want you to turn right around and leave my office. You and I are through, James. Don't call me again."

"You aren't gonna help me? What if I give you half? Is that what this is about, Dude?"

"No, Dude. This is about me trying to avoid killing you. Now get up and get out."

He stands and leans across my desk.

"You should watch that killing talk, cracker. You won't even believe where that kinda talk gets you with me."

"Forget it. Just leave."

He stands upright and points at me.

"You tell anyone I was here and you in a world of hurt, chump. Dig me?"

"I dig you. Goodbye, James."

"Yeah. And fuck you too, cracker man."

37

Danny and I await the arrival of Assistant U.S. Attorney San-Jish for my arraignment, set for ten o'clock this morning. It is the first of July and the day is already hot and humid. The air conditioners in this courtroom 9804 are working overtime to keep a chill in the room. Involuntarily, I shiver and Danny, next to me at counsel table, gives me one of her quizzical looks. I tell her it's nothing, that my body temperature has trouble modulating since I was burned. She is quickly picking up Mrs. Lingscheit's ways, however, because I don't think she believes me. She asks if it's not because I'm just a little bit frightened; I don't know what to say. Maybe she's right; maybe I am frightened. It's not every day I'm arraigned in U.S. District Court for a crime I didn't commit.

Finally, the AUSA appears, alone, Nathan Fordyce nowhere in sight, nor did we expect him to be. Judge Delores S. Sappington takes the bench and peers down at us over her reading glasses. From where I sit, her nose is long and aquiline, and her graying hair lays flat on her head, a sign that it is thinning with age. She is known as an exceptional jurist, and I am glad for that, but she is also a graduate of the U.S. Attorney's Office where they turn out these District Court judges like Denny's does pancakes.

Judge Pennington isn't here, nor should he be. He's already been arraigned. Today is my arraignment.

Judge Sappington calls the court to order and asks whether I have a copy of the indictment. I stand and reply affirmatively. She asks do I understand it? I answer in the affirmative yet again. She then reads the charge, despite my offer to waive reading. The indictment consists of two counts, one under the intimidation/threat portion of 18 USC 1512, and one under the harassment portion. The former can result in a penitentiary sentence of twenty years; the latter can put me away for only three years. Only three years, I think; how inured I have become in such a short time to the prospect of spending my days in some rank federal prison in lockdown twenty-three hours a day and glimpsing the sunlight through a window only one hour a day. The reality of it makes me shiver again, and Judge Sappington concludes the reading. I feel like I am going to vomit when she's done, and I swallow hard.

"Are you going to retain counsel, Mr. Gresham?"

"I am acting as my own lawyer, Your Honor."

"Well, you know the old saying."

"I do. And no one has ever called me a fool inside a courtroom."

The judge then asks for my plea. I inform the court that I will be pleading not guilty. AUSA San-Jish shoots me a look out of the corner of her eye from counsel table, but I ignore her reaction. We are beyond being intimidated by the awesome power of the U.S. Government in criminal prosecutions. We are prepared to stand and fight back. My Rule One of trial practice comes into play: no matter how many of them there are, they can only talk one at a time. And I can keep up with anyone if it's one at a time. So my back straightens, and I suck in a deep lungful of air and dare my body to shiver again. Next time I won't allow it. No fear.

The court then asks the clerk for a trial date and the clerk reports the trial date as September 15. We will have a pre-trial conference in thirty days. And that is all; the judge leaves the bench as Danny and I stand, and we begin putting our papers away.

Ms. San-Jish appears at my side. "Would you like to talk?" she asks.

"Go ahead," I say. "Danny is assisting me with the case. Feel free to speak in front of her."

"Would you be prepared to discuss a plea?"

"Such as?"

"Plead guilty to the lesser charge, one-year incarceration, three years probation."

I turn to face her. "You know," I say, "that's a fair resolution, and I appreciate your willingness to talk. But the truth? I didn't do anything wrong. A plea of guilty to a felony guarantees the loss of my law license and ruin of my business. I'm not financially able to do that, to walk away from what I've built up over the last thirty years. So no, I won't be interested in pleading guilty to a felony. Not any felony."

"Well, there are not appropriate misdemeanors, and I wouldn't recommend a misdemeanor to the U.S. Attorney anyway."

"Your boss must be appeased. I understand that. So thanks for talking, but no thanks."

"I won't be agreeing to any trial continuations."

I give her a hard look. "Neither will I. Be sure you're ready on September fifteenth. You and Agent Fordyce are about to get the living hell kicked out of you in this courtroom where we're standing."

She smiles and tosses off a light laugh.

"Of course," she says. "Of course."

"He's serious," Danny adds. "He won't countenance *any* plea offers. So please save your breath. We're going to trial."

I turn to look at her from beneath raised eyebrows. We won't countenance *any* plea offers? Really? I guess Danny's made up her mind, too.

Danny and I leave the courthouse on the Dearborn side and begin walking up the street. Marcel has joined us outside the courtroom and accompanies us, his eyes often darting to the street as he surveils the passing traffic. At the corner City Java, Danny asks if I'd mind stopping so she can get a coffee. I tell her that does sound good. Marcel says he will wait outside. He is restless and watchful this morning, and I am glad he's nearby.

We decide to sit and kick back after we have our orders. Danny has a mocha latte, and I have gone for my old standby, the venti bold. An empty table with two chairs beside the window catches our attention and we hurry over before the crowd can beat us.

"So," I say to Danny once we're seated and sipping, "you're from Alton, and now you're living in Mt. Pleasant?"

"Yes, but I'm thinking of moving closer. Something downtown, if the price is right."

I study her without trying to stare. She's a charming woman who has yet to show wrinkles around the eyes and mouth. I think she is forty-two or -three. I wonder about previous lives, whether there are children or ex-husbands, but I decide to stay away from the personal stuff. She'll tell me these things if and when she's ever ready. But then she catches me staring: Her dark blond hair is brushed back on the sides and brushed over on top, giving her the look of a college senior, and I realize I am smitten. I almost cannot believe myself. The natural color in her cheeks, the blond hair, the first attraction is there. Plus I am leaning on her now to some degree since she's helping me defend myself. I couldn't tell you why, but that fact alone makes her even more attractive to me. I'm prepared to do something stupid like ask her to dinner when Marcel suddenly leans around and knocks on the window from outside. He points at his wristwatch. It's 10:45 and I cannot understand why he's pointing out the time. Then he points at his mouth. I had forgotten: he has a dental appointment at noon. I wave at him as if waving goodbye, and mouth the words, "Take off now!" and he gets the gist of what I'm saying. He holds up a hand goodbye and saunters off down the street. He will retrieve his truck from our underground parking and make it to his appointment with time to spare, as it's on the near west side.

Back to my coffee date.

"So," I say, despite my earlier admonition to myself, "do you have children?"

She looks at me and giggles. "No. No kids. Do you?"

"No, and now I'm divorced and probably won't have any. Besides, I'm too old. I'm fifty-five."

"Nonsense," she says with a tilt of her head and bright smile, "I think Clint Eastwood was seventy when he had another baby. Mick Jagger was ninety!" She laughs at her joke. But the point is made: I am not ruled out of the baby-having class. Interesting.

I am silent. I've told her my age. Maybe she'll reciprocate.

"What was that U.S. Attorney even thinking, asking you for a year's incarceration. I almost pushed her down!"

"Don't do that. Those people are very touchy about such things. You would find yourself on the wrong end of some horrible indictment for some esoteric area of federal criminal law no one knows about."

"Yes," she says, "that's how it goes with the feds. Mucho laws."

She holds her cup and swirls the liquid inside. Clearly she is not going to tell me her age. Time to move on.

"I'm forty-one," she says. "In case you're wondering."

"I was, and I'm surprised. I would have guessed thirty-two or -three."

"You're a cunning man. But no, forty-one. Married once at nineteen to an air force pilot. We did a full tour of duty, and I found out he had a girlfriend in every port. Airport that is."

"So you left him?"

"Actually, he left me. For another man. Now that, my friend, was one helluva surprise. It was also no contest. I couldn't compete against smelly gym socks and a jockstrap."

We both laugh.

I am melting. It is time to move along and let this poor woman get on with the business of finding someone her own age, someone whose face isn't modeled after a recent assault, and get on with her life. Maybe have a baby. It's not too late for her.

"So, you about ready?" I ask, turning in my seat as if to stand.

"Yep. We've got a lot to do. Would you mind when we get back if we review the contents of the file Ms. Quinones returned to you?"

"Great idea. Let's get after it."

"Thanks for the latte."

"Yes, thanks for the laughs."

She smiles and tosses her head. "Maybe it's not too late for you. Your sense of humor will get you far."

38

"Hello, Mrs. Lingscheit!" I call out as Danny and I pass through the outer office. We're both carrying our coffee cups, just a little bit wired, and ready to dive into the file Valentine Quinones turned over to me.

Then I hear behind, "Hello, Mrs. Lingscheit!" and realize Danny is mimicking me. Good, there's that sense of humor again, and I like it. I like it a lot this time.

We go into the conference room and plop down the file on the table. She takes one side; I take the end next to her. She begins pulling file folders out of the Redrope file.

"Okay," she says, "this CD is marked 'gas pump.' Any idea what that means?"

"Yes, the judge was videoed at a gas pump within a mile or so from a San Diego hotel. The theory is that he was there in the vicinity of Tijuana. The up-close view is this was taken at or near the time he arranged for the murder of James Joseph Lamb."

"Good. The next CD is marked 'judge/hotel.' I assume they obtained surveillance video where he was staying in San Diego."

"Must be. Haven't heard anything about it yet."

"Okay. I'll go over it when we're done here, and I'll give you a report on the contents of both CD's."

"Perfect."

"Then we have a file marked 'Transcript- Pennington Dismissal Ramon Case.'"

"That would be the transcript of Judge Pennington when he dismissed the case against Emmie Ramon."

"The godfather's son."

"Exactly. The theory is Judge Pennington gave the kid a break on a drug trafficking case in return for the father and son agreeing to murder James Joseph Lamb."

"Sweet deal, if you're the judge."

"Well, money must have changed hands, too."

"How do you know that?"

"Hmm. I guess I don't, actually. I'm just guessing."

"Let's keep guessing to a minimum, shall we?"

I look at her. My first appraisal of her as a complete novice is rapidly fading. She is becoming someone with some judgment that I might actually trust. That's very rare for me.

"Then we have a file with a transcript in it. This one says it's Michael Gresham's recording from Raul Ramon's voice mail. So this is their smoking gun on you?"

"Yes."

"Can you give me some background?"

"Judge Pennington and I decided, during the course of my defense of him, that the cartel boss had been threatened by the FBI. We decided they were being forced to fabricate a story about the judge in order to convict him because the FBI wanted him so badly."

"So you decided to call the cartel guys and ask them about it. Not my move, but, hey, what's done is done."

I blush. "I know. But believe me, I really trusted Judge Pennington. Never in my wildest dreams did I imagine he would actually conspire to kill someone."

"Even the guy who murdered his wife? You didn't think that might happen?"

"Like I said, I believed him."

"Next, we have a copy of what must be the judge's letter to the Ramons. Here's where he incriminates you, correct?"

"Yes. He tells them that I helped plan my own client's murder by revealing to Judge Pennington where he is living now. Of course I would do that, I mean what lawyer doesn't want his client dead?"

"Ridiculous."

"You know, the judge wasn't stupid. He knew his mail was being intercepted and read. That's always done on people on federal bail."

"But why does he want you involved? You were doing your best to save his ass?"

"That's just it. It's always been about the fact I at one time defended Lamb. The judge has never forgotten that or forgiven me. He's out of control, Danny. That's all it is. The murder of his wife has driven him mad. Who wouldn't it make crazy?"

"All right." She pulls out two more files. "Statements. Father and son."

"Summarize and report."

"Check. Then we have FBI activity reports."

"Same thing."

"Check again."

"Now. What's happening with my civil case against MexTel for injuring me?"

She smiles. "See the Litigation File on the server. It's captioned *Gresham v. MexTel*. There's a forty-four count complaint."

"Federal court?"

"Right here. Chicago."

"Is it ready to file?"

"Just read and review and I'll get it filed and served."

"Do they have a registered agent in the U.S. for service?"

"Yes. One of the corporations will accept service."

"Fine. I'll review that next, print and sign, and let's file it yet today."

"Done."

"Now let me talk to you about affirmative defenses. We are going to defend this under the statute that says any prosecution for witness tampering can be justified by a defendant having the sole intention to encourage, induce, or cause the Ramons to testify truthfully."

"So you're going to admit the phone call, of course. But you're going to say it was done because you were afraid they were going to lie."

"Yes, that the FBI had induced them to lie."

"Wow. I like it."

"Take a look at the federal rules. See if we're required to disclose it as an affirmative defense in any pleading."

"I think we are. But let me double-check."

"Before digging into the file from Quinones, I would also like you to prepare and file with the civil complaint a request for documents directed to MexTel."

"What do you want me to request?"

"I'll give you a paragraph in an email. Basically, I'm looking for files that indicate MexTel had prior knowledge of toxic groundwater spills when it was constructing new towers and right of way. The smoking gun files."

"Sounds great, Michael. You want them to deny there are any such documents because you know you already have them."

"Yes. They'll realize that if they deny having them, we'll simply produce our own and run over to court and tell the judge they're lying, and sanctions for lying should include a judgment in our favor for ten million bucks. On the other hand, if they produce the records they know they're going to lose the litigation that Arnie was defending them on where thousands of Mexican citizens are suing them for diseases caused by toxic groundwater."

"So, either way, they lose."

"Exactly."

"Unless they just settle quietly with you."

I smile. "That will work to keep me quiet. But only to a point."

"What point is that?"

"Time will tell."

"I've never seen you smiling like this before. What's that mean, 'time will tell?'"

"Let me answer that with a question. All right?"

"Fire away."

I gather my courage. "Do you like Jazz?"

"I love jazz."

"Would you like to go sometime to a new jazz club?"

"Would I? With you?"

"Uh-huh."

"Are you asking me on a date?"

"I'm asking you to go listen to jazz with me."

"Sounds like a date, Michael."

"It would be."

"Hey, would I have to get dressed up? I'm kind of a jeans and sweaters girl."

"It's down by the University of Chicago. No high-flyers allowed."

"What time are you picking me up?"

"Seven."

"Saturday night?"

"Saturday night."

"Jeans and sweater?"

"It's summertime, almost. No sweater required."

"I'll be waiting at seven."

I almost stagger out of the conference room, swelling up with this huge feeling of relief she didn't tell me no.

"You're a funny man, Michael Gresham," she calls after me. "You know I could sue you for sexual harassment, right?"

"Yes."

"But I won't. Not if you'll let me buy the first round."

"Bring ten bucks. Sounds like a very reasonable settlement to me."

39

"Hey there, cop killer!"

I am walking along the slant to my parking slot in underground parking, deep in thought, when I'm suddenly jarred by the epithet. I turn and can't quite make out the person. He draws nearer, and I realize it's Nathan Fordyce. He looks very dark, almost malevolent here in the dim basement. This is not the same squeaky-clean FBI agent I saw in the office of AUSA San-Jish.

He's wearing a black suit, white shirt, black tie, and Ray-Bans. I cannot see his eyes and I'm wondering why the Ray-Bans when he suddenly whips them off and gives me a glassy-eyed stare as he jerkily approaches. I am about to open the driver's door on my SUV when he puts his hand on my forearm and jerks it back.

"Easy, Hoss," he says. I can smell the overpowering smell of alcohol on his breath. Suddenly I'm on full alert.

"What is it?" I ask. "Am I being arrested again?"

"Not yet! I'm just here to ask you why you killed my partner?"

"Your partner's dead?"

"Last night. Shot outside his home in his own driveway. Where were you last night, Mr. Gresham?"

"I was with my ex-wife eating dinner," I tell him, knowing that Sue Ellen would actually cover for me if push ever came to shove. The truth is, I watched the Cubs lose to the Brewers last night, alone, in my own home.

"Well the SAIC has the case. I'm not actually assigned, you'll be glad to know, or I'd run your ass downtown."

"Well, I'm glad for that, then," I say, and allow an easy smile.

Which relaxes him somewhat.

"Seriously," I tell him, "I'm terribly sorry to hear about your partner. I really am."

The agent looks at me and catches himself as he sways on legs that are slightly out of control.

"Whoa," I say and extend my hand. He waves it off and catches himself on the side of my SUV.

"Jim Burns was his name, in case you forgot. He was driving the car the day I shook you down."

"I remember."

"He was with me when we got the indictment against you."

"Well, there you are then. I know he was just doing his job."

He pushes away from the side of my car and raises a finger and points it at my forehead. "Not so! Nobody's just doing their job. The Bureau isn't like that, sir. We believe you're guilty, and it's our duty to act on that. You called those bastards in Tijuana and conspired with them to change their story! We have a recording of that. If that's not good enough, MexTel has a recording too."

This last phrase hangs in the air like a plume of breath on an icy day. Then the words suddenly explode in my mind. MexTel has a recording.

"MexTel has a recording? How does MexTel have a recording?"

"Oh, no, brother. You're gonna have to ask MexTel about that!" He leans closer. "Do I really look that stupid to you?"

"No, sir. You don't look stupid at all. I'm just wondering how you found out MexTel was recording the cartel's phone call with me."

He points to the side of his head, and his eyes light up. "We have our ways," he says. "Your FBI doesn't miss anything!"

"Does MexTel have other recordings?" I know I'm going for the gold here, but, hey, it never hurts to ask.

"What recordings?" he says with a sneer, suddenly very crafty. "Did I say MexTel has recordings?"

"Yes, you said MexTel has recordings."

"All right, then. Go ask them. Bunch of goddamn Mexicans anyway." He makes a swipe at me with an open hand, groping for my necktie. I jerk back, and he gathers the lapel of my suit and wads it in his hand, pulling me toward him. He puts his face inches from mine and whispers, "Don't fucking move."

"Hey, what's this about?"

"You shot my partner last night, didn't you?"

"I've never killed anything or anybody. That's not who I am."

"Bullshit. It was you or the Mexicans. And I think they're too goddamn stupid."

"Would they have any reason to murder your partner?"

"MexTel?"

"No, the cartel."

He gives me a long, studied look. It's as if he's considering that I might actually know something.

"That's the question," he says. "I'm working on that."

"I see you are. Hey, are you driving today?"

"Naw, too drunk to drive. My new partner's waiting up at the pay booth."

"Okay, good. Well, go some place and coffee up, huh? Then go sleep it off, Agent Fordyce."

His eyes narrow and he gives me a dagger look. "As if you really give a good goddamn. You criminal lawyers are all the same. One of us goes down; you celebrate."

"Hey, I'm not celebrating. In fact, your partner getting murdered is sad."

"Then you might be one of the good guys. I'm going to let you go now, counselor. We'll talk again."

"All right, Agent Fordyce. I'm sorry about Jim Burns."

"Yeah. Me too," he says and manages to turn and lurch off toward who knows where.

I open the door to my SUV and climb in. When I start it up, I am grateful for the backing-up camera. Nothing would be worse than running over a passed-out FBI agent. Especially the one who's investigating me.

Halfway home to Evanston, my cell phone beeps. Marcel.

"Hey, Marce. What's up?"

"You headed home?"

"I am."

"Good. Stay there. I'm headed up."

"I'll put the coffee on."

"Thirty minutes, Michael. Don't go anyplace else."

"All right. Can you give me some clue—"

"Go straight home and don't leave."

We hang up, and I find myself checking traffic out of my rearview mirror. I even reach and point the rearview down so I can check the backseat of my SUV. A shiver works its way up my spine, and I realize I am terrified.

I want to go someplace safe.

40

Marcel calls me when he's two blocks from my house. He tells me to open the garage, that he's coming in. Two minutes later I've got the door up and he's rolling inside.

His first words to me, as he's coming up the stairs out of the garage: "Never ask me to go to Tijuana again, Michael."

"Too dangerous?"

"Border crossing is three hours coming back. Homeland Security at work. Some woman ahead of me in line had evidently had a heart scan done. You know, radioactive isotopes injected into the blood stream. So she sets off Geiger counters at the border crossing from ten cars back. All these little soldiers in blue uniforms are running up and down the line of cars with Geiger counters. Then they find her and half-convince her that she's a terrorist. She's in her seventies, and they're holding her in secondary while they're passing these wands all over her body. Last I hear, she's laughing and telling them she gets to choose who does the body cavity search!"

"No way!"

"Way. Anyhow, the whole trip wasn't nearly as much fun. Those are some serious *narcotraficantes* down there, Michael. The upshot is, yes, they've been harassed by the FBI and promised the moon if they testify against Judge Pennington. You, you're a gnat on their radar screen. Here's the best part. They've broken off negotiations with the FBI, and they're not going to testify at all. Never were planning to testify. The FBI has been spoofing everyone."

"That's good news, right? They're not going to testify against me?"

"Good as it comes, I'd say. But they did tell me one thing about you."

"Yes?"

"Judge Pennington tried to buy a hit on you. This was during Lamb's trial. These guys refused, lucky for you."

"So why did they tell you all this?"

"Because they remember my name from Interpol. I called the dogs off them at one time years ago, and they haven't forgotten."

"One small question. Was it these guys who burned me?"

"No. They don't burn and extinguish. With these dogs, they burn, and you die. No, it was MexTel who did all that."

"I told you I heard Fordyce that night."

"Maybe him too. I can see him helping MexTel."

"What about getting to Arnie through me? Would the FBI be helping MexTel get Arnie's file away from him?"

"Entirely possible. MexTel is a tremendous intel source for our triple alphabet: FBI and CIA and NSA. Wouldn't surprise me for a second to find the FBI in bed with them."

"He threw the lighter on me. I know it was him. I heard him."

"Maybe, maybe not. We'll probably never know."

"Did you ask Ramon about it at all?"

"No. These guys aren't working you, Michael. You're nothing to them."

"Okay. Now tell me about this new thing with the judge. Should I be worried?"

"Only if he's managed to buy off some other hitter. Short version: hell yes, be worried. Until something happens and he's trucked off to prison or the narcos kill him, you've got me on your six every second."

"You're taking this all the way serious."

"That I am, Señor Gresham."

"All right. So how do we work it? You know what? Screw this! I'm going to go over to this crazy bastard's house and confront him!"

"That would be a terrible idea. He'd shoot you and get away with it. Slow down and think: local lawyer accused by judge is shot trying to break into judge's house. Not your best headline. Or obit, depending on how good a shot he is."

"I hear he practices every week. He's probably quite good."

Marcel places his shoulder bag down on the table we've arranged ourselves around. There is a light overhead in a brass fixture, and the light burnishes the silver of the gun as Marcel draws it out of the bag and places it in front of me.

"Nickel plated Colt .45," he says, a hint of wonder in his voice. "Colt Series Seventy."

"This is for me?"

"That, and this," he says, and slips an ammo clip out of the bag. Next comes a shoulder holster, and he inserts the ammo clip into a small case attached to the shoulder holster. Then he takes up the gun, releases its clip, works the slide to show me it's unloaded, inserts the magazine, works the slide once again to chamber a fat forty-five round, and slides the loaded weapon in the shoulder holster. He holds the unit out to me and motions I should put it on. I shrug into it, and I am impressed with the weight of the gun and bullets. I know I must look like something I've seen on TV ten thousand times, but that's good. I find that I am comfortable being armed and, because of all the rounds we've shot on the range, I feel quite comfortable in the rig.

"Nice," I say and pat the gun. "Good fit, too."

"This gun is now yours, Michael. Never sell it; it can't be replaced."

"I won't. I'll treasure this. How can I thank you? Do I pay you or what?"

"Don't insult me. This gun is a gift. And it's a necessity right now with John Dillinger alive and well on the streets of Chicago again."

"Not to change the subject. Have you heard about Jim Burns?"

"Fordyce's partner? Not only heard about it, I know who did it."

"Judge Pennington?"

"Naw, he's too fucking smart to kill a Fibbie. Now this was a TJ whack job. The cartel got him."

"But why?"

"He was down there last week threatening them with a busload of hurt if they didn't agree to come to Chicago and give testimony to a new grand jury. Evidently they were adding more charges against the judge."

"What about against me?"

"Not included this time around, mister. The Fibbies got a recording from MexTel. The recording was the call from Judge Pennington to Raul Ramon where he's offering the guy a hundred grand to murder you. Mr. Ramon laughed at him and said he makes a hundred grand every hour, and he never has to leave his TV set."

"That is scary. It was me he was trying to have killed, you're sure?"

"That's why I'm here, Michael. Anyway, long story short, the cartel doesn't like being threatened. They had a local thumper hit Jim Burns outside his home. Some guy on a bicycle of all things."

"Oh my God."

"Yes. The good part is, you're clear with the TJ guys. They've got nothing for you. But you're not clear with Pennington, and you're not clear with Nathan Fordyce."

"How do you know that?"

"After Burns got shot, Fordyce calls Raul Ramon and cusses him a blue streak. Evidently Fordyce is drunk and threatens Ramon too, if they won't testify against you."

"So are they going to come here and testify against me?"

"What do you think, Michael? These people are wealthy beyond Bill Gates, and they're anybody's worst nightmare. They're not under the FBI's thumb or anyone else's thumb. Sorry to let you down, kid, but you basically don't amount to shit with them. Nope, they won't be coming to your anointing on September fifteenth when you begin your trial."

I gasp and release an enormous sigh of relief. My head is just about spinning with all this, some good, some frightening.

"I should send you to TJ more often, Marcel."

"Never going back. While I was waiting in line at the border, I bought a four-foot statue of Elvis, two pork tacos, and a guitar made out of pressed fiberboard. There was nothing else to pass the time."

I'm laughing now and about to offer my poor, overworked bodyguard a drink. Or offer to take him to dinner.

He reads my mind.

"I'm taking the couch tonight. I've already told Evie I have your ass covered."

"Really? When were you talking to Mrs. Lingscheit?"

He winks and rolls his eyes. "When aren't I talking to her, you mean. Love that gal, Michael. All woman. All German, all hard-working and hard-saving. My kind of gal, that one."

"Okay, okay. I'll order in some Chinese. You grab the TV remote and see who's playing who tonight. Do you like the Cubbies?"

"You kidding? I'm a working stiff. White Sox for me."

"All right. Let's see who's on."

"I'm on it. Hot and spicy General Tso's Chicken for me, Michael."

"I already knew that. You've been here before, Marcel."

"All right! I knew you were good, kid, I just didn't know how good."

41

Sunday morning Marcel has insisted I go spend time at the shooting range. Last night, Danny and I went out to the jazz club, and it was quite a letdown. A letdown because Marcel tagged along. He had a man follow us and he stayed right with us. Did it cramp my style? That question assumes I even have a style. After a few lame attempts at having some laughs with Danny the tension finally got the best of both of us and we went home early. We dropped her at her place and drove home in silence.

The shooting range sounds uninteresting to me, but I go along with it because Marcel says I need to. While I'm there, and I'm armed, he will take his truck in for maintenance at QuikLube. The range outside Palatine is built on the back end of a firearms store that at one time was a barn on the Hosea Johnson King Seed farm. At least according to the sign along the highway as you enter the parking lot. There are maybe a dozen cars snuggled up along the first parking lane. Marcel pulls up, engine running, and I climb out carrying my utility bag with my gun and enough ammo to keep me squeezing off rounds for an hour or two. I slap the side of his truck, and he pulls off.

I go inside and examine the pistols in the display cases and ask to hold two of them. One that I like is the Glock 26 with the fifteen round magazine because I have large hands, and it fits me better than the regulation magazine. The other one I like is the hugely popular Glock 19. It's made for self-defense and has a history of reliability as good as any gun ever made.

After my window-shopping, I pay for my alley, select several targets, and walk through the north door into the shooting range. My earmuffs block out most of the sound from the dozen or so shooters in various stages of shooting, retrieving and replacing targets, reloading, cleaning, and taking cigarette breaks. It is loud and noisy and intense. As I'm walking along to my alley, I suddenly realize I'm looking at the back of the head of Francis Pennington Jr. He is standing at my right, directly facing his target and using a two-handed grip. His shooting glasses are yellow, and he is wearing in-the-ear hearing protection. He doesn't see me.

I pause and watch him shoot. Before he's emptied the magazine, I realize the judge is probably the best shooter I've ever watched. His groups are tight and centered, his trigger action is fast, and he's shooting without aiming so much as just looking. He seems to have mastered the sport. I realize he's shooting his regular Sunday morning box of 1000 rounds. He doesn't see me but neither do I want him to feel my eyes on his back, so I move on along. When I stop, there are four individuals in between us and I relax, knowing he very likely won't notice me because he would have no reason to approach my end of the shooting gallery.

Loading my pistol and affixing my target to the frame, I am keeping one eye on Judge Pennington. A shooter that was between us has shut down and left; now there are but three separating us and I'm only just beginning. Hopefully, the two remaining women and one man won't wrap up soon.

I quickly put a hundred rounds through my Colt. It is a heavy gun, and I'm impressed with how much of the recoil the gun eats up, not transferring it into my hands. I have nine empty magazines and pause to reload. To my right, I realize there are but two people standing between the judge and me. He is still shooting—very quick shots, tat-tat-tat-tat-tat, and repeat—and I'm quite certain he hasn't noticed me. Now I find myself praying the two shooters between us stand their ground. I am rewarded when a third shooter shows up and begins organizing her practice between us. At one moment Judge Pennington looks directly at me, but I believe he fails to recognize me thanks to my cap, muffs, and amber lenses.

Thirty minutes go by. I put hundreds of rounds through my weapon, stopping when I must to reload and wipe the barrel and have a drink of my Orange Crush. During one of these breaks I ease my gaze over to the right and discover Pennington is nowhere to be seen. I turn and face that way, removing the shooting glasses from my face, and just as I do he comes bursting through the far door, lugging a case of ammo under his arm and carrying his gun in his hip holster. He sees me, and he freezes. I don't turn away, and it is a standoff. For the first several moments I am numb. I am holding my gun, but the magazine is on the small wood ledge to my left. His right-hand moves down toward his gun and, almost unbelievably, he draws and aims the muzzle directly at me. He smiles evilly. I panic and fall to my left, behind two other shooters,

and my hand flops around on the ledge above me in a futile
effort to locate a loaded magazine so that I may defend myself.

Finally, I secure a magazine that I had been loading. It is
about half-full but I insert it into my Colt and slam it home
and in the next moment I rack the slide and lodge a bullet in
the chamber for firing. Ever so slowly from my crouched
position, I edge my head out to look for the judge. At first I
don't see him, so I come out further. Now other shooters are
noticing me in this crouched position, and they are looking
left/right and left/right trying to understand what I'm doing
kneeled down on the concrete floor. So I act as if I have
misplaced something and slowly begin to stand, all the
while looking carefully to my left to see if I can locate the
bastard who pointed the gun at me.

Now coming fully upright I step into the aisle and, to my
enormous relief, see that he has left the area. Just at that
moment, Marcel comes through the door. He is wearing his
gun in a shoulder holster and carrying a large storage box of
ammo, evidently intent on taking the space just beyond me
and firing off a few hundred rounds.

He approaches me and sees that I am broken out in sweat.

"What?" he says.

"Pennington was here!"

"Here, here?"

"Yes, four units down. He pointed his gun at me."

"What?" Marcel is moving back toward the door he just
came through, obviously after the judge. He shoves ahead,
scattering two shooters who are trying to enter, and disap-

pears as the door closes. Again I am alone, and I'm loading my magazines as fast as my fingers and hands will work. One fully loaded magazine replaces the partial magazine I had inserted earlier. New rounds are stuffed down inside the magazine and soon every magazine I have is fully loaded and ready to fire. These are target loads but believe me, they will do more than tear a target to shreds. A man would quickly die from just one well-placed round.

Five minutes later, Marcel returns. He shrugs as he comes toward me.

"You're sure it was Judge Pennington?"

"Of course, I'm sure. I've known the guy a dozen years or more."

"And he aimed a gun at you?"

"Yes."

"Then we need to call the police and file a report."

"No. He'll just deny it. Nobody else was looking. One on one."

"Okay. How are you feeling?"

"Scared. I'm not going to be a combat shooter. That became very apparent to me."

"Well stand back because I am and I'm not leaving you alone again for one minute."

"He lives in Barrington. This must be where he shoots on Sundays," I say lamely, still trying to believe it just happened that we ran into each other.

"Small world when it comes to ranges. I always see lots of gun owners I know."

"Marcel. He *aimed* that thing at me."

"Next time, aim back and pull the trigger. That's called self-defense."

"He's good. I saw his grouping."

"He probably is. Now get back over here and let's light up some targets. We've got a lot of work to do to get you up to speed."

"I think I'm done. I think there has to be another way for me to handle this thing with him."

"Oh yeah? Care to share your idea?"

"I don't know."

"So belly up here and let's shoot."

"All right."

But my heart isn't in it. I already know I'm not going to shoot someone.

I'm in way over my head.

Way over.

42

I deposited my five-hundred-thousand-dollar home equity check in my personal account, and I wrote a check for ninety-thousand dollars to Sue Ellen. Sue Ellen sends Eddie to pick it up. She says they're both delirious with joy, and she's on the way to the pharmacy to pick up the first round of injectables. It will be expensive, but my money gives them a shot at a new life with a new baby. So be it.

Eddie comes into my office looking hangdog and embarrassed and thanks to my new face and scars I can relate. So I know I can't have that. I decide to welcome him into the fold, try to make him comfortable while he's with me.

"Eddie, thanks for coming. Let me show you what I need Sue Ellen to sign," I say, and extend my hand with the paperwork. He glances over it. "This is a happy occasion, and I'm glad to be a part of it, you and Sue Ellen launching down this new road together."

His tan reddens. He is blushing and I wish he weren't.

"I'm amazed you're even talking to her after she left you high and dry, Michael."

I brush away his words. "We had both been unhappy for a long time. It was a good decision on her part, and I harbor zero animosity. In fact, I'm glad she found you. You seem to make her very happy."

He beams. "Well, hey, man, that's really cool of you. There's another thing, too. I was wondering how interested you might be in investing in an excellent business opportunity."

I should have known better. It's always something. My recently-found faith in humanity is quickly unraveling. But I plunge ahead.

"What opportunity might that be, Eddie?"

"It's actually a house washing service. I can get a franchise for twenty-five thousand."

This really throws me. House washing? Seriously?

"So what does house washing—what exactly is it?"

"Well, after a long, hard winter all the houses in Chicago are dirty. There's mud, soot, road salt, cinders—all the stuff that makes winter winter. So I come along with my van, and it's equipped with a five hundred gallon high-pressure water system that forces compressed water and soap up as high as three stories. I blow the dirt away and leave you with a sparkling house. If you're up for it, I'd even do you free for the next ten years."

"That's hard to turn down, Eddie. The franchise is twenty-five thousand?"

"Yes. Plus another twenty for the van. Forty-five total."

"And how much of this are you looking for me to invest?

"All of it. Forty-five grand."

"Wow, I don't know. I was thinking of putting my money into a SEP-IRA with Fidelity. Something to help me retire."

"You know, Michael, have you thought that in a way you're going to be related to my baby? I mean, Sue Ellen being the mother and all?"

"How exactly am I related? I mean it's a beautiful theory, but legally—"

"I'm thinking more like a godfather. Someone who will come to the christening and make a promise to be there for the baby if something happens to me and Susie."

"Susie." Good for him; he's learning. "Well, that's a real honor. Have you discussed it with Sue Ellen? Me being the godfather?"

"Sure, it was her idea. She's still got a soft spot for you, Michael. She still loves you in a way. My own feelings for you are growing that way, too. You're all but family."

"All but family. I'm not sure what that makes me, exactly, but okay, I'll be the godfather to your baby. It would be an honor."

He leans back and strokes his chin. Eddie has the thin waist and wide shoulders of a top-flight swimmer—damn him. Not really. He is wearing half-laced Nikes, navy shorts, and a sleeveless shirt that says, "Where's the Beach!" He repeatedly spins a rabbit's foot keychain around and around his index finger and, with the free hand, strokes his chin as if expecting new growth at any moment. In a way, he's endearing himself to me. But in another way, I want to leap across my desk and choke him to death for stealing Sue Ellen. She was my cheerleader first, damn it, I want to scream at him.

But I don't.

"You're certain house-washing is where it's at for you?" I ask him.

"Being my own boss. That's what I'm after. I can make enough to take care of Sue Ellen and my baby. And even pay you back."

"Even pay me back? How much would you be paying?"

"I'm thinking a grand a month. Possibly. Maybe a little more, maybe a little less. Until I get rolling, anyway. Then I would double down on it. Amortize the hell out of it."

"Amortizing debt is good. Good for you, Eddie. Tell you what."

"What?"

"I'm in. It sounds like an excellent opportunity for you and Sue Ellen."

He leaps to his feet, leans over my desk and begins pumping my hand. He is quite strong, and his shoulders knot up under the sleeveless shirt as he thanks me. I can see why Sue Ellen would throw me over for the guy. He's hard all over, and I am soft. He has perfect, berry-brown skin and I am scarred and road-weary. What's the old saying, he was rode hard and put away wet? That's me.

"I'll send you a check, Eddie. For the full forty-five thousand.

There will be an IOU with it. Just sign that and send it back. Okay?"

"Absolutely, Michael. Oh, my God! I'm gonna be self-employed!"

"And don't forget this." I pass him the envelope containing Sue Ellen's ninety thousand dollar check. "Tell Sue Ellen to sign the consent agreement and I'll get the judge to enter it. It will release me from all further alimony obligations. Make sure to remind her, okay?"

"Okay, okay, okay!"

He slips the envelope into his front pocket and begins backing out of my office. At the door, he raps the wall with his knuckles, points at me with a smile, pumps his fist, and he's gone.

Mrs. Lingscheit replaces him in my office.

"What was all that? That young man was walking on air when he left!"

"I just paid off my alimony, Mrs. Lingscheit."

"That was it?"

"And I just paid my child support, too. In the grand scheme of things."

"You don't have kids. How can you owe child support?"

I think of all the times Sue Ellen begged me for a child. I remember how often I said no.

"Trust me. I owed."

43

I am sipping coffee and ruminating about Sue Ellen and her baby. I sincerely hope it works for her. If there's anything else I can do to help, I will. Which is when my phone rings, when the angels in the air know I'm in a helping mood.

"Yes, this is Michael?"

"Mr. Gresham?"

I know the voice. It can't be.

"This is James Lamb. I need you to come down and get me outta jail."

"What is it this time, James?"

"They're hasslin' me, man. The cops won't let me alone. Just get me outta jail and I'm leaving town. You can tell them that."

"What are you arrested for?"

"They say I sold drugs to an undercover narc."

"Did you?"

There's a long silence.

"Dude, don't be asking that kind of shit over the phone. This is bugged, dude."

"Sorry, James. This time, I'm out. Call someone else."

I hang up and feel like I've come out the other end of a fire pit. Putting that kind of evil out of my life is good. He's someone else's problem now, and he's probably going away for a long time, according to what it sounds like. Sold drugs to a narc? Please take a ticket and go away for twenty years. I know the prosecutors won't cut him a deal. Not after the Pennington case. Good. I'll never have to deal with his ugly face and gold teeth again. For a moment I am nauseous. Just talking to him makes me sick anymore. Good riddance and goodbye, James.

44

I've done some looking into and here's what I've been able to piece together about James Joseph Lamb.

Bottom line, Lamb is a nobody. His name, his character, carry no weight among the denizens that freely roam South Chicago. When he is around, he's in someone's face and is out of control and frightening. Then he is a somebody.

South Chicago is a shooting gallery. Guns and gangbangers have turned that free-fire zone into the place in America where you are most likely to be murdered with a gun if you are black, under the age of twenty-five, and walking along a street. Why walking? Because the trademark assassination in South Chicago is the drive-by. Lamb and his fellow Crips have a year-round open season on all citizens. They shoot at will just for notches.

This is Lamb's modus operandi:

A pimped out low-rider careening around the corner at the other end of the block and you are walking along with your head down, hands in pockets, minding your own business. Riding shotgun in that lowrider is James Lamb, a street punk of twenty-five years with a rap sheet that completely fills a computer screen of the fifteen-inch variety, two-columns. He is angry—always—and mean. He is the kid who loved to torture cats and dogs with matches and pliers. He is the kid who at the old age of fourteen was raping nine-year-old girls whose mothers had left them alone in the projects. No boundaries restrain him—not ethical, financial, relational, or social; there are no rules that he won't break and no allegiances strong enough to keep him loyal to anything for very long. And tonight he is drawing a bead on you from the operator's end of an AR-15 assault rifle as you are walking along after a night at the school library.

It is ten p.m. And you wish you hadn't stayed so late. But your Black Studies paper is due tomorrow at the community college, and you need an "A" if you really do plan to go to law school.

Driving the car in which Lamb is riding is Johnny Rouse, a black kid all of nineteen years who has spent the last nine in juvenile prison in Kewanee Youth Center, the place where they send kids with severe mental health issues, kids who commit violent crimes, and sex offenders. Johnny Rouse is all three of these, so he fit right in during his stay there.

As you walk along, the Rouse car pulls abreast and slows to keep pace. You speed up; it speeds up. You slow down; it slows down. All the while, James Lamb is keeping you within the sights of his assault rifle, studying you. If you're a Crip, they will pull away and leave you alone. But if you're a Blood, brother, you won't be making it home tonight. And if you're neither, if you're a freshman at your local community college trying to study your way out of the projects—you're fair game. You're the young, six-point buck the deer hunters hotly pursue to mount on their wall.

He thinks he might just fire off one round into your lower body just to hear you scream. He does, and the bullet strikes you in your upper left thigh. It passes through the soft tissue there, impacts the thigh bone, and ricochets forward, ripping through your testicles and crumpling you to the ground. As you lie there, screaming and pleading, the car comes to a complete stop. Lamb throws open the door and walks up to you.

"Quit that fuckin' cryin'," he orders. "Yo, fool, take it like a man."

You are afraid to look up at him, afraid to make eye contact, but you are able to restrain your cries. Now the only sound is a low moan deep in your chest, and you try to shut that off too but find you're unable, that that sound is a bodily process you cannot control any more than you can control the rate of blood pouring from the wound in your scrotum.

"Stop that," says Lamb, and he lifts the assault rifle to his shoulder and takes careful aim at your head.

"Please," you say, and lift a trembling arm up to him, "I just wanna—"

But you don't get to finish because Lamb has just executed you.

He riffles through your pockets, finds a five and some change, and kicks you in the head in disgust.

"Fool," he sniffs, then spits.

Sirens can be heard a few blocks over on Dorchester and so Lamb sidles back to the car driven by Johnny Rouse and slides inside. He takes the assault rifle and works it down to the floor between his seat and the door. Out of sight to any cop who might look inside from the driver's side of the car.

He bumps fists with Rouse, who punches the gas and the lowrider surges ahead into the night.

He is everything you and I loathe.

Loathe and wish dead.

45

I t is midnight, and I have just gotten off the phone with —are you ready for this?—Judge Francis Pennington Jr. We have talked about James Lamb. The judge called me; I didn't call him. Ever the lawyer and ready to settle disputes, I accepted the call, and we talked. While I am enraged at the guy and really want nothing to do with him and don't trust him any more than I trust boneless fish, I talk. Evidently the Instagram pictures that Lamb posted online have found their way to the Chicago Police Department. An investigation took place, and it was confirmed; the pictures were original. Only someone at the murder scene could have taken those. That someone, the consensus is, is James Lamb. But as we all know, the judge says, Lamb is immune from prosecution.

So Judge Pennington asks me for help.

Have you ever cared for a sick animal that later you had to put down? The criminal justice system in Chicago is like that: you take care of your own and begin to develop a kind of proprietary feeling toward the defendants who cross through the courtroom. Some you like, some you hate, some need to be put down. James Lamb has become one of the latter. No matter how much the system—and all participants in the system—try, Lamb isn't going to get better. It is time to act.

Pennington and I meet the next morning early, six o'clock, at a Denny's on the north side. We don't shake hands; we hardly look at each other. He hates me, and I am up to here with him. Marcel, who has violently opposed my meeting the judge, has driven me today. He wants to accompany me to the meet, but I refuse. I am armed under my windbreaker; the silver Colt is riding shotgun. By now, I've fired it enough that I've become quite good. I feel like I can defend myself.

We talk. While the judge hates me, it is a mutual hate, and it will continue. But for now, we are forced to work together. He outlines what he needs from me. It means I will have to gain Lamb's trust—at least for a short time. Frankly, I'm so sick of Lamb that it is almost easy for me to agree to help.

The plan is agreed to, and we shake.

Then we each enjoy a Grand Slam Slugger breakfast.

All eating, no talking.

Still only $7.99.

Marcel stands beside our booth on the other side of the window, ready to draw down on Pennington for the slightest wrong move.

What a friend.

And what an enemy.

46

After Denny's, I show up early for work and begin drafting a paragraph to add to Danny's request for production of documents to MexTel. We are filing the civil suit against them today for harassment, assault and battery, kidnapping, and several other counts. The point is, Arnie and I have been harassed, kidnapped, burned, run off the road and injured, and we're both going after MexTel for restitution, medical bills, pain and suffering, and punitive damages. We know they will laugh at us and tell us we have no case. But that's not the point. The point of the lawsuit is to get them into a United States District Court where their assets can be attached.

Because, brother, do I have a surprise for them.

In the request for production of documents, I carefully list each and every document by name and date that exists in the smoking gun file Arnie made off with. MexTel still has all documents hidden away on its computer, and we know that. We also know they will deny that, because in the underlying litigation that Arnie was defending for them they have already said, on the record, subject to charges of perjury, that they didn't have foreknowledge of the toxicity of the chemicals they were dumping into the groundwater across Mexico as they laid their lines and built their towers and stored their petroleum products. They said they had no way of knowing ahead of time that they would injure and sicken and send to their graves with cancer thousands of citizens of Mexico and Latin America. They swore this under oath.

But we know better.

Now we ask them, in our lawsuit, to admit they do have such records. Which leaves them with two choices, as I see it. One, they can deny the records exist, but they don't dare do that because they know I will attach those identical records to a contradictory pleading in federal court and seek huge damages and criminal penalties for their lying. Or, two, they can come crawling to me and ask me how much I'll take for my injuries, Arnie's injuries, and damages for the wrongful death of Maddie to be paid to her family. In return, they will receive the smoking gun file, and we'll go away.

At least, that's what they'll think they've bought when they've paid each of us twenty million dollars. That's my asking amount. If they refuse, I'll go to twenty-five million.

You can see where this is going.

~

LESS THAN A WEEK LATER, MexTel, through a series of phone calls and conference calls and meetings with Sam Shaw at Arnie's old firm, settles with us. Twenty million for me, for Arnie, and for Maddie's family. The money arrives in their lawyers' trust account twenty-four hours later and by the next day, the three plaintiffs have each received their settlements.

But it's not quite time to celebrate. Not just yet.

Imagine MexTel, sitting down in Mexico City, relieved to have purchased our silence for only sixty million dollars when they're fighting for their existence in the original lawsuit that seeks in excess of a billion dollars in damages. Imagine the corporate looks on their corporate faces when I click ENTER on my keyboard and, from their own servers, the entire smoking gun file is off-loaded and a service then emails their ten million subscribers.

I have Arnie to thank for that. He hid the documents there while defending MexTel. He knew where they were. And I simply acquired a one-time VPN and safely browsed over to MexTel's server and emailed their documents to all telephone company subscribers in Latin America by clicking one button on my keyboard:

ENTER

47

D anny has agreed to go with me to the House of Jazz to drink a toast to Maddie. It was Maddie's last stop before being hit from behind by MexTel's thug and forced off the road to her death.

We take Lake Shore down to Ellis and Ellis over to 59th and northwest. It is Saturday night, around nine, when we arrive. Valet parking takes my keys, and we are swept inside the club. Playing tonight is the Mark Kent Trio, consisting of bass, keys, and sax. It should be quite a show as these two guys and one gal are packing them in at every stop on their tour. I've made reservations and made a little payoff, so we're shown down front, directly in front of the bandstand.

Danny is excited to be out and listening to jazz. Her favorite of all musical instruments is the saxophone, and her favorite music is jazz. So we should be good to go, and we're both smiling ear to ear. We order drinks—her a Black Russian and me a Pepsi. It's time to sip and savor. We don't talk, as the trio is in the midst of what sounded like *Moonglow* when

we first came in, but now I must admit I'm a little lost—
although there are refrains that make me think I know the
song.

We talk about the Notice of Dismissal that hit my desk
yesterday morning. It seems like Marcel had it right about
the Tijuana factor. Neither Ramon will come to the U.S.
voluntarily, according to the U.S. Attorney's paperwork.
They're afraid of being arrested for narcotics trafficking
across and beyond the U.S. border with Mexico. Their
American law firm filed a motion in the federal criminal
case for a cease and desist order against the FBI, the agency
that was trying to force the Mexicans to come here and
testify against Judge Pennington and me. They put their foot
down and without their testimony freely given the Justice
Department has no choice but to dismiss the charges
against both of us. The letter that Pennington wrote to the
Tijuana cartel? I don't know how that played out; nobody
asked me. But I suspect there was a huge insider deal being
cut between Justice and Pennington for that to have
happened. One thing: Pennington has agreed to resign from
the bench. My tiny ears out on the street tell me the U.S.
Attorney for Chicago is up for appointment to the departing
judge's seat on the federal bench. It's a lifetime appointment, the pay is excellent, there are no politics and there is
no way to be deposed. Unless you send a letter to Mexico
asking for help in killing someone. I guess that's one way.

We've ordered appetizers when Danny reaches across the
table and puts her hand on top of mine. Frankly, I am
shocked. But she doesn't take it away. She leaves it there and
turns her attention to the trio. I am immediately flooded
with a thousand different feelings and images and hopes for

a future, but I act nonchalant as if this happens to me every night of the week that some beautiful female a dozen years younger than me makes the first move. Sure, Michael, I'm thinking, sure it happens. Like never.

For appetizers, we have chosen Veneta Mussels prepared with white wine - Chablis, fennel seed and tomato *concasse*. The dish and two plates arrive, and we find we are starved. She removes her hand for something as mundane as using it to eat, and I am disappointed. I had already made a life-time commitment, and I have to tell myself to slow the hell down and not scare anyone off with my drama.

Because we don't want to mix foods, we order vegetarian for our entree: the Malezana Sandwich, consisting of grilled eggplant, red peppers, zucchini, and brie cheese. Appetizers and entree take us about forty-five minutes to devour, as we are talking and joking the entire time we are eating. First, Danny tells me about her worst law school professor, and then I regale her with my version of Dr. Dandle, the woman who taught legal history to a hundred and eight unworthy freshman law students in one giant hall. She was a character, and I love her to this day. I think we all got more out of her class than any other during our three years in law school.

Talk turns to more serious office matters, too, though I wish upon wish that it didn't have to. Still, Danny seems to want to move our talk in that direction, so I don't resist.

"James Lamb has turned out to be a rather revolting character. Too bad, after all you did for him."

I pause and dab my mouth with a linen napkin.

"Not really all that bad. I don't vouch for these people Danny. I only defend them. Whatever they do after I'm through with them is really none of my concern."

"Come on, Michael, you know he beat his wife to death in that alley. That doesn't make you want to throttle him?"

"What do you mean, throttle him?"

"You know" — she raises both hands and makes a wringing motion.

"You mean do him in. Yes, I do have those thoughts. But no, that would never be me. I don't even kill spiders in the bathtub or mosquitoes in the summer. I'm a softie."

"I like that about you," she giggles. "Some of the nice-guy things I see you do. Giving people a partial refund so they can pay private school tuition. You really did that!"

"You heard about that? They were good people, Danny. It was the least I could do."

"And agreeing to pay your ex-wife. What was that you told me, ninety thousand dollars so she could have a baby with a younger man? Wow! You are some kind of easy, Michael."

"Yes, I suppose I am. I've never handled guilt very well. I always capsize under that kind of emotional load. Maybe someday I'll toughen up."

She reaches over and again rests her hand on mine.

"Oh, I didn't mean to hurt you. Did I hurt you?"

It is all I can do to let it pass by. She'll never know how happy I actually am to get the hell rid of Sue Ellen's alimony. For now, I'll let her think it was guilt. That certainly won't throw a damper on the evening and might even have a positive effect.

"No, you didn't hurt me. Sue Ellen deserves everything she gets. And so does James Lamb. All right, can we talk jazz now? It seems like the perfect place for it."

"Certainly we can. Do you want to talk about Thelonius or Louie?"

"Neither. I want to talk about you and why you love jazz. That's what I want to hear about."

After dinner, we drive leisurely along the lake. I've had several espressos at this point, so I'm wide-awake and ready to carry on until late. Danny is curled up in the passenger seat, leaning as near me as she can with the console blocking her, legs tucked up under her, slowly tapping her fingers on my shoulder in time to the twelve-speaker sound system. Bose—one word says it all. If that's not their motto, it ought to be.

And an hour later we have exhausted ourselves on each other in my bedroom, and it's not even midnight. So we make love a second time, and I am amazed at what I can still accomplish in bed, given half a chance. But it's easy. This woman is the most beautiful creature I have ever seen, especially without clothes, and I want the night to last forever.

She confirms my own sensuality when she says, softly, "I don't want tonight to end. Let's go in and go through your records and find our favorite song. We need to start building a history together right now. That is if you're ready."

I am above her and looking into her eyes.

"Absolutely," I tell her and lower myself onto her.

Thirty minutes later we are in the family room, on the floor, both wearing bathrobes from my health club, surrounded by records and CD's.

History, one might say, is being made.

T
he Department of Corrections provides a bonding
facility controlled by the Clerk of Cook County to
accommodate family members of incarcerated
detainees to post bond on site by means of credit card, cash
or certified check from 9:00 a.m. to 8:30 p.m. Roland Lamb
accompanies me to that location.

Fifty thousand dollars in cash has been sourced. It has been
provided to me by Judge Pennington. James Lamb's brother,
Roland, is given the money, and I take great pains to explain
to him exactly what steps he needs to take to bail his brother
out of jail. Then he is to bring James around the corner to
my car, where I'll be waiting to take him to my office. This is
to protect him against more police harassment. Roland
understands, and he goes into the jail to post bail.

I wait an hour. Two hours. Finally, at nine-thirty at night,
around the corner comes Roland Lamb with his brother,
James. They start to get in. I stop them. Only James is to ride
with me; it's too dangerous for Roland to go with us. I slip
Roland a hundred dollar bill and tell him to call a cab. He

looks puzzled but then shrugs and walks off, stuffing the bill into his pocket.

James Lamb stinks. Of foul breath, body odor, and cigarette smoke. Evidently the CCSD doesn't require an inmate to take a shower before turning them loose on bail. I think there ought to be such a law.

We start to back out when Lamb suddenly reaches across and turns off the ignition on my car.

"Hold up! Last time we talked you wanted to kill me. What's changed? Why are you bailing me out?"

"Because there's real money to be made, James. I've been working a case for you."

"For me?"

"Uh-huh. Against the cops that busted out your teeth.

"Oh yeah? Like what? They gonna pay me or something?"

"Three hundred thousand dollars."

He whistles and slaps himself. "Wake up, dude. This honky man done you right!"

I smile. "Of course, I'm doing you right. Haven't I always? But there's one catch James. I get one-third of the money because I got it for you."

"That's cool. How much is one-third?"

"Hundred grand."

"So's I know: I get two hundred grand, you get one hundred? That's the deal?"

"It is."

"Who's doing' this?"

"Well, that's just it. This is being done on the down low, little brother. So no one finds out you've been paid off. The other part of the deal: once you have the money you have to immediately leave for Los Angeles."

"I gotta leave Chicago?"

"Right."

"That's cool. Maybe I swing by and get the twenty grand for my baby on the way. You know them fuckin people stiffed me?"

"Make them pay up, James. They owe you big time."

"You know, Mr. Gresham, you all right. Shit, I thought we was done, man. But here you are."

"Always taking care of you, James. Plus myself. A hundred thousand dollars is a lot of money to me."

"I don't feel bad. I owe you for gettin rid of that murder beef they put on me. We only paid you a couple thousand. This is better."

"Deal?"

"Deal."

I turn the ignition key, and we finish backing out and drive away on California Avenue. Four miles southwest, there's a park. We're headed there.

It isn't long before I say, "This is Haley Park. We meet them here."

"We be meeting who, dude?"

His eyes are cutting all around as he tries to understand the plan. On the one hand, he is very suspicious. On the other, he is already somewhere over Colorado on a straight-through to L.A.

"Okay, we turn in here. There's a bench down here by the duck pond. That's where we get out."

"Where someone else?"

"On the way. We're a little early. Ten o'clock."

We park and exit my car. We step up onto the grass and walk down thirty yards to pond-side. A green bench is placed so visitors can sit and watch the water and the ducks and toss them breadcrumbs.

"We need breadcrumbs," I say to James as we sit down. I am on one end of the bench; he is on the other. He keeps looking around, and I can tell he wants to run but, damn, he also wants that windfall, that two hundred thousand dollars. After all, he's got it coming to him and he knows it.

"What for breadcrumbs?"

"Feed the ducks."

"I don't see no ducks."

"See that tall grass? That's where they nest at night."

"How you know that? You been here before, dude?"

"Sure. Lots of times. It's very peaceful here."

At just that moment, headlights come winding up the road, and a car pulls in behind mine. The car remains running, and a door opens and closes. In the flash of the ambient light, if you were watching, you would see the decal on the driver's side: Chicago Police Department. James turns around and sees silhouetted in the light a rather tall man carrying a bag. He is certain his money has arrived.

He remains swiveled on the bench as the man approaches. Then he sees and realizes.

It is Judge Pennington.

Pennington reaches into the bag, removes a pistol with a silencer screwed on the end of its barrel, and points it at James Lamb's face. "PSSST!" the gun hisses. Lamb is blasted backward off the bench, a huge round hole in his forehead. Judge Pennington squeezes off two more shots into his heart and drops the gun on the newly deceased murderer of Pennington's wife.

Then Pennington looks at me for the first time. He removes his gloves and places them in the pocket of his dark pants. He fidgets. He begins to stoop down as if to pick up the gun.

I tell him, "My bodyguard has you in his sights right now. You would do well to just turn around and leave the same way you came."

Pennington turns around and takes a step away. Then he pauses and turns back.

"He was after me for more, you know?"

I don't know what he's talking about.

"Lamb? After you?"

"Oh, yes. He was paid in full when he killed my wife. I held up my end of it. But then he got greedy. He came back for more. Now look at him."

"You paid him to kill your wife? Now I get it. You needed him dead to protect yourself."

"Michael, you're amazing," he says sarcastically. "I think you've finally got it."

Pennington turns Lamb's head with the toe of his shoe. He shakes his head in disgust.

"I had them send the confession to you. You know that?"

"No," I tell him. "I didn't know that."

"Oh, yes. The video was part of the deal. It saved his life. I needed him out of jail."

"Wait. Are you saying that Fordyce and Burns—"

He raises a hand. "No more, Michael. Stay clear of this."

He pulls a pack of cigarettes from his breast pocket and lights up. He blows a long plume of smoke across the night air and I can see his troubled eyes in the glow of his ember. Suddenly I want to run, to get away from this person. But I force myself to stay. Running would be a terrible mistake.

"I owe you, Michael. I won't forget tonight."

"Call off the dogs," I tell him.

"Consider it done."

He reaches out to shake my hand.

But I turn my back instead and begin walking slowly back to my car. I have crossed a line, and I will never be Michael Gresham again. Not the Michael Gresham that drove in here.

It is hot, and I am tired and need to just go home and go to bed. I am walking so slowly that Pennington strides past me and climbs back into the cop car. I don't even look up to see who's driving. I no longer care. Then they are gone.

I start the engine of my SUV and turn around in the narrow street.

As I am leaving, I think I hear a duck quack.

Or maybe not.

It's hot, and I'm so tired.

Sleep. I just need to sleep. Without my gun underneath my pillow.

It will be good to be free of that inconvenience.

49

One day in August I fly with Danny to Lafayette, Louisiana, where we rent from Hertz and drive thirty minutes north of town. I have twenty thousand dollars cash in my briefcase. It is my own money, and I am happy to be able to spend it like I'm about to.

The house is a broad, sloping wood frame with green shingles. There is a sweeping front lawn with magnolia bushes everywhere. We park out front and go up onto the porch and knock.

It's all prearranged. Without ten words, I hand them the briefcase with the twenty thousand dollars. They carefully count it. Then the woman goes into a back room and returns with a baby. There are tears in her eyes and in the eyes of her husband, too. But there are laws against this kind of thing that has happened, and I have gone over those laws very carefully with their attorney. They decided, in the end, to return James Lamb's baby to his family rather than return to Chicago and face serious federal charges for human trafficking.

The money is all there, and the baby is in Danny's arms. She covers its face with the light cotton wrap, and we step out into the bright August sunlight. There are no goodbyes, no promises of meeting again. We are here and taking this baby away because the law says we can. Without that, the man inside that house would have gunned us down with his shotgun. But he wasn't given that opportunity. He got his money back and got to remain outside the walls of some horrific federal penitentiary.

At O'Hare, we are met by both grandmothers. They are Sylvia's grandmother and James Lamb's grandmother. It has all been arranged over the months since James' death and wouldn't have happened if he hadn't given me the name and phone number of the couple who bought little Thel—short for Thelonious. The grandmothers asked Danny what she would like to name the boy, given that she had done most of the workup on the kid's retrieval.

At least, that's the middle name and not the first and not the last. The kid won't have to start fighting in kindergarten because of his name like Thelonius Monk must have done. I have nothing to back that up; I'm going strictly by human nature when it's six years old.

On the wide-body jet back to Chicago I sat next to the window, Danny and the baby were on my right. As I watched the sun quicken in its descent below the horizon, I saw in that light the Michael Gresham I had always been. To him, I apologized for my role in the extinction of James Lamb. And you know what? He immediately forgave me. Forgave me and took me back.

50

Twelve months have gone by, and I find myself in one of those buildings I rarely frequent—a church. It is not a great cathedral, and it is not a small church in the country. It is in the Northwest 'Burbs, and it is non-denominational.

Sue Ellen looks resplendent in a light knit summer suit topped off with a wide-brimmed summer hat. She is holding a bouquet of daffodils—I don't know why, custom at one of these gatherings, maybe. Beside her stands Eddie, the successful entrepreneur and owner of three house-washing franchises that are quickly cornering the market in this area of town. He is holding their son, a blue-eyed, very light-skinned baby that, if I were describing it I would only say, looks very fragile and very needy. It sucks quietly on one of those rubber nipples and occasionally opens its eyes to look around and frown. His name is Michael, although I'm told they will call him Mick.

Seated to my left are Esmeralda and her baby girl, and to her left is Arnie, who can't quit twisting his hands as though he's washing them. Esmeralda said something about Arnie having forgotten to take his OCD meds and today wanting to wash and re-wash his hands at every stop. My poor dear brother and all the rest of the people who suffer such unfathomable torture. I love him even more because of his ailments, never less.

And finally, to my right is my best friend in all the world, Danny Gresham. She is holding my right hand with her left, and I can hardly keep my eyes off the ring on her hand; it set me back twenty-five thousand dollars and at times I wish I had spent twice that for her. She's worth everything I have or ever will have. Again the shades of my dark house are raised, the curtains are open, and she has me out in the yard cutting the grass and trimming the bushes while she's inside cooking and taking every possible vitamin and mineral and supplement that her well-baby doctor says she should be taking. She is four months along, and our baby girl's name will be—you ready for this?

Dania. Just like her amazing mother.

Arnie has reminded me that Clint and Mick did this fathering thing in their seventies, and I am supposed to somehow feel unburdened by that.

I don't. I worry about college funds and freshman visiting day when her father shows up in a wheelchair with an oxygen bottle strapped above the rear-mounted electric engine.

Dania tells me that's all in my head.

And it might very well be. But I've given up my two-a-day habit.

Cigarettes are kaput.

51

On the day I am to take Danny to the hospital so labor can be induced (we have a baby who is resisting this world), I receive a call from Sam Shaw over at Arnie's law firm.

He is breathless.

"Michael," he rasps into the phone in that senior partner voice of his. Off-putting to some, mildly humorous to nobodies like me who will never go up against him. "Have you seen Arnie?"

"No, Sam. I haven't seen Arnie. Why?"

"He hasn't been in the office two days in a row. He is missing depositions. Is he sick or something, do you know?"

I pause to reflect. "You'll have to call him, Sam. I don't do Arnie keeping anymore."

"I'll keep trying his cell, Michael, sorry to bother you."

I had to turn off the snowblower to take the call when I felt the cell phone vibration in my pocket. I replace the phone and am about to start up again when the phone begins vibrating a second time.

"Hello?"

"Michael, Esmeralda. Have you seen Arnie?"

"No, why?"

"He's gone. I was up at my mother's visiting, and I thought he was home. I got back an hour ago, and I cannot find him and he's not answering his cell. I've called everyone. Nothing."

"Well, you know how Arnie can be."

I am ready to fire up the snowblower and continue with my own driveway in front of my own house and leave Arnie and his problems on the other side of town.

"Michael," she says before I can say goodbye, "the handcuffs are gone."

I stop. I cannot move.

I begin shoving the silent snowblower toward my garage.

The search is on.

THE END

UP NEXT: SECRETS GIRLS KEEP

"When you are looking for writing excellence you cannot go wrong with John Ellsworth!"

"How you weaved together their lives and circumstances were spellbinding and kept me turning pages to the end."

"Many twists and turns and a few great surprises."

"This book starts out fast and furious...and then the suspense and drama get moving even faster."

"Once again, John Ellsworth has written a winner. I have read all of his books and they have all been very good."

Read Secrets Girls Keep: CLICK HERE

ALSO BY JOHN ELLSWORTH

THADDEUS MURFEE PREQUEL

A YOUNG LAWYER'S STORY

THADDEUS MURFEE SERIES

THE DEFENDANTS

BEYOND A REASONABLE DEATH

ATTORNEY AT LARGE

CHASE, THE BAD BABY

DEFENDING TURQUOISE

THE MENTAL CASE

THE GIRL WHO WROTE THE NEW YORK TIMES BESTSELLER

THE TRIAL LAWYER

THE NEAR DEATH EXPERIENCE

FLAGSTAFF STATION

THE CRIME

LA JOLLA LAW

THE POST OFFICE

SISTERS IN LAW SERIES

FRAT PARTY: SISTERS IN LAW

HELLFIRE: SISTERS IN LAW

MICHAEL GRESHAM PREQUEL

LIES SHE NEVER TOLD ME

MICHAEL GRESHAM SERIES

THE LAWYER

SECRETS GIRLS KEEP

THE LAW PARTNERS

CARLOS THE ANT

SAKHAROV THE BEAR

ANNIE'S VERDICT

DEAD LAWYER ON AISLE 11

30 DAYS OF JUSTIS

THE FIFTH JUSTICE

PSYCHOLOGICAL THRILLERS

THE EMPTY PLACE AT THE TABLE

HISTORICAL THRILLERS

THE POINT OF LIGHT

LIES SHE NEVER TOLD ME

UNSPEAKABLE PRAYERS

HARLEY STURGIS

NO TRIVIAL PURSUIT

LETTIE PORTMAN SERIES

THE DISTRICT ATTORNEY

JUSTICE IN TIME

ABOUT THE AUTHOR

For thirty years John defended criminal clients across the United States. He defended cases ranging from shoplifting to First Degree Murder to RICO to Tax Evasion, and has gone to jury trial on hundreds. His first book, *The Defendants*, was published in January, 2014. John is presently at work on his 31st thriller.

Reception to John's books have been phenomenal; more than 4,000,000 have been downloaded in 6 years! Every one of them are Amazon best-sellers. He is an Amazon All-Star every month and is a *U.S.A Today* bestseller.

John Ellsworth lives in the Arizona region with three dogs that ignore him but worship his wife, and bark day and night until another home must be abandoned in yet another move.

johnellsworthbooks.com

johnellsworthbooks@gmail.com

EMAIL SIGNUP

Can't get enough John Ellsworth?

Sign up for our weekly newsletter to stay in touch!

You will have exclusive access to new releases, special deals, and insider news! Join today!

Click here to subscribe to my newsletter: https://www.subscribepage.com/b5c8ao

AMAZON REVIEWS

If you can take a few minutes and leave your review of this book I would be very honored. Plus, your support will help me write more books.

Made in the USA
Monee, IL
24 August 2022